CW00558129

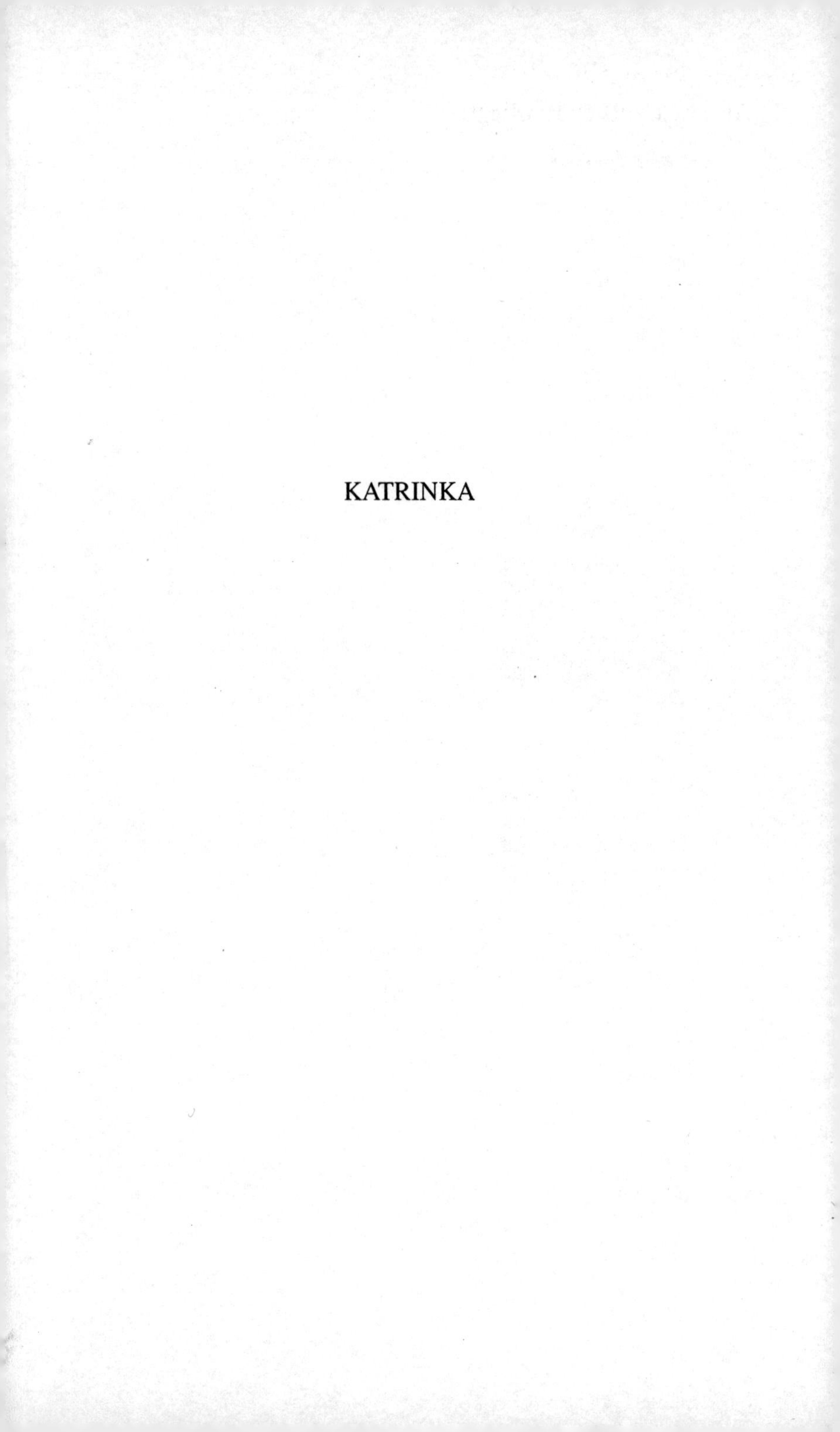

KATRINKA

Also by Geoffrey Rawlings:

Tolcarne Merock

KATRINKA

Geoffrey Rawlings

To PETER
WITH BEST WISHES
Geoffrey Rawlings

UNITED WRITERS
Cornwall

UNITED WRITERS PUBLICATIONS LTD
Ailsa, Castle Gate, Penzance, Cornwall.

British Library Cataloguing in Publication Data:
A catalogue record for this book is
available from the British Library.

ISBN 1 85200 120 8

Printed in Great Britain by
United Writers Publications Ltd
Cornwall.

To my children
Leo and Carol
who have helped to make
my life complete.

Prologue

I shivered as the screaming wind threatened to rip the coat from my back. My ears ached with the roar of the Atlantic Ocean as its waves relentlessly pounded the rugged Cornish cliffs. Sometimes the wind would whip up the foaming surf and carry it across the golden sands to half a mile inland, where it would be flung and scattered with vicious contempt, and appear to the onlooker as a carpet of cotton wool snowflakes which clung precariously to the tough winter grass on the fields of my farm. With my head bent low I forced my legs to move against the wind's strong invisible hands, and slowly crossed the bleak and open farmyard. Just a few yards ahead of me stood the graceful old granite farmhouse that was my home. The soft, warm light spilling out from the kitchen window beckoned me to hurry indoors, but first I had to check the animals in the cowshed. Then my day's work would be done.

Relieved, I stepped into the back kitchen and firmly closed the door behind me. A few years ago I would have easily taken the harsh weather in my stride, but now, in my sixties, these battles with the elements were beginning to take their toll. Wearily I sat down on the seat just inside the door and rested my arm on the still washing machine. Beside it, the tumble dryer was emitting a lazy drone as it slowly dried a load of my farming gear. It was a good, hard-working friend in the short days of the winter months. Elizabeth, my wife, had long ago come to the conclusion that the wind's favourite playthings were the freshly-laundered garments that she pegged with pride on the washing line. With a fiendish giggle it would invariably snatch the pristine garments from the line and dump them one-by-one in the muddy corner of the field.

Poor Liz, I can see her now, stomping back indoors with the basket of muddied clothes that had to be washed all over again. I think they were the only times that I have ever seen her really angry.

Bending forward to remove my wellingtons, I grimaced as a searing pain shot up my right leg. I paused for a moment or two with my stockinged feet resting on the cold slate floor, waiting for the pain to subside. I knew that rest would be the cure. But the aches and pains were getting worse, and I cursed the advancing years. I could hear Elizabeth clattering around in the kitchen and knew from the aromatic smells that she had been baking. There was nothing wrong with my appetite.

Slipping my feet into my old slippers, I followed the smell into our cosy kitchen, warmed as always by the Aga stove. Elizabeth was standing in front of the kitchen sink, her arms immersed up to the elbows in soap suds. Even at sixty she still has a trim little figure, and after forty years of marriage I still feel an excited little flutter whenever I look at her.

She turned to me and smiled, her rosy cheeks explaining the racks of saffron buns that lay on the surface of the scrubbed wooden table. 'You're early tonight,' she said, glancing at the clock on the wall. 'The pasties aren't quite ready yet.' She sounded apologetic.

I gave her a squeeze from behind. 'Don't worry,' I said, my mind already feasting on the trays of freshly baked buns. I sat down at the table and helped myself. The bun was still warm. It looked mouth-wateringly delicious with its deep yellow colouring and crusty brown top; a few sultanas shyly peeking out here and there. I took my first bite and knew at once that it tasted as good as it looked. Elizabeth, her work finished at the sink, brought over two mugs of steaming hot tea and sat down on the seat beside me. I wrapped my hands around the mug and sipped the warm soothing liquid. Yes, life is good!

Elizabeth's voice broke our contented silence. 'You haven't forgotten that I have to go out this evening, have you?'

I shook my head, but in fact it had slipped my mind. I felt a sudden pang of loneliness; the house always seemed bare and empty without her.

She smiled, as if reading my mind. 'Why don't you light the fire in the front room? There's a big stack of logs all ready. You'll be much more comfortable in there.' She rose to check the pasties in the oven. 'It will be warm and cosy for you by the time you have eaten your tea.'

She was right, as always, so I finished the mug of tea and went through to the front room. It was a spacious room with a low, beamed ceiling, and a large window which gave us extensive views over some of our fields. The old-fashioned grate was pleasingly large, which it needed to be in order to warm the whole room. I lit the fire and left it to burn.

By the time I had washed and shaved and eaten my pasty, I was beginning to feel human again. The log fire in the front room was burning brightly. I settled comfortably into my armchair and rested my aching leg on a low stool. It was sheer heaven. I only hoped that there would be no cause for me to have to venture out again that evening. As my eyelids grew heavy, I soon surrendered to a blissful sleep.

Vaguely, somewhere in the far distance, I heard the sound of a man's voice. My senses sharpened. I sat up, alert now, and listened. Then I relaxed and sat back in my chair. It was only Garth, talking to Elizabeth in the kitchen. We had known Garth for a long time. He was employed as a salesman for a corn merchant and called on us every month without fail. Over the years we had become firm friends.

Elizabeth brought him into the front room.

'Ah, so here you are . . . skiving as usual I see, Pete!'

'Shut up and take a seat,' I told him. 'I've several things I want to order from you this month, so that should please you.'

Garth was short in stature, but he was quite portly. His face was creased but kindly, and the dark-rimmed glasses he was forced to wear rested with perfect ease on his large red nose. His sparse grey hair was flattened damply to his head, permanently squashed by an old flat cap which was worn everywhere but indoors. He settled down into the armchair opposite to mine and took out his order book, then rummaged in his pocket until he found a small stub of pencil. He brought the pencil closer to his glasses to check if the lead was adequate for order writing. Apparently it was, as he then licked the tip and held it poised over the page. 'There now, I'm ready, Pete. I seem to be always losing my pencils – still, I think this will do the job. When you're ready, my friend.'

The pencil scratched away busily and recorded my order in his notebook. 'I think that's about it for this month,' I told him, but I knew that Garth, as always, would be holding another selling card up his sleeve.

He rested his pencil for the moment and relaxed back into the chair. 'I noticed when I was driving down here along the cliff road, how rough the sea looked. You will have to keep the steers' bellies full this winter if you want to market them in the spring.'

I waited for the usual following hard sell, and wasn't disappointed. Garth's pencil was already hovering over the pad again as he gave me a look of eager anticipation.

He said, 'We have a new lot of sugar beet pellets in at the moment . . . just the thing for hungry bullocks – that is if you would like some delivered?'

As always I ended up ordering more than I had planned, but it was always put to good use. We chatted for a while and he mentioned that he was living alone now that his mother had died. 'You'll have to find yourself a woman and get married,' I remarked half-jokingly, but it failed to raise a smile.

'I think I've left it a bit late for that now, Pete.'

'Get on with you – it's never too late for that.'

At that moment Elizabeth came in with two steaming mugs of tea. Garth always enjoyed tea with us on his monthly visits. Elizabeth offered him a pasty which was going spare. 'Gosh no,' he said, 'I couldn't take your pasty.' But, as always, he ended up eating it, and a couple of saffron buns as well. Elizabeth threw me a secret grin as she left us to it.

A little later, Elizabeth's head appeared round the door. 'I'll be off now. I expect I will be quite late coming home, so don't worry.' She gazed longingly at the cosy fire, but she had to go; she was babysitting our grandchildren some ten miles away. 'Bye.'

'Drive carefully,' I said, before returning my attention to Garth's news and gossip from all over Cornwall. It was quite amazing what he learned on his travels. I eased my leg off the stool, trying not to show the discomfort I was feeling as I replenished the fire with fresh logs. The room would soon turn chilly if I allowed it to lose its steam. We both sat quietly, contentedly watching the flames licking the crisp new logs, nothing to break the silence but the hissing and crackling of the pine wood as it shrank and withered in the intense heat.

I reached for my cigars, which was the signal for Garth to stoke up his pipe. He was soon puffing away merrily. 'What is actually wrong with your leg, Pete? Arthritis, is it?'

'No, my friend, nothing like that.' I paused for a moment as my mind raced back over my life with astonishing clarity. Garth was clearly curious as he waited for me to continue. 'It's a long time ago now,' I said. 'I was stabbed.'

'Stabbed!' Garth sat bolt upright in his chair, his face contorted with concern and amazement. 'Where? When? How?'

'Germany – just after the war. I was just nineteen. A skirmish with three local ruffians. Anyway, like I said, it was a long time ago, and it's a long story.'

He was still on the edge of his seat. 'You've never mentioned a word of this before.' He drew excitedly on his pipe and sent a cloud of blue smoke billowing up to the beams. 'You must tell me.'

I looked across at Garth's kind and honest face. I think I needed to tell him. A secret weighs heavily; maybe the time had now arrived to share it, and lessen the load. I threw him a smile. 'In that case we will have a drop of malt together,' I said.

I hobbled over to the stone-built bar I had in one corner of the room and gathered up a couple of glasses. Carefully, I reached for the whisky. 'I have a good one here – saving it for a special occasion,' I confided. 'I had it for my birthday back in July.'

'Sounds good.'

'Should be.' The top was secured by a strong lead seal, which I managed to prise off with the pocket knife I always keep handy. I gave the cork a turn and gently pulled, until a mouth-watering aroma escaped into the air with a pleasing whoosh. I savoured the soft, velvety gurgle as I filled the glasses. To my mind whisky has a special gurgle of its own, perhaps because I don't hear it very often. I handed a generously-filled glass to Garth, then went back to collect mine, along with the remainder in the bottle. It would be nice to have it handy, just in case . . .

Garth studied his whisky, holding it aloft, almost drinking it in with his eyes. 'It looks as if I'm eating and drinking you out of house and home, Pete.'

'Nonsense, my friend. I look forward very much to your monthly visits. So much better than this newfangled idea of telesales, or whatever it's called these days.'

Garth twirled the amber liquid around the glass before reverently raising it to his lips and taking a delicate sip. Then he gave a contented smile and said, 'I'm all ears, Pete.'

Chapter One

I think it's best if I start at the beginning. I was brought up in the St Austell area of Cornwall, amongst the clay-works. Like a lot of youngsters in my village I used to enjoy football and was lucky enough to play for my home team. I also loved boxing. Once a week I would go to a local farm, where the farmer's son happened to be a professional boxer. They had successfully converted an old disused barn into a gym, which proved to be perfect for our needs. And we were extremely lucky to receive our training from a retired Cornish champion. He was a hard taskmaster but he was good. I really enjoyed it, but little did I realise at the time that one day I would have to fight for my life. Many times since have I thanked God for that early training.

On leaving school I worked for an oil company, until I was called up for the army. I was the youngest of five children. My father was born on a farm but spent most of his life mining tin and clay. When he was just nineteen he was awarded the DCM for gallantry in the First World War while serving as a private in the Duke of Cornwall's Light Infantry. My mother was a small woman but her size didn't hinder her in bringing us all up. She had a big heart and there were times when I felt she was ten feet tall.

I vividly remember the day when I arrived home from work, and my mother pointed to an official government-stamped letter propped against the clock on the mantlepiece. There was sadness in her voice as she said, 'A letter for you, my son.'

My heart was in my boots as I took down the brown envelope and reluctantly opened it. Sure enough it was my call-up papers. The unfriendly words glared back at me:

Report to the Duke of Cornwall barracks at Bodmin, 3rd September 1952.

The third of September was a pleasantly warm and sunny day, which failed to lift my spirits. I ate only a little of my shredded wheat that morning and just moped around, not wanting to leave, yet wishing I was gone. The bus was due at eleven in the morning, and as the journey to Bodmin was just ten miles, I would be there in no time at all.

Finally, at 10.45am, I picked up my case. 'I had better go now in case the bus is early.' I tried to sound cheerful, without much success.

My mother hugged and kissed me. It was hard for her; her baby going away. My father came over and put his arms around me, then he shook my hand. 'Obey all your orders and keep out of trouble, then you will do fine,' he said.

I put on a brave face. 'So long . . . I'll see you in a few weeks.'

I turned quickly and hurried out before I had the chance to make a fool of myself. After a short wait the Western National bus appeared around the corner and shuddered to a halt beside me. I jumped aboard, and in little more than half an hour I stepped down into the little town of Bodmin.

I walked nervously up the road to the barracks. Guarding the outside was an impressive sculptured monument of a British Tommy. I glanced up at his noble face and felt a sudden twinge of pride. Yes, I too was going to be a British soldier!

I paused at the main entrance. Facing me was a very large door with the badge of the DCLI proudly displayed above it. Set in the door was another smaller one; I gingerly stepped through it. I had taken about three strides when a voice roared, 'Name, boy?'

I looked up to see a corporal glaring at me. I snapped to attention. 'Peter Rundle, Corporal.' He pointed to another doorway. 'Go through there, Rundle, and get registered.'

I did as I was told, and emerged some three hours later a soldier in the DCLI. I had been kitted out with a uniform, two pairs of boots, kitbags, lots of belts and straps made out of webbing, a knife, fork and spoon, mess tins, and numerous other things which completely baffled me and all of the other chaps who had come in on the same intake. We were then taken to our billet. It was one great room furnished with about thirty beds in all. Stood in the centre was an ugly big black tortoise stove, which I imagined would have a hard struggle to keep its occupants from shivering. I picked a bed in one corner and gratefully dropped my kit down. It barely touched the floor before a sergeant came roaring in.

'Men! Come here! Watch closely, and see how to make your bed properly army style!'

I had never seen so much bullshit in all my life, but from then on that was the way it had to be done. In six weeks they had made soldiers of us. We had a passing out parade, then, thankfully, we were off home for two week's leave.

Chapter Two

When we returned from leave we found that the majority of us were being sent to a battalion in West Germany – a place called Minden. I for one felt excited, even though I was apprehensive. On the fifth of November we had an early breakfast, then started to pack all our kit together for our new billets in Germany. The corporal had advised us to keep our greatcoats handy. He explained that we would be travelling mostly by night and the troopship and transit camps could be extremely cold. At last we were ready. We stood laden down with all our military kit while eagle eyes swept over us to make sure everything was in its right place, then we were marched the few hundred yards to the railway station.

The train was already in and waiting for us. It was a special military train, comprising just two carriages and the engine. At the next station the two carriages would part company with the engine and be connected to the main line train which would take us to Paddington in London.

We stood to attention on the platform while the sergeant gave us a few parting words of advice. 'Do not forget you are soldiers of the DCLI. You will act like one at all times!' He bade us farewell and we fell out to board the train.

We arrived at Paddington just as it was getting dark. I had never seen such a big frightening place – so many platforms and so many people hurrying this way and that. One of the NCOs in charge ordered us to keep together and to follow him closely. 'We don't want anyone getting lost!' His voice hardened. 'Or deserting!'

A few of our chaps lived in London, so I suppose there was

good reason for those in charge to be a little concerned while we were on their home patch. I made sure I kept up with them. I was out of my depth and terrified – this was all very different from the one platform station at St Austell. I slung my large pack on my back and carried my heavy kitbag in the upright position as I shuffled along behind the others, slowly weaving my way endlessly along and then finally down to the underground station.

I felt lost, as if in a dream, as I boarded the waiting train. The deafening noise and the stark artificial lighting served to add to the unreality of the situation. But as soon as we were all bundled together inside, our own kind talking and laughing together, the feeling of normality slowly returned. Our train took us to Liverpool Street, then it was up again into the fresh air, where yet another train awaited us. This one would take us to Harwich.

The station in Harwich seemed almost calm and relaxed after the bustle of London. Gradually though, the platform filled with troops as they spilled out from the numerous carriages. Orders were given and we dutifully filed into our respective groups and followed our leaders down and out on to the docks, where we were led into a huge transit shed in order to be fed.

Once inside, I just stared open-mouthed. I had never seen such a large building in all my life. Running down one side were several desks with army personnel busily writing. On the other side was the cookhouse, fronted by a long servery and manned by scores of cooks. In front of this were hundreds of tables and chairs which were already starting to be filled. I joined the queue and expected a long wait, but the cooks were experienced in their job and very soon I was sat hungrily tucking into a plate of delicious bacon and scrambled eggs. As soon as the meal was finished we were ushered outside, then before we knew it we were marching up the slippery gangway of the troopship. We were directed down below by one of the many sailors who stood awaiting us on the upper deck.

Clumsily I made my way down several metal stairways until I reached my allotted deck. Hundreds of three-tiered bunks stretched out in front of me. Choosing the nearest bottom one, I gratefully dropped my heavy gear and fell with some relief on to the mattress. As I lay with my eyes closed, I could feel and hear the huge engines throbbing – so much noise as the ship filled up with its human cargo. After a short while the Tannoy system crackled into life, and the voice of the Captain echoed around the ship:

'Each man must stay on his bunk We are now casting off.'

The ship steadily settled into its gently rocking rhythm, and I knew we were now sailing out on the high seas. Confirmation of this came over the Tannoy, as we were informed that we could now leave our bunks, if we so wished.

I sat on the edge of my bunk and gazed around at the unfamiliar surroundings. I think I would have started swimming for home if it wasn't for the chap who was lying on the bunk above me. As luck would have it we knew each other by sight. His name was John Osborne, and he came from the St Austell area. His family were also clay miners, so we had something in common. I think we both felt we each had a little bit of home beside us.

Suddenly I felt the need for some fresh air. 'Fancy a stroll on deck?' I shouted up to John.

He jumped down from his bunk, stretched his long legs, and said, 'Sure do. I was afraid to go on my own in case I got lost.'

We walked between the rows of tiered bunks. Some of the men were smoking, some were looking wistfully at loved one's photos, while others were merely lying there, just staring into space, probably wishing they were back home with their families.

There were some who had made the trip many times before. These were the ones who remained relaxed, either playing cards or reading, evidently feeling quite at home. On reaching the foot of the stairway that led to the upper deck, we both made a mental note of our own deck number, just in case we had difficulty in finding our way back.

The wind chilled our faces as we emerged from the stairway onto the bare, windswept deck. We ambled to the rail and peered over the side. Everywhere was jet black, but in the far distance we could see the twinkling lights that we were leaving behind. We rested our arms on the rail and listened to the heavy swish of the water as we ploughed through the North Sea, bound for the Hook of Holland. John tried to light a cigarette, but the cold, salty wind soon put a stop to that. We wandered around a little until we found a temporary shelter. It looked like a life raft of some sort, but it served our purpose as we both sat quietly smoking, each with our own thoughts of home. It wasn't long before our warm bunks beckoned us back below, so we descended the stairway, our hob-nailed boots clanging and echoing with each step we took. Even this sounded alien to me. It was as if someone else was crashing out these thundering footfalls I was hearing. Not me.

We soon found our deck, but we weren't so quick in finding our bunks. The trouble being they all looked the same. When we did finally locate them I sat down and took off my boots to let the air get to my feet – a practice I kept up all my army life. Then I settled into my bunk, snuggled under my greatcoat and closed my eyes. It was lovely and warm but sleep evaded me. No matter which way I turned, I couldn't block out the persistent dull throbbing of the engines. And my mind was working overtime, wondering about Germany, then the next minute racing back to my family at home.

I must have dozed a little. When I looked at my watch it was four-thirty in the morning. I yawned and turned over. But any further sleep was out of the question. The best thing, I thought, would be to go and have a wash and shave; at least I would probably have the place to myself at such an early hour. I ran my hand over my chin; it felt like sandpaper. My hair was very dark, almost black, and my beard grew like wildfire. I had always needed to shave twice a day. Fumbling in my small pack, I found my shaving gear and green army towel. I slung the towel around my neck and pushed my feet into the cold, hard boots and headed for the doorway which I hoped would lead me to the washroom. I stepped out into a long deserted corridor and for a moment wasn't sure of which way to turn, when a sailor suddenly appeared from somewhere behind me. I asked him if he could direct me to the toilets. He looked a little perplexed for a moment. Having repeated myself, it finally dawned upon him what it was that I wanted.

'You mean *the heads*,' he laughed, and pointed the way. My broad Cornish dialect didn't help. He didn't have a clue what I was talking about at first. I think it was the green towel that eventually did the trick.

Off I went, and about fifty yards along the corridor I came to an open doorway. I peered in, and sure enough there were about twenty sinks in a line. On the other side was a row of lavatories. I had to high step through as there was a bottom on the doorway to enable the door to be sealed off in case of an emergency.

Everything went smoothly until I started with the razor. I realised that with the movement of the ship, shaving was going to be a nightmare! I managed to get the job done in spite of scores of painful little nicks, which I had to cover with toilet paper. When the bleeding eventually stopped, I gently eased the bits of paper off my face. Glancing back in the mirror, I looked better than I felt – anyway, it would have to do. Gathering up my bits and pieces, I hurried back, hopefully to find my bunk.

By this time most of the men were awake. There was confusion everywhere. Men hunting for kit, coughing and swearing; general pandemonium. Then sudden silence as the Tannoy spluttered to life.

'*We will be docking in approximately 30 minutes. Gather your kit together and remain by your bunks until we have docked. No one will be allowed on to the top deck until further notice.*'

As soon as the message faded away all hell broke loose again. Everyone seemed to be heading for the toilets. I was pleased to have beaten the rush.

After a while I noticed that the engine-note had changed. There were a few grinding bumps, then silence. The next Tannoy message was loud and clear:

'We have docked. Stand by your bunks until your deck number is called!'

John just made it. He came scurrying back with his face covered in bits of paper. By the time he had picked up his gear, our deck number was being called.

When we emerged on to the top deck I was surprised to find that it was still dark. There were four gangways down to the quay and the troops were streaming down them and straight into the big transit sheds right on the dockside. We were soon swept along with all the others, and when I found myself on the gangplank with so much kit to carry I found it quite tricky to keep my balance. At the bottom our sergeant was waiting for us. As we entered the transit shed he was yelling, 'Keep together lads! Stay in line!'

Once again I gazed in awe as I entered. This one was as big as the last, with the same layout. Cooks and tables on one side, desks and administrative personnel on the other. But there were literally thousands of troops here. The masses of tables that fronted the canteen seemed to be littered with dirty mugs, plates and overflowing ashtrays. It was chaotic to say the least. John gave me a rueful look as we took our place at the end of a very long queue. We were feeling hungry and it looked as if we were in for a lengthy wait. But our concern was unfounded. These cooks were as experienced as those in the previous transit shed, if not more so. The speed with which they dished up the meals was amazing; not one minute was lost. We were soon pushing the dirty dishes on a free table to one side to make room for our own.

After we had eaten, John took out a Woodbine and lit-up. Settling back into his chair, he gave a contented sigh and patted his stomach. 'Just what the doctor ordered,' he grinned. 'I needed that.' His repose was short lived. The dreaded Tannoy couldn't be ignored:

'*Prepare to embark on the colour coded trains to your final destinations.*'

John took one last puff before dropping the half-smoked Woodbine onto the concrete floor and crushing it flat with his heavy boot. We gathered up our gear.

Outside, numerous groups of men gathered together in order to be marched to the station which was situated a little further along the dock. As I approached the platform, I saw the very long trains that were waiting for us. They were sporting markings of different colours: blue, red and green. These coaches would take our troops all over Germany, and some as far as Austria. We learned from the Tannoy that the green train travelled to Osnabruck, Minden, Hannover and Berlin. This one was ours; we were earmarked for Minden.

It took a bit of manoeuvring to squeeze inside with all our kit, but we managed it. Then doors were being slammed, troops were running up and down the corridors in search of seats, while others, their heads hung out of the windows, peered anxiously up and down for their missing mates.

Then the whistle blew and we were off. A chap returning to Minden after a spot of leave told us that we should arrive at our destination by about nine o'clock that night. We settled down for a very long ride.

Chapter Three

After an hour or two the train stopped at Arnhem station. There was a buzz of excitement all through the train. Everyone knew of the Battle of Arnhem and several of us had known friends and neighbours who sadly had lost their lives there. We journeyed on for maybe twenty minutes or so, then the train once again jolted to a stop. John looked out of the window and relayed back to us what was happening. 'Nothing very exciting,' he said. 'There's just three railway blokes walking alongside the train. One of them has a hammer and is tapping each wheel as he goes by.' We presumed they were carrying out a safety check and soon lost interest. Everyone settled back into their seats, all eager to be on the move for the next stage of the journey The sound of the tapping hammer faded as the men slowly made their way to the end of the train.

Our sergeant poked his head round the door and informed us that we were now at the Dutch-German border, and that very shortly the customs would work their way through the carriages. 'Don't worry about it,' he grinned. 'They won't bother any of you lot – they know you haven't any money to buy anything worth smuggling!' Sure enough, when the two customs officers arrived, they just glanced into each compartment and went on their way. With a flutter of excitement I realised that I was now in Germany.

Some of the chaps who had left wives and girlfriends behind were still upset. We sang everything from *Bye Bye Blackbird* to *Going up Camborne Hill Coming Down* to try to cheer them up, but with little success. It was a timely relief when a steward came along and told us to make our way to the dining carriage for the second sitting of lunch. We didn't need to be told twice. Everyone was starving, as well as being glad of the respite from the singing.

All of us first-timers had a shock as we entered the dining area. The carriage was laid out like a posh hotel. I had no experience of such a place; a fish and chip café was about my limit. Once we were seated the stewards worked like clockwork. First, serving us all with a welcome glass of beer. Next came the soup and a crusty roll. I glanced nervously at the array of sparkling cutlery placed before me, then someone to the side of me hissed, 'Start from the outside and work your way in!' So I was through round one – I knew what to eat my soup with.

We had barely finished the last spoonful, when all the dirty dishes were expertly whisked away. Then came the roast beef with three veg. John grinned as he swallowed a large mouthful. 'I'll be signing-on if all the grub out here is as good as this,' he laughed.

We finished off with spotty dick and custard, and a choice of either tea or coffee . . . lovely.

As soon as we had finished we were politely but firmly ushered back to our own compartments, as they had several more sittings to contend with. We arrived back feeling fat and full. Even the soldiers who were feeling low were looking much better. Now, as I looked out at the passing countryside, I could see that it was beginning to look much colder here. Snow was lying on the ground, and the huge dark pine forests were sprinkled with sparkling frost. The few people we saw were well wrapped up against the cold, just glancing at us for a fleeting second as the train sped by en route to Berlin.

As the hours and the miles rolled by, most of the chaps lay sprawled around the carriage, sleeping or smoking. We were all pretty tired by now, as we had been travelling for almost thirty hours. I could no longer see out of the window. Darkness had fallen, relieved only once in a while by the glittering lights of a town or village. I decided to stretch my legs for a bit. My chin was beginning to feel prickly, so armed with my shaving kit, I headed for the wash-up.

Confidently, I lathered my face. There was a slight sway with the movement of the train, but compared to on board ship this was going to be child's play. But it wasn't to be; my razor was blunt! It pulled out more than it cut off. This painful experience taught me that I would need a new blade each day if I didn't want to torture myself. Feeling a little more awake, I sauntered back to my mates. It was now 6pm. Two more hours and we would be in Minden. Excitement was running high as we neared the station. Cases and kitbags were hoisted down from the luggage racks and lined up in readiness, leaving hardly an inch of spare floor space between us.

A corporal appeared in the corridor. 'Come along! Smarten yourselves up! I don't want to take a lot of zombies into the camp of the DCLI.'

Someone muttered cheekily, 'What's a zombie?'

The corporal turned on him. 'You will bloody-well find out tomorrow morning, lad,' and, with a face of stone, wandered off to threaten the men in the next compartment.

The train slowed to a grinding halt. Minden at last.

'Right, you lot, out you all get. Pronto!' came the order. And I took my first step on to German soil.

The station teemed with soldiers. The majority of them were from the South Staffordshire regiment and the Royal Engineers. The Duke of Cornwall's chaps could easily be identified by the green berets of the Light Infantry. Whereas all of the other berets were black.

A corporal shouted to us from the end of the platform: 'Make your way to the side entrance,' and waved his arm to point the way. Once there, we found five trucks ready and waiting to take us to our new residence. We noisily climbed aboard and set off in convoy through the town of Minden.

It seemed only minutes before we were going through the gates of the barracks. The sentry on guard duty looked blue with cold. It was freezing out there. The ground was tightly packed with snow, and icicles hung like sharp, glistening barbs all along the gates. The trucks came to a halt in front of a massive block of billets. Tired, shivering, and feeling far from home, we were led inside, then up to the second floor, where we were told to grab a bed space.

John managed to secure a place beside me. We were glad to have each other's company. Before we had time to remove our great-coats, a corporal informed us that there was a hot meal awaiting us in the cookhouse. 'It's the big block at the end of the square,' he told us. 'And don't forget, you are in "A" Company now . . . I don't want any of you getting lost on your first night here.'

We made our way to the cookhouse, our boots crunching and slipping on the freezing snow, and the cold biting into our bones. We were glad of the warmth as we entered the huge building. We learnt later that it seated a thousand men.

We hesitated as we stepped inside, feeling a bit lost. A cook called out to us, 'Over here! We've been waiting for you lot. We want to finish and be off, so get a move on!'

We quickly lined up with our plates and received mashed spud from one cook, corned beef from another, and peas from yet another. A fourth cook ladled custard into a bowl and dropped a spoonful of red jam into its centre.

At the end of the long counter stood an oversized urn of sugary tea, from which we all helped ourselves. It wasn't as sumptuous as our last meal on the train, but we were all very hungry, so it went down a treat.

In small groups we left the cookhouse and found the way back to our new billets. We each had a steel locker for our kit, and a small bedside table with one drawer and a cupboard beneath. I unpacked my kit and put it away, then hastily made the bed. By that time, the bugler out on the square was blowing 'Lights Out'. I scrambled into bed and promptly dropped off to sleep.

The next thing I remember was the bugler playing reveille and someone going from room to room shouting, 'Wakey, wakey! Out of bed!'

After breakfast we were all ordered to the gym to be allocated our respective duties. Officers from different platoons were there to determine our suitability for a wide range of military tasks. It was a little like a slave market, I thought. I could ride a motorbike, so the captain from the mortar platoon in 'Support Company' bagged me for a dispatch rider. My mate, John, was to be a 3-ton lorry driver. We grabbed our gear and reported to 'S' Company, which was to be our home for the next twelve months.

I settled into army life and quite enjoyed it. Every week we had a cross-country race of about ten miles or so. Everyone in the camp, including the officers, was expected to take part. It was on one of these runs that I managed to finish twelfth. I was tired and exhausted, but felt very proud. There must have been at least eight hundred men running that day, so I felt that I had excelled myself.

When the CSM handed me my finishing disc and asked my

name, he enquired whether I was a brother of Jack Rundle. I replied that I was. Apparently, he had been Jack's sergeant in Greece some years earlier. Jack had been one of their finest runners. The CSM probably had the same high hopes of me, but sadly I was nowhere near Jack's class. 'We will soon have you up with the leaders, my boy,' he said confidently.

I smiled but said nothing. My love was boxing, not running!

My mother wrote to me about every ten days or so. Every so often I would find a neatly folded seven-and-sixpenny postal order tucked inside the letter. It wasn't easy for her as times were hard, but I was extremely thankful. At that time I was earning just three pounds a week. And one pound of this would be put into an army saving scheme, which was called 'Credits'. Our savings could be drawn at a week's notice, which at times came in very handy.

I remember on one occasion I was bawled out for wearing a dirty belt on parade. I thought my turnout was immaculate, which it probably was, but there was some labouring to be done down in the gym. Four of us failed the inspection and were ordered to report there at 1800 hours. Our task was to clean the floors, for seven nights in a row. On the second night I was on my knees scrubbing, when the staff sergeant strode in with a boxer in tow. Following along behind them were two more men dressed in track suits. The boxer moved away from the rest of the group, shrugged off the towel which covered his muscled shoulders, and started to give the punch-bag a hard time. I watched him carefully, whilst keeping one eye on my scrubbing brush. After a few minutes he moved on to do some shadow boxing. This fellow was good. The chap working beside me whispered, 'He was an ABA champion in civvy street. He's training for the BAOR finals.'

The scrubbing brush was soon forgotten. My whole body tingled with excitement as I watched him duck and weave, and throw powerfully sharp punches at an imaginary opponent. I froze for a moment as the sergeant's loud voice brought me guiltily back down to earth. It was only when I realised that he was not interested in me, but was addressing the boxer that I began to breathe more easily.

'It's getting late. He's not coming.' The sergeant glanced at his watch, then picked up the boxer's towel and handed it to him.

The boxer slung the towel over his shoulder and glared at the sergeant. 'But, I must have some ring practice! What does he think he's playing at?' he growled.

Without really thinking, I rose from my knees and, in a voice which sounded alien to me, said, 'I'll volunteer to spar with you.'

There was a stunned silence as they all turned to stare at me. The staff sergeant was first to speak: 'What's your name, lad?'

'Rundle, Staff.'

He stepped closer. 'Can you box?'

'A little. I did some boxing in the army cadets and I trained with a professional for a while.'

One of the track suited characters spoke up: 'Have you any experience at club level?'

'No, but I have been in the ring many times with a Cornish professional.'

'And where, might I ask, would this have taken place?'

'In a converted barn.'

He started to turn away before I had finished. I stood with humiliation written all over me as the sporting group spoke softly together. I was about to drop down on my knees to resume my scrubbing when the staff sergeant called me over.

'Let's have a good look at you. What's your weight, lad?'

'Ten four, Staff.'

'A welterweight, eh? Hmm, you aren't afraid to tackle our champion then?' He studied me from top to toe.

Averting my eyes from the men in track suits, I smiled gratefully. 'No, Staff. I'll do my best.'

'I'm sure you will, my lad. Strip down to your vest and we'll put the gloves on you.'

I knew then that I would soon be facing the champ, which would be better than scrubbing floors. Or would it?

The sergeant acted as referee. He called us to the centre of the ring and said to me, 'Any time you want to quit, just raise your right hand. I will then stop the fight. Understood, Rundle?'

Nervously I nodded. The ref moved out of the way and ordered the fight to begin.

Almost at once the champ caught me with a stinging left to the side of my head, just to let me know who was boss in there. I backed swiftly away, making sure my chin was safely behind my guard. Just in time, he was back after me in a flash. Left and right to the head, and a stabbing jab into my ribs before he eased back a little. I sprung forward with a straight left to his head, closely followed by a right hook into his midriff. We were now in close, pulling and shoving, neither of us willing to let the other one go until the ref decided it was time to pull us apart. We had tested each other, and for the rest of the round we swapped punches and treated each other with a little more respect. Especially as we both now knew that we were quite evenly matched. I was glad to hear the bell.

As I sat in my corner, trying desperately to get my second wind, I noticed the champ receiving advice and getting all the attention. I was just the humble sparring partner. My scrubbing pals gave me the thumbs-up and grinned enthusiastically. At least I had someone on my side. The ref called the second round.

Before I could get my rhythm going again, the champ showered me with several stinging blows. I breathed deeply and managed to gain my composure enough to force him back and onto the ropes. The ref intervened and parted us. Then the champ was charging towards me like a raging bull. From deep within my mind I heard the voice of my old Cornish trainer: 'Hit him when he's coming forward and you'll hit him twice as hard.' I unleashed a vicious straight left at the same instant as he was going to land one on my shoulder. It caught him full on the nose and stopped him in his tracks. I sprang forward to maximise my advantage but the staff was between us like a flash.

'Stop!' he yelled frantically.

My opponent was standing with blood streaming down his nose and chin, looking shocked and sheepish.

'That's it for tonight . . . we can't take any risks. The finals are in just over a week's time. Oh, and by the way, well done, lad. You've proved you can box.' The sergeant shook my gloved hand before hurrying over to tend to his wounded champion.

The men in the track suits seemed friendlier now and helped me off with the gloves. I dressed back into my work clothes and picked up my scrubbing brush to carry on with the floor cleaning. Then a timely word from the sergeant came as a great relief:

'Leave that, lad. Get yourself a shower.'

'Thanks, Staff.'

'And I don't want to see you down here with that bloody brush again, right?'

'Right, Staff.'

As I passed my busy workmates their good-natured gibes of 'crafty bugger' and 'bloody shirker' brought a smile to my rapidly stiffening lips. Saluting them with my upturned thumb, I headed for the shower room.

Chapter Four

The days and weeks hastened by and I was well on my way to becoming a trained *Infantryman.* Each week, through some strange quirk of luck, and perhaps a lot of effort, I managed to get placed among the first twenty of the battalion's cross-country runners. It was hard work though. I felt that I wasn't really cut out to become a runner.

One day, while reading the Company orders on the noticeboard, I had a shock. The names of the men picked to run cross-country in Berlin were proudly displayed for all to see, and down at the bottom of the list I became aware of my own name silently staring back at me. In disbelief I looked again. Yes, there it was; my eyes hadn't been playing tricks with me. Admittedly, I was placed in the reserve position, but at least I had the pleasure of an exciting trip to look forward to.

The next few weeks were filled with regular and strenuous training for the chosen men. Even when the great day arrived most of it was spent working out. But eventually, at eight o'clock that evening, we were all paraded outside the HQ block where we were picked up by truck and taken to Minden railway station. From there we would catch the troop train coming from the Hook of Holland.

The train slithered and steamed its way to a standstill. We all stood back while a myriad of troops spilled out on to the platform, shivering and pulling their coat collars up tightly to their ears against the bitter cold. Some would glance hesitantly this way or that, before scurrying off along the platform; others strode out with confidence, having done it before. As soon as the open carriage doors came into view we all made a dash to get aboard and out of the piercing cold. There were plenty of empty seats waiting for us, and I for one was glad to sit down and make myself comfortable. The compartment felt homely and lived in, as the presence of its last occupants was still with us in the warm, stale and smoky atmosphere. I closed my eyes to savour the moment, and felt the trembling of the train as it slowly steamed out of the station. As usual, some of the men started to play cards. It seemed that wherever they were they could produce a pack, and in no time at all would be playing in earnest. Outside it was dark. I couldn't watch the countryside go by, so I closed my eyes and was gradually lulled to sleep by the rhythmic motion of the train.

I was rudely awakened by the screeching of brakes. The train had stopped. One of the card-sharps had wiped a section of condensation from the window, and with his hands cupped to shield his eyes from the inner light was peering intently into the blackness.

'Nothing to see,' he reported, but we heard a commotion in the corridor. It was two stewards, working their way through the train, pulling down the blinds as they went. They informed us in no uncertain terms that we were not to touch the blinds again until we were through the Communist sector and safely in West Berlin! It was with growing trepidation that we continued on our way.

'What if we break down?' some joker piped up. 'We'll be stranded in the midst of all these Russians.'

As we rumbled on into the night, I noticed that the cards were put away. We were all feeling distinctly uneasy. Some of the old hands enjoyed telling us weird tales of what went on in countries such as this. I did wonder whether it was all true, or whether their imaginations were working overtime. Then the train was slowing to a stop once more.

We all sat quietly waiting; no one felt like talking. I strained my ears, listening for anything that might provide a clue as to what was happening.

After a while our curiosity got the better of us. The chap next to me volunteered to take a sneaky look out from under the blind. Stooping low, he carefully inched up the blind to give himself the merest of cracks to see through. 'Hell!' His voice was a shocked whisper. 'What a grim looking station. It's deserted!'

'No wonder,' I replied. 'It's nearly two in the morning.'

He was about to pull down the blind when something caught

his eye. 'Wait a minute,' he said. 'Two soldiers with guns are walking along the platform!'

I couldn't constrain myself any longer. I had to take a look. Crouching down beside him, I squinted through the tiny gap. I saw what he meant. Grim wasn't the word for it. It looked freezing cold and evil out there.

Looking tall and forbidding in greatcoats which almost touched their ankles, the two armed soldiers were nearly upon us. Their heads were encased in thick fur hats, and the hands which menacingly gripped the rifles across their chest were covered in the same black fur. A shiver went through me as an image of a werewolf passed through my mind. Hastily we leapt back from the window, for fear of being spotted.

After a few minutes, with our heartbeat returning to normal, we ventured another peek. The Russian soldiers had passed us by, and behind them the scene was left as deserted and forbidding as before. We were kept waiting at this desolate spot for ages. Although it probably seemed longer to us because we were all keyed up and nervous. Eventually the train started to move. Everyone gave a sigh of relief, and within the hour we were in West Berlin.

The city's drab, wet streets were deserted. It was still early morning and the inhabitants were probably still enjoying the comfort of their beds. It saddened us to see the havoc that had been caused by the allies during the war. The grey bomb-blasted ruins told their own pitiful story. The bus fell silent as we all reflected on the stark realities of the Second World War.

The bus drew up in front of a spectacular white-pillar-fronted building. We had been informed earlier that our billets would be in the competitors' quarters of the 1936 Olympic Games stadium. We had expected something special, but we weren't prepared for this. It was magnificent, and I for one felt very privileged to be staying there. We entered the spacious foyer and were led immediately up the grand stairway to our rooms.

I washed and shaved in the luxurious warmth of the bathroom, then met up with the rest of the team for breakfast in the dining room. After we had eaten, the officer-in-charge of our party came in with a list of the names of those who would be running. I was more than grateful to find that I was still listed as a reserve.

An officer gave the usual pep talk to fire-up the runners, then, informing us that the race would start at noon, gave us permission to walk around the stadium. Most of the team decided to explore, even though they would need every scrap of energy later on. It was too good a chance to miss. Tagging along with the others, I was dumbstruck most of the time. Never had I seen anything on such a grand scale as this. We passed sports fields, running tracks, swimming pools, and tennis courts, each one more immaculately kept than the last. Eventually we came to the perimeter wall of the Olympic Stadium itself. We walked up a ramp and peered through the huge iron gates. A shiver coursed through my body as I gazed in wonderment at the sight before me. The stadium was a vast and daunting place. Empty and silent now, but as I stood there I could imagine the roar of the crowds. The atmosphere was still electrifying. I will never forget that moment.

Sadly for us, the DCLI failed to perform well in the race. My name wasn't called to run, so all in all I had enjoyed a cushy trip. In the early hours of the next morning, with our tails between our legs, we were on our way back to Minden. Over the next few months the usual training exercises continued. Sometimes we went up north to open country, where the forces had huge firing ranges and training grounds. At times our stay would last for two or three weeks, firing three-inch mortars and taking part in manoeuvres with other regiments.

On occasion I would be sent back to our base camp for the mail. By evening everyone would be eagerly awaiting my return, hoping that I would bring them a letter or parcel from their loved ones at home. When we weren't training our weekends would be spent in the barracks.

Sometimes on a Saturday I would take a walk down the hill to the town of Minden. It was a quaint old place with bumpy cobbled streets. The first thing that struck me was the atmosphere which was always thick with the pungent blue smoke of cigars. It seemed that no self-respecting adult would dare be seen without the comforting long cylinder of tobacco between his lips. The River Weser flowed through the town, and its banks were lined with poky little old-fashioned shops. My favourite shops were those that sold cuckoo clocks. They would be displayed all over the walls of the room, without an inch to spare. Every tiny bit of convenient space held a work of art. Hand carved, each one was slightly different from the rest, but the chorus of chirpy cuckoos that rent the air from time to time were all of one voice. Tobacconist shops, as to be expected, also abounded in this picturesque little town. Their speciality was weird and wonderful smokers' pipes, handcrafted out of wood. I made up my mind to select one as a present for my father when I went home on leave.

On the eve of that great day I was pleased to learn that another chap from Camborne in Cornwall was also due home, so I would have a travelling companion for the entire journey. That evening I went down to the town to buy one of those special pipes for my father. The rich aroma of cigars and tobacco greeted me as I entered the warm, homely shop. The shopkeeper was busy serving a handful of customers, which gave me a wonderful opportunity to browse. It took me a good half hour to select the pipe, but I enjoyed every minute of it. The proprietor told me that he had been to England many years ago and had many fond memories of his stay there. I was telling him about my home county when his wife brought him out a cup of coffee. He was so wrapped up in our conversation that he asked her to fetch another cup for me. As we drank our coffee, I asked him who had made the many pipes which adorned his shop. Proudly, his eyes swept the room. 'I make the pipes. All my own work!' Pointing to a door behind him, he said, 'That is where I create my supplies.' He placed his cup on the counter and proceeded to show me a very long stemmed pipe with exquisite carvings on the bowl. He caressed it with his long fingers. 'Cherry wood . . . yes.'

I nodded as I ran my fingers over his masterpiece. It was superb.

Carefully, he put it back in its place, and I was then treated to a private display of many more of his superb products. Our conversation turned to cigarettes. I took out a pack of *Senior Service* and offered him one. I wasn't a heavy smoker but I always carried a packet or two with me, as our cigarettes were eagerly sought after by the Germans. They were duty free and we had a ration of six packets a week from the NAAFI. He took a cigarette and sniffed the tobacco. 'Very good,' he remarked gratefully.

I helped myself to one and patted my pockets for a match. The pipe-maker indicated a large wooden pipe resting in a stand on the counter. When he pressed the side of the bowl, a flame appeared – yet another clever idea from the master craftsman. To my surprise he then beckoned for me to follow him through the back door and into his workshop.

The room was small and dusty, but here, as in the shop, no space had been wasted. The small, high placed window was opaque with years of dust and grime, but with the flick of a switch, a powerful bulb which hung over a well-worn and littered work bench soon illuminated the room's deep secrets. My feet sank into the springy carpet of sawdust and wood shavings as I followed my host into his special domain. Over the bench were scores of racks from which hung an array of narrow strips of wood. 'For the stems,' he proudly informed me.

Another wide shelf accommodated scores of crude little bowls, all waiting their turn to be carved into something special for the discerning customer.

In the far corner stood an old stove with a heavy black saucepan on top. The sickly, sweet smell of glue that was simmering away merrily in the pan made me feel slightly nauseous as I passed by, but the feeling soon disappeared as I was led onwards to see the pipes that were near to completion, and the special tobaccos that would eventually fill their bowls. Smelling the tobacco, I was reminded of the time when I was a boy, and of sailors coming home on leave with plugs of tobacco which they had made out of leaves and rum. These would be held together and tied with cord. They smelt nearly as bad as they looked, and I remember how my eyes would water and my throat would sting if I was anywhere near them when they lit up.

When it was finally time for me to take leave of that little shop, I think the pipemaker was sorry to see me go. He had enjoyed showing me around his kingdom, as much as I had enjoyed the privilege of being there.

I set off back up the hill to the barracks, clutching the paper bag with the precious pipe inside. There weren't many people abroad that night. Just a sprinkling of soldiers who passed me by on their journey down to the town, probably with the hopes of having a few beers in one of the local taverns. Walking alone up the hill after dark was a strange and eerie experience. On my left was nothing but a dark wilderness, but across the road, tram garages spewed their lights to illuminate my way for a few yards. Then, abruptly, it was pitch black again – just a long and lonely stretch of waste ground. My boots clattered hurriedly onward until a little further in the distance I could see the welcoming lights of the Military Police headquarters. It was just a rather large house, with usually a few open topped jeeps waiting outside at the ready. Normally the place would give me the shivers, but tonight I was glad it was there.

Some minutes later, having passed the redcap's HQ, I thought I heard someone shouting up ahead. I stopped for a moment to listen, and my heart started to thump wildly as I realised, with all the yelling and shouting that was going on, that there was a serious fight taking place. Almost on tip-toe, so as not to be conspicuous, I edged slowly forward, and as I drew nearer, my fears were realised. This was no innocent skirmish. In the gloom I could just see the figures of four men. They were oblivious of me as they kicked and shouted at a shapeless lump lying on the ground beneath them. My instinct told me to keep walking, then I happened to see a beret lying nearby. The victim was one of us! Without thinking, I was halfway across the tarmac; in seconds I would be amongst them. My brain started to race. How best to attack them? Which one first? My fist had automatically clenched as I drew alongside.

Sensing my approach, one of the louts turned to face me. I realised these bullies were German youths when he called to his friends for assistance. For a split-second my eyes rested on the lifeless bundle on the ground. The battered face was streaked in blood. With sickening horror I realised they may have killed him! In a blind rage, I swung out my arm and caught one of them on the side of his face, sending him sprawling. Grabbing another tightly round the neck from behind, I yanked him backwards and held him in an iron grip. He would serve as protection for the front of my body. The other two were now somewhere behind me. I gasped for air as I swung my captive this way and that in order to dodge the stinging kicks which tried to knock my knees from under me. I held my ground and tightened my grip on my German shield. The blows from behind suddenly ceased, and they both stood silent and evil in front of me. My blood turned to ice as a knife was expertly drawn from its sheath and pointed to my face. My mouth grew dry, as even in the gloom I could see the glint of the cold, razor-sharp blade. Fear made me swing my captive assailant into the path of the weapon as it lunged towards me. He squealed with fright and jabbered hysterically to his mates, who regardless of his desperate plight, never gave an inch.

From the corner of my eye I saw that the first thug I had hit was now on his feet. My heart sank. I couldn't hold out much longer.

Suddenly the scene around me seemed much clearer and more distinct. Relief flooded my body as I realised the light came from a vehicle's headlamps, still distant, but approaching rapidly. I was not the only one who had spotted that we were expecting company. I was dimly aware of a sharp pain in my leg, then I felt a heavy blow to the back of my head and fell forward into a bottomless black void.

'Lie still, soldier.' The echoing voice vibrated through a long tunnel. I needed to move; my whole body felt stiff. A hand was gently placed on my arm. 'Lie still, soldier, an ambulance is on its way. You have a knife wound in your leg.' The voice sounded closer now. Then it all came rushing back to me. I opened my eyes. A medic was bent over me. 'You are in an ambulance, on your way to the RAF hospital in Rintein. You're lucky – you have a stab wound in your leg but you'll live to tell the tale.'

'The other chap! How is he?' I was almost too afraid to ask.

'I'll be OK, Pete.'

The voice from the other stretcher sounded weak but vaguely familiar. 'John, is that you?'

'Yes.' His voice faltered. 'The sods would have killed me if you hadn't turned up when you did.'

'You're both damned lucky,' the medic said.

We both spent a few weeks in hospital. Initially we felt the pain and soreness of our wounds and were content to just lie down and be pampered. But as our scars and memories faded, we couldn't wait to get back to our usual routine. There were several visits from both the German police and the Redcaps. Statements had to be made. Forms had to be filled in. Descriptions of our attackers were required. We weren't much help in that quarter though; the cover of night had made sure of that. We learnt that the headlights which had shown up at that vital moment belonged to a jeep driven by one of the MPs. We couldn't have been in better hands, although by the time the jeep had arrived at the scene our assailants had vanished into the darkness. Our rescuer came to see us. Although we were pleased to be able to thank him personally and were both very grateful, it didn't alter the fact that both of us felt uncomfortable in his presence. I was just wishing he would leave when he drew out a small and tatty brown paper bag from his pocket. 'Does this belong to either of you?'

In his hand was my father's pipe. Gosh! I had forgotten all about it. I told him that it was mine, and recounted the story behind it.

He studied it carefully. 'I can see it's a good one, but I'm afraid the stem has been broken.' He showed me the damage, then asked me the name of the shop. Then, much to my surprise, he promised to take the pipe back to the shop to have it mended. And it was a promise he kept.

So some of the Redcaps were human, after all.

Chapter Five

It was a time of change. Some sixth sense told me that everything would be different after that night of violence, but just how different was to prove a shock even to me. Much to the chagrin of our workmates, John and I were put on light duties for a couple of weeks after we had been discharged from the hospital, then I was due a spot of home leave. After a pleasant but all too brief interlude with my family and friends in Cornwall, I returned to Minden to learn that my battalion was being posted to the Caribbean. The downside of this was that those of us with only twelve months to serve were to be transferred to another regiment in Germany. After another medical to see if I was fit enough to stay in the infantry I was passed Al, and John and I joined a unit of the King's Shropshire Light Infantry at Gottingen, some sixty-five miles south of Minden.

Our new billet was divided into small rooms, each of which slept four men. I was placed with three chaps from Shrewsbury. I noticed a wireless in the room, and was informed by my new room-mates that it was rented from a shop in the town. It cost them three marks a week, and if I paid a share it would cost each of us seventy-five pfennigs. They were all more than pleased when I told them that I would gladly pay my share.

A week later I heard on the grapevine that our storeman was soon to be demobbed. It was a job which I had always fancied, so without too much hope I put my name forward for the vacancy. The stores were situated in a large cellar, and housed everything the army required. Even the three-inch mortar guns were stored there, under lock and key. The storeman's job was to sleep in the stores and keep his eye on things. It was quite a responsible job.

The army would have taken a very dim view if anything went missing. Much to my surprise I was chosen for the job, and within a matter of days I had moved into my solitary billet. The one thing I really missed was the company of the wireless. There was no way I could have afforded all of the rental by myself, so after almost being driven mad by the silence, I decided to pay a visit to the wireless shop in the hope of finding something really cheap.

I was lucky. Understanding my predicament, and after much mumbling and sighing, the shop-owner pulled out a rather dilapidated specimen from underneath the counter. He brushed away the cobwebs, and gently blew at the dust which had settled heavily into its cracks and corners, then turned the switch. Amazingly it worked, and sounded every bit as good as the one back in my old room. I was delighted when he told me I could rent it for one mark, fifty pfennigs, which I was just able to afford.

I quite enjoyed being on my own down in the stores. The days proved busy but I swiftly adapted to my new routine and actually enjoyed the change. Little did I know then that much more drastic changes awaited me.

From time to time I would visit the chaps back in my old room for a good old gossip and chin-wag. It was on one of these occasions that someone mentioned that they were a few weeks behind with the wireless rent. Mine too was due to be paid, so I volunteered to take their monies and settle both accounts at the same time. The next day was a Saturday, so I would be free to take a stroll down into the town and get the rents sorted out.

So the following morning I checked my cap badge and the brasses on my belt, making sure they were gleaming. Everyone had to book out at the guardroom before being allowed to leave the camp, which meant passing the Guard Commander's inspection. On that particular morning my turnout was up to scratch, and twenty minutes later I found myself wandering the streets of Gottingen. It reminded me very much of Minden. Several cuckoo clock shops, and tobacconist's by the score. Even the smoke-tainted air smelt the same. We had been warned to keep to the main thoroughfare when alone. It could lead to bad trouble if we ventured into the dimly-lit back streets. I would certainly take heed of the warning; I had already had my fair share of street problems.

I came upon a small kiosk selling a variety of newspapers,

books and confectionery. Glancing through the magazines, I found they were all foreign to me – except the girlie pin-up mags, which look the same in any language. There was one other person beside myself browsing through the papers. A down at heel, dowdy-looking woman. A shawl which had seen better days covered her head, and a long, dark grey coat which met with what looked like hob-nailed boots, encased her feet. I paid her scant attention as I pointed to some chocolate, then handed some money to the man behind the counter. He handed me my purchase and then the change. I had a strong feeling that I had been given the wrong change, so holding it in my hand, I studied it and tried to work out whether it was correct or not.

The woman beside me glanced quickly at the money, then pointing to my hand, spoke to the trader. I realised then, that she was just a young woman. The man angrily snapped back at her, and looked daggers at me. There was another burst of German from her, then he threw the rest of my change as hard as he could towards me, where it went spinning and rolling in every direction.

As I stooped to pick it up, the girl started to help me. 'He tried to cheat you,' she said, speaking very good English. She handed me the rest of the coins and started to walk away.

'Fraulein!' I called, moving to follow her.

She stopped and turned, her eyes flashing with disapproval. 'Not Fraulein . . ! I am Polish!'

I was taken aback. Quick – say something! My brain worked overtime. 'I wanted to thank you for helping me back there,' I stammered like a guilty child.

This time she smiled. Her smile was beautiful, in such contrast to the shabby garb she was wearing. 'I was happy to be of help to you,' she said.

By this time I was standing alongside her. I took her gloved hand. 'Thank you once again; it was kind of you to look after me.' I suddenly realised that I was in a strange part of the town and wasn't sure which street to take for the wireless shop. The name of the street and shop was written on the front of the rent book. I showed it to the girl and asked her if she could direct me there.

She studied the address and smiled again. 'Come with me. I too, also visit this shop.'

As we walked together along the cobbled street, I asked her where she had learned to speak such good English.

'In Poland, and in . . .' She hesitated, then said, 'My grandmother could speak English.'

We had turned down a side street, and just around the corner stood the dingy wireless shop. She stood aside for me to enter first. Then I heard my mother's voice, 'Ladies first, Pete.' I opened the door and gallantly ushered my new-found friend inside.

The shop was as dreary on the inside as it was on the outside. It was strange, but I hadn't really taken any notice of it before. There were bare boards on the floor, and a long dusty counter which also served as a workbench. Everywhere one looked, there were valves and odd bits of wire, and strewn here and there were skeletons of ancient wireless sets. The old man was absent today. Instead a buxom woman in a faded patterned apron, and with her grey hair combed into a bun which sat comfortably on the top of her head, waited to serve us. She looked as if she knew the girl, and spoke to her in German. The girl handed over three separate lots of marks which, after checking each pile, the shop woman entered into a well-thumbed ledger.

Then it was my turn. I passed over the individual cards and rents. All the while the two women were busy jabbering away in German. The shop woman marked the ledger and initialled my cards, then handed them back to me with a smile.

The girl said something to the woman on the way out, and I nodded my farewell.

Outside, the girl told me she had been acquainted with the wireless shop for a time. She had become quite friendly with the old couple. The lady who had served us was the wife of the proprietor. 'Sometimes I forget they are German,' she sadly added.

Suddenly I felt that I didn't want to leave this girl – not just yet. So, thinking quickly, I asked her if she would like a cup of tea.

'I am afraid I do not drink tea very often . . . unlike the English. But I would like some coffee.'

Feeling delighted, I asked her if she knew of a place that served coffee. She thought for a moment. 'Yes, I will take you there.' Self-consciously, we walked together in silence, until we came to what appeared to be an ordinary dwelling place. 'We go in, yes?' Her hand was already opening the door.

I followed her inside. Although it looked like a normal home, with a large open fire, and a sideboard littered with ornaments, a fine cuckoo clock taking pride of place on one wall, there were a few too many tables and chairs for the average household. There weren't many customers; just two old-timers sitting close to the fire, with their half-filled tankards of ale within easy reach. The girl motioned for me to sit in a corner of the tavern, a little distance away from the men.

My teeth juddered as we pulled out the chairs, and they scraped across the hard flagstone floor. When I had made myself comfortable, I glanced over at the two old chaps hugging the fire. They were peering at us thoughtfully. When I raised my hand to acknowledge them, they returned the gesture with a smile, then promptly lost interest in us as they reached for their glasses again. The landlord came over to take our order.

The girl whispered, 'I do not think you will drink tea here. Perhaps you will take beer?'

I told her, 'Yes, that would be fine.'

She ordered in German, and away he went.

I took out my packet of *Senior Service* cigarettes and offered her one. 'English!' she exclaimed. 'I cannot refuse one.'

It was a new packet, and as I have mentioned, I smoked very little and mainly carried them for barter. Consequently I was without matches. I glanced at the two across the room. They were now lustfully eyeing my packet of fags and almost drooling.

I pushed back my chair and strode over to them, holding out the open packet. Eagerly they helped themselves, and I indicated to them that I was without matches. One of them fumbled into his pocket and extracted an ancient lighter. With a shaky hand he proceeded to light my cigarette. I took a long puff to make sure it was alight, then returned to the girl waiting at the table.

I held my cigarette towards hers. As she leant across the table her hand gently covered mine to steady it. At the same time, her eyes met mine. They were a wonderful ocean green. She had draped her scarf over her shoulders, and her long blonde hair hung loosely down her back . . . and that smile! But she was painfully thin. My heart was beating overtime in that split second before she pulled away. The landlord was striding towards us with our drinks on a tray. He placed the coffee on the table in front of the girl, and the foaming beer was set down in front of me. I held out some marks and pfennigs in the palm of my hand

and the girl pointed to the coins I should give him. He dropped them into his apron pocket and headed over to his other two customers.

I took a sip of beer and lowered the tankard to the table. 'My name is Peter Rundle,' I told her. 'I am from Cornwall – a county in England.'

She smiled that wonderful smile again. 'My name is Katrinka . . . Katrinka Wazda.'

I took her hand across the table. 'I am very happy to have met you, Katrinka.' Reluctant to release her hand, I asked her if she was in Germany on vacation.

'No,' came her quiet reply, but she did not elaborate further. We chatted on with ease for a while, but I learned nothing more about her. I just knew her name and homeland. She finished her coffee and covered her head with the shawl.

'I must go now,' she said softly as she rose from her seat.

I followed her out of the tavern, nodding to the two old men who were still sat by the fire. They smiled ruefully back as their hopes of another English cigarette vanished through the doorway.

Katrinka took my hand. 'Goodbye, Peter. I thank you for the coffee.' She turned and started to walk away.

I called after her, 'I will be here next Saturday to pay my rent. Will you?'

She stopped and turned to face me. 'I will be here, if I have money.' Then she turned and hurried away.

Chapter Six

The first few days of the following week were taken up on a border patrol. We returned to camp late on Thursday, and spent all of Friday cleaning the scores of dirty pots and pans which had been used in the mobile cookhouse.

Saturday morning was the usual battalion parade. It was the Regimental Sergeant Major's favourite day. He would march up and down the ranks, his chest thrust out like a bantam cock, ranting and raving at all and sundry. On a bad day he would find an excuse to have one or two of the lads marched off to the guardroom and locked in the cells for a few hours. After the RSM had done his bit, the Commanding Officer would ride onto the scene and take the parade. Sitting stiffly on his horse, his steady gaze never missed a trick. You could have heard a pin drop in the silence of the parade ground, because we were all afraid to move a muscle, and hardly dared to breathe.

It was bitterly cold, but the parade was over by 12.30 and I headed straight for the wireless shop.

As I entered the scruffy little store my heart fell. It was empty except for the proprietor who was busy fixing something at his counter. I sorted out the different rents while he thumbed through the pages of his ledger. I was wholly engrossed in making the monies tally when a voice from behind me gave me quite a start.

'Good day, Peter Rundle.'

I swung round and there was Katrinka. She was sitting in a gloomy corner of the shop. How I hadn't noticed her, I can't imagine. My heart pounded with elation as I walked towards her. 'You came, Katrinka.' I took her hand in mine.

'Yes.' Her voice was the merest whisper as she rose from her seat. I stood transfixed in my own little world, just drinking in the beauty of the girl stood before me.

'It is polite to kiss a Polish girl's hand when you have meeting,' she said smilingly.

The wireless man broke into my thoughts with his broken English. 'Here we have it,' he claimed, tapping his ledger. And when I turned to face him, he grinned and nodded his head towards Katrinka, so I took her gloved hand and kissed the back of it. 'That is good,' he said, looking very pleased with himself.

I don't know who blushed the most, Katrinka or me . . . but it was nice. As we were leaving, the old German shouted and held up my rent cards. I had forgotten them in my excitement.

We walked round the town looking in the shop windows as we passed by. I didn't take in much of my surroundings, as I could think of little else other than the girl walking beside me. As in Minden, the place abounded with cuckoo clocks. They really did fascinate me. I said to her, 'When I have a home of my own someday, I will have a cuckoo clock to remind me of Germany.'

'And will it remind you also of me?' she asked coyly.

I looked admiringly at this shabbily dressed Polish girl. 'I will never need a clock to remind me of you, Katrinka.'

We came across a small park and rested on one of its cold wooden benches. Probably in the warm months this little park would come alive with many coloured blooms that struggled even now for life under the carpet of freezing snow. The few evergreens which were dotted here and there helped to relieve the starkness of this cold white world. We sat quietly for a while, watching the occasional warmly-clad passer-by, then Katrinka broke the silence. 'Will you spend your life in the Army?'

'Hell no!' I said. 'I am just a National Serviceman.' I explained to her that men of eighteen were required to enlist into one of the three armed services for two years. I told her that I had only just recently been posted here to the KSLI, and that previously I had been stationed in Minden. I added that I had now completed half of my service. I then asked her in what part of the town did she live. Did she live with her parents?

She told me her parents were killed in the war. Speaking in a whisper, she said, 'The Germans frighten me. My grandmother has looked after me and it was she who taught me to speak English.'

'She has done an 'ansome job,' I said.

She looked puzzled. 'I do not understand 'ansome' . . . what does it mean?'

'It's Cornish,' I laughed. 'Cornwall is right down at the bottom of England. We say funny things like that . . . 'ansome means it's lovely, like you.'

She blushed, 'I do not know of this Cornwall.'

I bent down and drew a rough outline of England in the snow. Then I pointed to the south western tip. 'That is Cornwall.'

Katrinka looked at the map, then at me. Then she burst out laughing. When she laughed her whole face lit up. 'It is 'ansome place, yes?'

It was lovely to see her happy. At times she seemed to have the weight of the world upon her slender shoulders. By this time we had started to feel the cold, so I took her hand and we strolled through the park and out into the street.

We were looking into a shop window when we were spotted by a corporal from my platoon, who happened to be passing with a few of his mates.

He looked directly at me, then glanced scornfully at the shabbily dressed girl by my side. Turning to his mates, he spoke in quiet undertones, to which they responded by laughing heartily. Then, glancing back in our direction and still highly amused, they continued on their way.

Katrinka's face looked troubled. 'That man – you are acquainted with him? I feel he is laughing at me.'

I felt mad, and I knew in my heart that it was so, but I tried to reassure her. 'No, of course not, they wouldn't laugh at you. But if he did, I can promise you that it will never happen again.'

When her eyes met mine, I saw her welling tears. I don't know what made me do it, but I took her in my arms and kissed her. I felt her arms going around my neck, my beret fell to the floor, then we parted for an instant, until I was kissing her again on her wet cheeks, her lips and her nose. I forgot where I was for a moment, until I suddenly felt the presence of a third party. Slowly and self-consciously we both turned to look. A cute, grubby-faced little boy was gazing up at us. He had picked up my beret and was patiently waiting for the right moment to hand it back to me. Digging deep into the pocket of my greatcoat, I found a mark which I placed into the palm of his tiny hand. He surprised me by saying 'thank you' before scooting off to the nearest sweetshop.

Katrinka said, 'Many children learn the English language.'

But I was still thinking of that wonderful kiss. 'I am sorry . . . I got carried away, I . . .'

She placed her hand to my lips to stop the words. 'Please do not be sorry. That was my first kiss, and it has been given to me by a Cornwall man.'

Laughing, I said, 'We are known as the Cornish.' Feeling dizzy with excitement, I took her hand and we wandered on our way. Several Germans eyed us with disapproval as we walked together hand-in-hand. They wouldn't know that Katrinka was Polish, and anyhow it didn't matter; nothing could banish the feeling of elation which was surging through my entire body. The air suddenly took on a pleasing aroma. Just a few yards ahead of us stood the source of the smell – a busy frankfurter café. Suddenly I felt hungry, and when Katrinka offered to buy me one I needed no second telling. I followed her in with undisguised eagerness. It was hot and steamy inside, which reminded me of our own English fish and chip shops. The lengthy counter stretched from wall to wall. Part of it housed a king-sized grill, from where thick clouds of greasy steam rose and buffeted the ceiling, before swirling back down amongst the customers, and then vanishing out through the open doorway. A tall man in a soiled, once white, apron, and with a face of a colour to match the well-cooked produce, stood behind the counter, busily tending to the spluttering cooker. Behind him were stacked heaped piles of soft, springy buns, all waiting their turn to encase the hot sizzling sausages.

Katrinka ordered for us in German, whereupon the man deftly made up the frankfurters, and we helped ourselves to some mustard. There was an array of pots of relish lined up on the counter, but not recognising their contents, I decided to stick with the mustard. Along another wall a wide ledge had been fitted, with high stools tucked neatly underneath. We availed ourselves of these and tucked in. The frankfurter was delicious, and the mustard, although milder than ours, really did it justice. In fact, I can still taste it . . . forty years on!

She put her hand in mine as we stepped out from the warm café. A little further along the street we came across one of the town's cinemas. Outside was a poster depicting a wild west scene and Katrinka asked if I enjoyed cowboy films. 'I love them,' I told her.

'You have seen this one?' she inquired. 'It is an English film with German subtitles.'

'No I haven't . . . so what are we waiting for, pard?'

'Dollars!' Katrinka said, as she pulled her hand out of her pocket, and opened it to reveal just a few pfennigs.

'How much is it?'

She studied the board of prices beside the pay-desk. 'One mark seventy at the front. Two marks fifty to have a seat further back.'

'And the back row?' I inquired with a cheeky grin.

She looked slightly bemused. 'It will be the same . . . in England it is different?'

I caught hold of her hand. 'Oh I'm just being silly. Come on, it will be nice to be inside where it's warm.' I started to lead her over to the pay kiosk, but she stopped and tried to pull back.

'I do not have money.'

'I have enough for both of us,' I assured her, handing the correct amount to the cashier. Katrinka was still protesting but the tickets were already shooting out of the machine towards us. She could do no other than hold my hand as we followed the usherette into the darkness of the cinema.

We clutched each other tightly as we stumbled down the steps. The beam from a torch displayed our two seats, about three rows from the back. It always makes me wonder why they have steps in cinemas, with it being so dark. I feel it's quite dangerous. The air was thick with cigar smoke. Even the projector light was struggling to penetrate the haze. When I glanced at Katrinka from the corner of my eye, she was watching me. I smiled and reached for her hand. She had taken her gloves off and her slender fingers felt warm to my touch. I held her hand throughout the film.

It was dark as we left the cinema. When I asked Katrinka if she would like another coffee, she declined at first, explaining that she had to get back. But my persistence paid off and we revisited the café we had patronised earlier. It was busier now, with the fireplace almost hidden by the warmth-seeking beer drinkers, but we managed to find a seat in a secluded corner, which suited us fine. We were happy in our own company.

Katrinka gave me a worried look. 'Will there be trouble for you, because of me?'

'Of course not,' I assured her. 'Anyhow, you are not German, are you?'

She was quite upset by that. 'Most certainly not! I have told you. Do you not believe me?'

'Of course I believe you. But the people who are in here tonight will know that I am English . . . do you think they will know you are Polish?'

She looked me straight in the eye. 'They will know what I am.'

The flustered landlord suddenly appeared, and Katrinka ordered coffee and a beer. I asked her what part of Poland she was from.

'Goleniow.' She spoke the word softly.

'Was it nice there?'

'I do not remember very much about it; I do remember it was close to the sea. I have not been there for a very long time. In fact my home is no longer there . . . it was destroyed in the war.'

Our coffee and beer was placed on the bare wooden table. Katrinka's coffee looked black and strong. She noticed me looking at it. 'Is English coffee different to this?'

'We put milk in ours,' I informed her.

She handed me her cup to take a sip. It was even worse than it looked. She chuckled when I grimaced. I took a big gulp out of my own glass. 'I'll stick to my beer,' I told her.

We sat cosily ensconced in the warm room, chatting and asking questions about each other, oblivious to what went on around us. But I was unable to discover where she lived. Whenever I broached the subject, she would skilfully evade it. Still, all in good time, I thought, she must have her reasons. The tavern was getting crowded and noisy with the effects of the many tankards of ale passing over the counter, so we decided it was time to go.

At the end of the street, Katrinka told me she would make her own way home. She seemed resolute, so I did not press her. But I was determined to try for another kiss. Taking her hand, I pulled her close. We were stood below an old gas lamp and in its peculiar light her lovely pale face was truly beautiful. She looked trustingly up at me as I bent towards her. I took it slowly this time, savouring every wonderful moment of her warm lips against mine. I wanted it to go on for ever, but all too quickly she broke away and said, 'I thank you, Peter Rundle, for taking me to the cinema, and for my time with you.'

The words came tumbling out of my mouth. 'It's Sunday tomorrow, can I see you in the afternoon? I don't have to work on Sundays.'

I felt like shinning up the lamp-post when she said, 'I will be happy to see you tomorrow.' Then she inquired, 'Do you go to church?'

I told her, 'Not normally, but when there is a church parade at the camp, we all have to go. Are you a church-goer, Katrinka?'

'Oh yes,' she promptly replied. 'I will be there early in the morning.'

I stole one last kiss, and we both went our separate ways.

Over the next few weeks we saw a great deal of each other. We were now hopelessly in love. There were times when things became awkward. Sometimes I was sent away at short notice and there was no way of letting her know. The army had to come first, but she understood my position and was always pleased to see me when I returned. When I wrote and told my family that I had fallen in love with a Polish girl named Katrinka, my mother answered my letter, saying how pleased they all were for me, but I was left with the impression that they all thought it was just an army romance.

The one fly in the ointment proved to be the corporal who had made fun of us in the town. He was forever taking the mick and saying things to annoy me. Because of his rank I could not retaliate, so the pressure between us was mounting. John warned me on several occasions, 'For God's sake don't hit him, or you will never be allowed into the town again.' That would mean I wouldn't be able to see Katrinka, so I had to control my fists, but it wasn't easy.

Our platoon sergeant had sensed that something was wrong. One day when we were all working out in the gym, he put the two of us together in the ring. We were well matched, both welterweights, but that wasn't why he paired us off. A buzz went around the gym. Most of them knew there was no love lost between Corporal Mulholand and myself. As I ducked through the ropes, I saw Mulholand grimly waiting for me in his corner. He was part Irish, from Liverpool. The both of us were typical Celts – dark, thickset and hairy. The PT sergeant, who was acting as ref, handed us our vests. Blue for me; white for him. By this time word had got round about the fight, and there was quite a crowd gathering. Some of the men had even sneaked off from their work, and I noticed a couple of cooks, who should have been in the kitchen, were stood in the front row, eagerly awaiting a bloody battle. The ref called our names and we both stood to attention in the middle of the ring. He told us to keep it clean.

'Go to your corners and come out fighting,' he ordered.

In the brief seconds that I waited for the bell I thought only of Katrinka, and of her beautiful smile. It didn't matter to me that she was poorly dressed. 'Now I will get my own back, my 'ansome,' I muttered to myself, then the bell sounded and Mulholand was at me like a roaring bull. A left and right to my head, even before I raised my guard. I back-pedalled furiously but he kept on coming. It was as if he had no boxing sense whatsoever. He fought like Rocky Marciano, his two hands held low, relying on his strength. As he ploughed straight into me I knew that I had to use the ring and box. Otherwise he was going to knock me senseless. The next time he rushed in, I sidestepped and managed to get to the middle. I had just managed to get my chin safely tucked behind my right guard when he was coming at me again. I rammed a straight left smack into his face. That gave him food for thought, but I still felt the force of his two punches on my shoulders. I knew he couldn't do a lot of damage there, so the bout took on a pattern. I boxed, and he fought like a street fighter. When the bell rang, and we made our way back to our corners I was thankful for the cold wet sponge on my face, and as I looked across to my rival, I could see that he was also grateful for the magic sponge. I took several deep breaths, and then we were at it again. Halfway through the second round he trapped me in a corner and gave me a painful hammering. Right – left! Right – left! He pummelled me with his fists, and all the while glaring at me with cold hostility. I felt it best to move in close and hang on, which I managed somehow to do. With my chin on his sweaty shoulder, I managed to turn him around before the ref stepped in and parted us. I had gained the precious seconds that I desperately needed. Mulholand thought he had me and rushed in again. This time I was waiting for him. I caught him a thumping right hook on the side of his nose. He staggered away, dazed, as a fine trickle of blood ran down his chin. By this time our audience was going mad. Shouting, cheering, whistling and booing – even professionals would have been proud of a reception such as this.

The timely bell sounded, and we both flopped gratefully down on to our stools.

The cool, refreshing sponge was once more administered. This time I winced as the dampness stung my skin, but it had the power to wake my senses. 'Keep calm and box,' my second said. 'He can't keep this up.' Then we were facing each other again, for the last round. I still felt like killing him, and I knew the feeling was mutual. The gym was full of excited infantry men, all waiting for the kill. We fought as before, no quarter asked or given. I used all my experience to try and knock him out, but he was a tough-nut indeed. I could feel my left eye closing, and Mulholand's face was a mess. But it was now the dying seconds of the final round, and there was no way the ref was going to stop it. He was on his way in again, but a lot slower now. I clipped him on the side of the jaw. Then the final bell sounded. It was all over.

A tremendous cheer went up from the crowd. The ref came over, took our hands and held them aloft. The contest was pronounced a draw!

Our gloves were removed, and the sergeant motioned for us to stay put in the centre of the ring. He called out for silence, then turning to us he said in a firm voice, 'I hope that both of you have got whatever it was between you completely out of your systems. Now shake hands.'

We looked at each other and shook hands, both bloody and utterly exhausted. From that moment on we treated each other with the uttermost civility.

Chapter Seven

When I met Katrinka on the following Saturday my face was still marked.

'Your face! What has happened to you?' Greatly alarmed, she tenderly smoothed the bruises with her fingers.

I gave her a kiss. 'Come on, let's find a seat, then I will tell you all about it.' We walked to the park and were lucky enough to find a seat inside a draughty shelter, where I proceeded to explain about the fight.

She listened with growing concern. 'It is because of me you have been injured.'

I cuddled her tightly. 'You mustn't think that, Katrinka. There are some people in this world who enjoy being nasty. Anyhow, we both shook hands afterwards and any bad feeling there was between us is now over. It was a good thing that it happened.'

It was bitterly cold that day. Our shelter did little to protect us, so we decided to go along to the wireless shop and pay our rents. Afterwards, there was always the warm tavern. It had started to snow heavily again. The shops looked bright, warm and welcoming, but there was one in particular which caught Katrinka's eye. It was a ladies' clothes shop. We stopped to have a better look. Katrinka was admiring a shawl in the centre of the display. It was a beautiful red and gold – the type of covering she always wore on her head, but hers had long seen better days. As we stood gazing into the window, our own reflections looked back at us. Katrinka, with her long, drab coat and boots, a faded scarf covering her head – an appealing waif and stray. Me smartly dressed in my army uniform. 'Don't we make a fine pair!' I gave her a squeeze.

'A fine pair? I do not understand.' She eyed me quizzically.

'You will,' I told her, and guided her into the shop. 'Why do we go into this shop? It is for women only.'

'I know.' And with that, I pointed to the shawl in the window, indicating to the assistant that I would like to see it.

As the girl was retrieving it from the window, Katrinka whispered, 'I cannot have this, I have no money. I do not wish for you to buy it – you have no money to spend on me.'

'I can, and I will,' I told her. 'My mother sent me a postal order this week, so I'm in the money.' I knew the price of the shawl – five marks, ninety five – I had noticed the price tag as we were looking in the window. The assistant reached for a bag but I politely took the shawl and passed it to Katrinka. She was still protesting as she placed it over her head, but the look on her face was worth every penny.

As we left the shop she stuffed her old scarf deep into her coat pocket, and when she drew back her hand, something dropped on to the snowy pavement. She moved quickly, her hand covering whatever it was that had fallen, before hurriedly thrusting it back into her pocket. It made me wonder what it was to make her so self-conscious. I had previously noticed that she kept one hand tucked inside her pocket whenever she could. Strange! But no matter. What *did* matter was that Katrinka stopped to look at her reflection in almost every shop window that we passed. Her eyes shone, and her face glowed with joy as she lovingly touched the shawl. 'Thank you, my Peter,' she said.

I looked at the scene around me and thought how beautiful everything looked, just like a Christmas card. I was so happy.

As we walked, I thought it might be a good moment to ask her why she never allowed me to walk her to her home at night. 'Are you ashamed to be going out with a British soldier?'

'Certainly not ashamed, you 'ansome,' she laughed, then she ran off, playfully gathering up snow as she went to use for ammunition against me. I wasn't going to learn any secrets today. For a little while we had fun in the snow, then I guided her into a dark shop doorway that had closed up for the weekend. The snow was now falling so thick and fast that passers-by were hidden from sight until they were within a couple of feet from us. I dusted the flakes off my coat and beret, undid my buttons and drew her close to my warm body. As our eyes met, so did our lips.

We kissed and embraced and happily let the rest of the world go by. Katrinka wanted to know what a postal order was.

I explained, 'It is a safe way to send money by post. Because I am the youngest of the family, my mother tends to spoil me a bit.' Then she wanted to know what 'spoil' meant. At times it wasn't easy, but then again, I couldn't speak Polish or German. I felt lucky to have met someone like Katrinka.

'By the way,' I tendered quietly, choosing what I thought to be the right moment, 'what do you carry in your pocket that you do not wish me to see?'

She blushed and looked away. 'It is of no importance to you.'

'Show me.'

She withdrew something from her pocket, and as her fingers unfurled I noticed a string of beads lying in the palm of her hand.

'Is it a rosary?' I asked. I had never seen one before. There weren't many Catholics at home amongst the clay tips.

'Yes.' She averted her gaze. 'I am a Catholic. Now you will not want to see me any more.'

'Of course I do.' I cupped her face in my hands. 'Why should I worry about a few beads?'

Her eyes flashed. 'It is not just a few beads! The rosary belonged to my grandmother. It is very precious to me.'

I held her close. 'I am sorry, Katrinka. I didn't mean it to sound so trifling.'

Suddenly the moon shone brightly through the clouds. I looked up and said to her, 'Look at the moon, it's shining down on both of us. You a Catholic, and me a Methodist . . . I don't think God will mind what we are, do you? Next week will be Christmas . . . do you believe in Christmas?'

She nodded.

'So do I.' I tilted her chin and kissed her lovingly. 'As long as you want me, I will be here.' We moved along down the street and I told her I would be having a few days off over Christmas, and that I would be able to see more of her. She seemed more relaxed, and I was relieved that things were back to normal.

The moon had vanished behind some clouds and the snow had started again in earnest. I looked around for some shelter, to no avail. Then Katrinka pointed. 'There is a church over there.' Light was streaming out from its beautiful stained glass windows. I hesitated for a moment – I wasn't too familiar with holy buildings

– but she had already taken my hand and was leading me to the great arched doors. She turned the big iron ring and the door slowly opened. The sound of organ music greeted us. Very soft strains which seemed to sound from every corner of the church. My apprehension lessened slightly as I realised the church was empty, except for the organist who was sat high up behind the pulpit. Lost in his own melodious world, he was unaware of our presence. I felt completely out of place as Katrinka led me to a pew, and only remembered in the nick of time to snatch off my beret.

I sat, but Katrinka went down on her knees and crossed herself. Then she sat beside me and squeezed my hand. I think she knew just how tense I was feeling. We sat quietly listening to the organ. I wasn't familiar with the tunes, but it was nice to be inside and out of the cold. My fingers and toes were gradually coming back to life in the warmth of the church. The organist was still playing, and seemingly quite oblivious of the two intruders who sat behind him. Suddenly, I pricked up my ears. He had begun to play one of my favourite pieces – *Ave Maria*.

'I love this one,' I whispered to Katrinka, 'do you?'

She smiled knowingly, then startled me by singing the words out loud. I was dumbstruck. She had the voice of an angel. As I listened a thrill went through my whole body. Her clear, pure voice filled the church with its sheer magnificence, and I gazed on open-mouthed as she sang unfaltering through the verses. As the last notes died sweetly away, I shivered with emotion. I was spellbound.

The organist rose from his stool, then turned to us and bowed. 'Katrinka,' he said in acknowledgment, before departing through a door by the side of the organ.

I made to speak, but she put her finger to her lips and shook her head. We both sat quietly for a few moments, until she finally took my hand and led me back to the pavement.

Still snowing, it seemed even colder than before. Time to head for our favourite tavern, we decided, with its welcoming fire.

When we were comfortably seated inside, I asked her who had taught her to sing so beautifully.

There was sadness in her voice when she answered. 'My grandmother,' she told me. 'She was once an opera singer, many years ago. She sang all over Europe . . . even in London, I think.'

'Does your mother sing?'

Her eyes were filled with sorrow. 'I do not think so . . . I did not know my parents well. The Germans took them to a forced labour camp in what is now known as East Germany.'

'And you have never seen them again?'

A tear trickled down her cheek as she gave a quick shake of her head. I covered her hand with mine. Neither of us was able to speak for a moment or two. I would not have mentioned her mother if I had known of the upsetting circumstances. Seeking to ease the trauma, I reached into my pocket for my cigarettes. I lit two, then handed one to Katrinka. 'Come on, try one of these.'

My heart went out to her. She looked so defenceless as she dried her tears with a hanky, and I asked myself why a lovely girl like this would want to go out with a chap like me. Then another terrible thought crossed my mind! What if I am transferred to another unit? I was now realising just how much I loved this little Polish girl.

'Ouch!' While I had been daydreaming, the match had burnt back to my fingers.

Katrinka winced. 'You poor thing. What were you thinking?'

I tried to smile. 'I was thinking about you.'

She took my hand to see what damage had been done, then gently kissed the tip of each finger.

'I thought only mothers did that sort of thing,' I remarked jokingly.

Smiling a little now, she said, 'My grandmother would kiss my fingers when I hurt them.'

'When did your granny die, Katrinka?'

'It was one year since . . . I was sad . . . I was left on my own.'

I asked her if she had any relatives?

'No,' she answered despondently. 'There is now only me.'

We drained our glasses, then I beckoned the landlord over and ordered a refill for both of us. I had to shout to make myself heard. We had been so wrapped up with each other that I hadn't realised how noisy the tavern had become. Most of the people around us were in high spirits and seemed to be more than a little merry. A few standing around the fireplace had started to sing, and before long the other customers were joining in with gusto. As the evening progressed we found ourselves drawn into the warm and happy atmosphere, both of us humming and tapping our feet along with the other songsters. There was one song in particular that was sung with great feeling and emotion. I guessed it was the people's favourite. Katrinka informed me that it was called *O'Tannebaum*, and she joined in the singing along with the rest, while I struggled to keep in tune with my own discordant humming. The singing finally stopped, and it was time for us to go. As we departed, most of the revellers waved us goodnight. One of them even shouted 'Goodnight' to us in English. I almost felt as if I was stepping out from one of the pubs at home.

When we paused in our favourite shop doorway, I undid my coat buttons and she cuddled closer. With my coat wrapped around the both of us, I kissed her gently on the lips, then her arms were around my neck. Holding her warm body tightly to mine, I kissed her with more passion than ever before. I could feel her heart beating rapidly in time with my own, and aware, now, that we both wanted and needed each other, my kisses grew more demanding. But we were both starting to shiver with the cold and I had to get back before lights out. I kissed her goodbye on the corner of the street and she was gone, leaving me cold and desolate. I missed her so much.

The next morning I was up bright and early. I strolled to the washroom to shave and spruce up for breakfast. On Sundays the cookhouse was always nearly empty. Most of the lads would rather stay in bed, so there were plenty of buckshees going spare; the cooks were only too happy to get rid of all the eggs they had fried. It had stopped snowing, but the several inches that had already fallen had frozen over. Walking the pavements would be difficult that evening, when I was due to meet Katrinka again.

It was mid-afternoon when John came down to the stores to see if I was ready. I told him I wouldn't be long. I needed to give the brasses on my belt a polish. If I didn't do it I would only be sent back again.

He sat down on my bed to wait for me. Looking rather uncomfortable, he said, 'I'm a little broke, Pete. Any chance of loaning me a quid's worth of marks? Helga, my new girlfriend, drinks like a fish.'

I smiled to myself. Helga worked in the canteen, and I knew that John had been laying on the charm lately. Good for him, it must have worked.

I gave him what he wanted; I think it was about seven marks

to the pound. I didn't have to worry about losing my money; I knew he would honour his debt. He dropped the money into his pocket for its brief stay. One final examination in the mirror and we were ready to set off.

At the bottom of the hill we parted company and went our separate ways. Katrinka was waiting for me. Her bright new shawl was unmistakable, even at a distance. As I approached her, her face lit up with a lovely smile. 'Good evening, Private Rundle,' she said.

I took her into my arms and kissed her. Her face felt icy, and I wondered how long she had been standing there. I moved to kiss her again, when I was attacked by a frozen missile which caught me with a stinging blow on my right cheek. Spinning round, I saw three grinning boys scurrying off. We grabbed some snow and ran after them, making snowballs on our way. We exchanged rapid fire for several minutes, but gradually our assailants were being joined by their friends, so we deemed it time to beat a hasty retreat. Laughing and out of breath, we ran up a side street and managed to evade the playful snowball gang. We wandered aimlessly around. The raw, cold wind seemed to be everywhere. Cuddling her tighter to me for warmth, I said, 'It's so much colder here than in England.'

'Yes, I know,' she replied. 'The winds from Siberia sweep right across mainland Europe. In Poland it is even colder.'

After a while we came across a shop loading-bay which looked as if it could afford us some protection from the weather, so we hurried inside, grateful to be shielded from the icy blast. Cuddling her tightly, I asked her if the people she was living with had decorated a Christmas tree?

She hesitated for a moment. 'Today I think it will be done.'

'And where would that be, exactly?' I asked, hoping to catch her off guard.

'I do not think I will tell you, Mr Rundle.' She spoke as if she was teasing me.

'Are you afraid that I will turn up for my Christmas dinner, Katrinka?'

I detected a note of concern in her voice when she whispered, 'I do not know what to think.' So I was left none the wiser and I knew the subject was closed. I wanted to give her a Christmas present and had been trying to decide what to buy her. Then I suddenly realised that I had never noticed a watch on her wrist. If she didn't have one, it would make an ideal present for her. Thinking fast, I asked her the time, mentioning that I had forgotten to wind my watch that morning.

'I have no watch,' she said, 'but we can check with the town clock.' So my nagging problem was neatly solved.

The cold was really getting to us now, and there was just nowhere to go. 'I wish I could smuggle you into the camp with me,' I said, 'it's lovely and warm in there.'

She laughed. 'Yes, with so many men living there.'

Then I suddenly thought of the railway station. It wasn't too far away, and with any luck we might get a coffee there. So off we tramped.

Sure enough there was a little snack bar there, and it was heaven to get inside and out of the cold. We sat drinking our coffee and gradually started to thaw out. Katrinka said, 'Next year, at this time, you will be at home in your Cornwall. You will be out of the army . . . and then perhaps, I will be forgotten!'

'Oh no,' I said with great conviction. 'One day I was rather hoping to make you my wife.'

She gazed at me lovingly across the littered table. 'You would make me Frau Rundle?'

'No, Katrinka . . . Mrs Rundle!'

'I make joke,' she giggled. 'It is not Frau in Poland.'

We left it at that, but I knew in my heart that this little Polish girl had certainly stolen my heart.

She wanted to know all about Cornwall and the clay mining. She said, 'I try to picture this place in my mind, the big white pyramids, and the enormous deep pits full of bright green water. It sounds so wonderful . . . like paradise.' She listened avidly while I described my homeland to her.

'You miss your home very much?' Her eyes searched mine.

'I do, but I can't imagine returning to Cornwall without you.' With growing excitement I asked her if she would like to come to Cornwall for a holiday when I left the army. I leaned closer to her. 'You will be able to see it for yourself: my Cornwall, my home!'

She studied her coffee cup and whispered sadly, 'I do not think they will allow me to do this.'

'Who the hell are they?' I was disappointed and spoke harshly.

Fear flashed in her eyes as she quickly answered, 'No one, I am sorry. I make a mistake. We will talk of other things.' She remained silent as she lingered over her coffee. Then she completely changed the subject by asking, 'You will have extra time next weekend, for Christmas?'

'I think so, yes.'

She nervously jabbered on. 'How will it be in the camp? Will all of the soldiers drink too much beer?'

'Yes, I expect so.' My answer was curt, I felt let down. I had convinced myself that she would jump at the chance to come to Cornwall with me. Her negative response left me totally deflated.

All of a sudden we were aware of much bustling activity going on around us. A train had pulled into the station and people were dashing here, there, and everywhere, all of them intent on getting under cover, out of the cold wind. We sat watching with interest the comings and goings of the people, all heavily disguised in layers of thick clothing and fur hats, and showing just enough of their faces to prove they didn't belong to some wild ursine race. Then, as quickly as it had started, the hustle and bustle died away. Even the little snack bar seemed much quieter than before. One of the waitresses came over and spoke a few words to Katrinka in German as she collected our empty coffee cups. 'We have to go, Peter,' Katrinka told me. 'They're closing.'

I stood up to button up my greatcoat. 'I feel like a refugee, with no place to go,' I said complainingly. I didn't relish the idea of wandering aimlessly around in the bitter cold. Katrinka looked away as I was grumbling, but not before I had noticed a deep sadness which had crept into her eyes. Feeling like a worm, I put my arm around her. 'Come on, the main thing is that we have each other.'

Treading cautiously, we made our way along the slippery street. I tried to think of something that would cheer her up; she seemed so withdrawn. The only thing I could think of was the cinema, so that was where we went. It was a German film, which left me rather in the dark, but at least it was warm inside, and Katrinka could explain it to me later. I sat as close to her as the chair arms permitted, and as the film progressed she seemed to have forgotten the incident in the café. Despite my ignorance of the language, the film was surprisingly easy to follow, and after what seemed a short space of time we were once again outside, shivering in the cold. It was much later than we had realised, so after giving her a long lingering kiss, I arranged to meet her on Christmas Eve, at five o'clock outside the wireless shop. Another snatched kiss, and we both hurried on our separate ways.

On the way back to the camp I was thinking about how I was going to manage to buy the watch. I had only a couple of days to purchase one. But luck was with me. The next day, I got talking to a soldier whose father owned a jeweller's shop back home in Cornwall. He seemed very knowledgeable about the trade, so I ventured to ask his advice. I explained that I wanted a good one for my girlfriend.

'Have you got forty marks?' he asked.

I told him that I could probably rustle up that amount, and he went on to say that he would shortly be going down to Gottingen and would do his best to find a good watch for me. 'One that she will be proud of,' he added confidently. The man was a diamond.

Later that night I was in the church army café having my supper when he suddenly reappeared. 'So here you are,' he said. 'I was told I would find you here, stuffing your face.'

'Have you got it?' I could hardly contain my excitement. He proudly opened up a long slender box. 'What do you think of this?'

It looked lovely. She would be happy with this, I was sure. He went on to tell me that it was gold plated, with a jewelled movement, and that if it didn't fit her wrist the shop would fix it for her free of charge. Digging his hand into his pocket, he added, 'And I have some change for you, my lad!'

'That's an 'ansome job, and you can keep the change for getting it for me,' I told him cheerfully. I was more than pleased.

On the morning of Christmas Eve it snowed for a couple of hours. Then it cleared, leaving a bright blue sky. We worked until lunch-time, then we were off-duty for the whole Christmas period.

After I had eaten, I wrote a letter home, then generally lazed around for the rest of the afternoon, just whiling away the time until I met Katrinka.

She was waiting for me outside the wireless shop. Her nose and cheeks were bright red from the freezing air, and with her new shawl covering her blonde hair, she looked really cute. I had some rent to pay, and as we entered the shop the bell over the door clanged and trembled loudly to announce our arrival. I stood at the counter with my rent book and money in readiness, and after a few moments the owner appeared from the back room, his hands full of spare wireless parts. He smiled a greeting and looked hopelessly around for somewhere to drop his bits and pieces. Everywhere was littered with wireless parts, so Katrinka held out her hands to take it from him whilst he served me. He took the money and signed my rent book, evidently in a hurry to get back to his repairs. On our way out he said something in German. Katrinka smiled coyly. 'He is a nice German. He said *Merry Christmas, young lovers*!'

The tavern was to be our next stop. We had decided to go in for a Christmas drink, but when we stepped inside it looked as if the whole of Germany had been packed in there. The noise was deafening, and the air was blue with smoke. After waiting ages for one beer, we thought it best if we left. Also, we felt a little uneasy with so many Germans around us. We found ourselves once again aimlessly walking over the crunchy snow. As we neared the church we heard singing, and the haunting strains of the organ. Multicoloured light spilled out onto the snow from the stained glass windows. The building seemed peacefully magical in the dark, lonely street. 'They have the singing of carols,' Katrinka said excitedly. 'Shall we go inside, just for a little while?'

I saw that her heart was already in there, so once again I found myself in church. It was more than half full of people this time. We slipped into the back row of pews and Katrinka picked up a book from the little shelf in front of us. She leafed through the pages until she found the carol they were singing, and joined in. As she sang her free hand found mine and gave it a gentle squeeze.

After the carol, the priest read a scripture from a large, well-worn bible. I couldn't understand a word of it, but I took the opportunity to gaze around the church, and to study the congregation. Suddenly there was a stir as everyone dropped to their knees to pray. Katrinka, still holding my hand, gently pulled me down with her. They prayed aloud; it sounded a little like our *Lord's Prayer*, so I very quietly recited the words of that. Afterwards, as we rose to our feet, the pain in my knee made me gasp. I had forgotten about my stab wound. Kneeling in such a confined space didn't do it any good at all. The next carol sounded more familiar, then I realised they were singing *Silent Night*. Katrinka whispered, 'You know this carol; you can sing it in your English.'

I smiled ruefully. My singing voice was on the same level as a crow with a sore throat. In my case it would be much wiser to listen. There was another short prayer, then the congregation started to leave. The priest was waiting at the door to shake everyone's hand as they left the church. He spoke a few words to each one in turn, which made the long procession of people filing past our pew, very slow. Resentfully I thought, they will be going back to their warm Christmassy homes, whereas we would be left to roam the cold, deserted streets. At last I followed Katrinka out. The priest shook hands with her, then with me, and wished us both a very happy Christmas. We thanked him and followed the others out into the night.

The cold wind was still blowing in from Russia; it really made me cringe. It was certainly a night to be at home in front of the fire, rather than out braving the elements. A wild thought suddenly popped into my head. 'I know where we can go where it's warm and private.' I held Katrinka close and looked down into her trusting eyes.

Her expression brightened. 'Where?'

'In my store room, where I sleep in the camp.'

She looked at me, horrified. 'Oh no . . ! I will be put into prison, or shot!'

I tried to explain to her that tonight would be different, that most of the camp would be elsewhere, enjoying themselves.

She was still looking worried and shaking her head. But the more I thought about it, the more I liked the idea, 'You see, Katrinka, tonight there will be just three men on duty. The quarter guard at the main gate, and two more guarding the ammunition huts. I know of another way in, which means we won't even see them.'

She was weakening. 'We will not meet with the guards?'

'Of course not. My block is in the far corner of the camp, near the perimeter fence. There is a place where we can get in quite easily.' With growing excitement I explained to her that there was a dirt road which went all the way round the camp, and that if we head out of town and go past the displaced persons' camp, then turn left and follow the dirt road, it would lead us right up outside my part of the camp. 'What do you say? Are you game, Katrinka?'

A frown creased her brow. 'I do not wish to pass the refugee camp!'

'All right, we will skirt round it . . . please say yes. I promise no harm will come to you.'

She battled with herself, while I waited on tenterhooks. 'Well, all right, but I am very much afraid.'

So we set off on a mad scheme that would surely land me in deep trouble if I happened to be caught. As for Katrinka, she would just be shown out of the camp. But desperate people do desperate things!

Chapter Eight

We were on our way! By ten-to-eight we were scurrying feverishly up the dirt track that skirted the camp. The barrack rooms were brightly-lit, and the camp's tall, orange streetlamps gave the complex the look of a small town. We were almost at the spot where I knew we could get through the wire. 'No talking now,' I whispered in Katrinka's ear. 'I want to make sure I know where the sentries are.'

I heard only the wind as it whistled through the fence. The camp itself was reassuringly quiet. Hopefully, everyone was in the NAAFI, boozing. I told Katrinka to wait while I went ahead to check on the guards. As I neared the top of the track I heard voices. Peering into the shadows, I was able to distinguish the figures of two sentries. They were standing just inside the fence, conversing in low tones as they smoked their illicit cigarettes. They would clearly be unhappy at being on duty during the Christmas festivities. I didn't move a muscle. Luckily I was in the shadow of a tree. I could see them, whereas they were unlikely to spot me. And they were certainly less than vigilant as they finished their cigarettes.

After what seemed like an age, the disgruntled pair started walking towards the other side of the camp. Silently, I retraced my steps to rejoin Katrinka.

Katrinka's face mirrored her concern. 'I am so afraid in this lonely place,' she whispered. 'It's horrible.'

Giving her a hug, I assured her that everything would be all right. I took her hand and led her along the track to the flaw in the barbed-wire fence. As I stooped to slip through, she suddenly pulled back. 'Do they carry guns? Do they have bullets? I am so afraid of soldiers with guns.'

'You have nothing to worry about; these guards are unarmed.' I gave her a kiss to cheer her up. I didn't let on that the guard outside the main gate carried ammunition at night. For one thing she could innocently tell others the procedure of the camp, and for another, I wasn't ruining my chances now I had got this far. One last reassuring kiss, then we slipped through the gap and into the enclosure of my camp. Hardly daring to breathe, we waited, looking around us to see if the coast was clear. It was deserted, thank God. I pointed to the nearest billet block. 'That's where I live, in the basement of that building over there.' Luckily for us, the doorway was on our side of the block.

'Ready? We'll make a run for it.'

Grabbing her hand, I led her helter-skelter across the road and almost fell in the doorway, then down to the basement store. Both our hearts were pounding as I fumbled with the keys to unlock the door. It was pitch dark inside. I led her over to my bed and whispered, 'Sit down until I put my coat over the window.' That done, I locked the door and turned on the light. Katrinka sat on the very edge of the bed, pale and wide-eyed. I took her in my arms. 'We made it.'

Her eyes strayed over my shoulder to the rows of rifles that were stored there, and her body went rigid.

'Don't worry about those; they aren't loaded. They're as harmless as toy guns,' I said, trying to lighten the strained atmosphere, but she was shaking like a leaf. I thought perhaps if I showed her round, it might help to calm her nerves. Gradually she started taking an interest. She was amazed at the number of different cooking pans, and by the size of them. She remarked how clean and shiny they all were. We wandered around the store and I explained the usage of all the different things which filled the many shelves, until I felt she was back to her normal self.

I opened my locker and spotted the Christmas cake which my mother had sent me. Just the job; I was feeling peckish. Katrinka nodded when I offered her a piece, so I cut off a couple of large chunks and we sat down on the bed and tucked in. Katrinka looked at it very closely before nibbling a piece of icing. Having made sure it was as good as it looked, she attacked the remainder with gusto. Picking up an escaped crumb, she asked, 'Your mother make this cake? It is good. I have not tasted food like this before.' She rose from the bed and started to look around on her own. I had left my locker door open and she peered inside. 'You keep a tidy cupboard.' Then she spotted my spare flannel vest and pants. They did look rather old-fashioned. The pants came down to my knees, and the vests had half-sleeves in them. They were issued to us for maximum warmth in the winter months. She turned towards me, holding the long pants aloft to show them in all their glory. She giggled, 'Are you wearing some like this, Peter?'

I moved to grab them from her but she whipped them behind her back and raced round the other side of the bed. I leapt over the bed, caught her, and pushed her back on to the pillow. We tussled with each other, laughing and tugging on the garment until we were both out of breath. Finally, I managed to retrieve my misshapen underwear and we both lay back on the bed puffing and panting, completely exhausted. My breathing was just getting back to normal when suddenly I became aware of Katrinka's warm body lying beside me. With my heart starting once more to work overtime, and my eyes fixed firmly on the ceiling, I asked her if I should put out the light? Very softly she answered my question:

'The light – I think yes. You put out.'

I took her in my arms and kissed her. As far as I was concerned this girl was mine for life!

After what seemed to be a very short time, Katrinka stirred. 'The time . . . is it late?'

Glancing at my travelling clock, I nearly had a fit. 'Hell, it's almost ten! We'd better move now, before the drunks come back.'

There was just time to get her back to the town, and for me to return to sign in before eleven. I turned on the light as we dressed frantically. Then I pulled her close to me. 'I love you, little Polish girl.'

'I love you, too.'

I unlocked the door and told her to stay where she was, while I checked to see if the coast was clear. I crept up the main passageway and gingerly opened the main door. For a moment my heart was in my mouth; I heard several rowdy voices. Then I spotted them – merely a few of the lads somewhat worse the wear for drink. 'Quick, we have to hurry,' I called to Katrinka, and we slipped out of the door and up the road in record time.

I asked her if she had any regrets.

'No, but I will not visit your camp again. I am much too frightened.' She stopped to catch her breath. 'I am happy to have seen your bed-place; now I will see you there when I think of you.'

'I wish I could take you all the way to your home Katrinka, then I would know you are safe.'

'It is not possible!'

'Maybe one day?' I ventured.

'Maybe. I do not know,' she said.

I paused and embraced her. 'It was wonderful tonight; the first time we have been alone together.'

Shyly, she whispered, 'I will remember it for all of my life.'

We agreed to meet the following day – Christmas – at three o'clock in the afternoon, which was the earliest I would be able to get away after the camp's festive dinner. I blew her a kiss, and she vanished into the darkness.

I made it back with only minutes to spare.

Chapter Nine

'Open up, Rundle!'

I leapt up from my pillow with a start. Someone was hammering on my door. My heart was racing as I scrambled out of bed and staggered to the door. I inched it open and peered through the gap.

The sergeant was standing there with a big jug of sweet tea. 'Your early morning cuppa, Rundle,' he said, with an uncharacteristic smile. It was a long-standing army custom. The officers and senior NCOs would wait on the lower ranks on Christmas Day. Like a zombie, I fetched my mug, and he poured in the pale, hot steaming liquid and wished me a Merry Christmas. It was certainly strange, being pampered by him, but it made a welcome change. And it wouldn't last long. Tomorrow he would be as hard as nails, and today's little treats would seem like a dream.

But the 'dream' wasn't over yet. Just a few hours later the Christmas dinner was great. Served by the officers of the regiment, we all dined in style. The usual turkey with all the trimmings, christmas pudding, and all washed down with a fine bottle of beer. We lads could hardly move when we had finished . . . just like home!

A little before three in the afternoon I found myself looking in the full-size mirror which adorned the wall outside the guardroom. It was there for the men to double-check their appearance before being inspected by the Corporal of the Guard. Actually it was quite handy, as many is the time I would have been sent back for some trifling detail that I'd missed in the smaller, defective mirrors on the inside. Scruffy soldiers were never let out of the gate. I straightened my beret a little, then marched into the guardroom.

I was surprised to see that the officer of the guard had some company. Standing beside him was the Provost Sergeant, whose duty it was to police our camp. And like all coppers, he seldom missed a trick. 'And what have we got here?' he growled, as his beady eyes searched me from top to bottom. 'Going out on our own on Christmas Day, are we?'

'Yes, Sergeant.'

'Wait a minute . . . aren't you the boxer chap from Mortar Platoon.'

'Just a storeman, Sergeant, although I have boxed a little, yes.'

'Just a little, eh? I heard it was a ding-dong fight you had with Corporal Mulholand. A pity I missed it. Tell me, will there be a return?'

'I don't think so, Sergeant.'

He looked rather disappointed at that, but he allowed me to sign myself out. As I passed the sentry on duty, he muttered under his breath, 'You were lucky to get past him – he must have had a drink or two.' I gave him a cheery wink.

Walking down the hill to the town, I felt in high spirits. I patted my breast pocket to check Katrinka's watch was still there. I couldn't wait to see her face when I gave it to her. It was a lovely sunny day. Although still very cold, the sun made everything look brighter and more welcoming, I enjoyed picturesque scenery as I walked. Over to my right stood a gently sloping woodland and I spotted something glinting in the trees. I stopped in my tracks for a better look. The glare was so bright that it brought tears to my eyes and I had difficulty in making out what it was. In the end I decided it was the turrets of a castle. It seemed quite exciting and I made a mental note to go and explore there one day.

As I approached the town, it struck me how quiet and deserted it was. Katrinka was waiting at our usual meeting place. She came towards me with her arms held out. 'A good Christmas Day to you, Private Rundle.'

I clasped her in my arms and kissed her lovely Polish lips. 'A very good Christmas Day to you also, my darling.'

She was bubbling with excitement as she took my hand and placed a small package into it. 'It is a gift for you, my Peter.'

She watched me as I carefully peeled off the wrapping paper. It was a cigarette lighter.

'Thank you, me 'ansome. I will treasure this always, but you shouldn't have wasted your money on me.'

'You like it very much?'

'I love it,' I told her truthfully, and her face glowed. 'Now I will be able to light my cigarettes whenever I want to. I will always carry it with me.' Then I reached into my tunic pocket and brought out the special gift I had for her. Now it's your turn for a surprise,' I said, my own excitement matching hers.

Eagerly, she tore off the outer wrapping. 'A watch . . ! A Swiss watch!' – tears were slipping down her cheeks – 'It is so beautiful. Now you have spent all of your money on me.'

I put the watch on her slender wrist, then she put her arms around me and hugged me tightly. 'I will remember this Christmas for the rest of my life!'

Between our kisses I murmured, 'And so will I, my darling.' Then I suggested we have a cigarette, so as to try out my new lighter. Katrinka looked proudly on as the flame shot out with the merest flick of my thumb. We stood for a bit while we enjoyed our cigarettes, but the cold was beginning to seep through our bodies, so we thought it wise to move on. Where to go was the problem. The whole town would be closed. Everyone would be at home, in front of their log fires, eating, drinking, and making merry. 'Where can we go, Katrinka? What can we do? Any ideas?'

Still looking at her watch, she slowly shook her head. While I was thinking hard, I heard a car approaching. As it drew nearer I saw that it was the Commanding Officer's staff car. Everyone in the camp was familiar with his posh Opel. As it drew closer the driver flashed his headlights to tip me off that the colonel was aboard. I quickly stepped away from Katrinka and threw up a smart salute. Sitting upright on the back seat, the colonel noticed me and returned my salute with military precision.

Katrinka looked on in wonder. 'Who is this man?'

'That was the boss, Colonel of the Regiment,' I told her.

'He looked very . . . how do you say? – stern!'

I agreed with her. 'Yes, he's stern all right, but we'll forget about the army for now, and think about what we are going to do. I suddenly remembered the strange, dazzling light that I had noticed in the woodland. Describing what I had seen, I told her how I thought it might have been a castle, and asked her if she

d

would like to help me find it. Anything would be better than hanging around in the cold. With a cheerful nod she tucked her arm in mine and off we set.

Eventually we found a track which led into the woods. The thinner layer of snow beneath the trees had frozen over, leaving the surface very slippery, so we were happy to steady each other as we continued our exploration. It seemed much colder than before. The trees grudgingly sifted just a little sunshine through their heavy branches, and every so often, just for spite, dropped little showers of snow on to us. We walked quite a way, but there was no sign of a castle. We hadn't met with a single person since entering the wood. It was so quiet, we felt we were the only two people in the world. Every few yards we would stop for a kiss and a cuddle, even though our faces were numb with the cold. It was lovely. After a time we came across a clearing. Several trees had been felled and the wood had been cut in lengths the size of pit props. All were neatly stacked and ready for collection. The sun shone more brightly here, so I found a suitable log, brushed off the snow, and we made ourselves comfortable. It was good to rest our legs and have a breather. Katrinka sat quietly thinking, then wistfully she said, 'Your mother and father – they will be celebrating Christmas in your home?'

I drew her close. 'Yes, right at this moment they will probably all be sitting cosily in front of a blazing fire. All my family will be there. Dad with his pipe, nodding off every few minutes. My mother, still with her apron on after cooking the turkey, reminiscing about when we were all young. I expect she will talk about me, and have a tear in her eye because I'm not there with them. I expect they will also talk about you, wondering what you are like, and whether, one day, they will be able to meet you.'

'It is good to have a family,' Katrinka said, trying to hide the tremble in her voice. I gave her a kiss, and thought it best to be moving on.

A little further on we came across a farmyard. It was strange to suddenly find evidence of human habitation in this solitary place. We stopped and studied it from the road. There was an open-sided house with cattle busily feeding inside. Next to it was a hay shed and a few other buildings which looked ready to collapse at any minute. I could see no farmhouse, and there was certainly no sign of a farmer. I took Katrinka's hand and led her over to watch the animals munching on their hay. One nosy creature came over to join us and began to smell and nibble at my coat sleeve. Katrinka looked horrified. 'It will bite you,' she gasped, jumping back.

'They won't bite us,' I assured her. I took her hand and gently smoothed down the animal's nose. Whereupon he shot back to the safety of his own kind. 'You see, they are much more afraid of us. There is nothing to worry about.'

The mangers looked as if they had recently been filled with hay. I suspected the farmer had visited his herd, fed them, and had now returned to his home. He probably wouldn't be back for several hours. The hay shed looked very inviting. With a little coaxing, Katrinka sat down beside me. It felt warm, and the sweet-smelling hay was a delight in itself. 'It reminds me of home,' I told her, as I tenderly eased her back to kiss her.

'Do you take the English girls into the hay sheds when you are in England?' she wanted to know.

Teasing her, I answered, 'No, they are crafty . . . they won't go.'

'Are the English girls 'ansome – more 'ansome than I?' She studied me with open concern.

'No, of course not. You are my only 'ansome.' Playfully, I started tickling her. She tried to move away, but the more she laughed, the more I tickled. In the end I had to kiss her to stifle her giggles. I realised that if the farmer did come back, he would wonder what on earth was going on. We lay in each other's arms, oblivious of our spartan surroundings. Content to just be with each other. The next hour sped passionately by, then we decided it was time to start on our journey back.

We were just leaving the shed when we heard the throaty chug-chug of an approaching tractor. There was nowhere to run to, so we guiltily stopped in our tracks to confront the farmer. He jumped down from his tractor and strode towards us. Flustered, I told Katrinka to tell him that we were out walking and had stopped to admire his cattle.

He listened patiently to her excuse, then pointed to the flattened hay. With a broad grin, he said, 'I speak a little English, I was a prisoner of war in England. Thank you for admiring my cattle.' He gave me a knowing look and returned to his duties. Meekly, we waved goodbye and started back to the town.

The light was starting to fail, and it was dark when we arrived in Gottingen. The shops were closed and the streets were deserted. Sadly, I had been detailed for guard duty the next day, so in the circumstances I thought it wise to head back to camp. All my kit needed polishing, and the session in the hay hadn't done any favours for my army greatcoat. After saying our loving goodbyes, and receiving an extra hug from Katrinka for her watch, we parted company and regretfully went our separate ways.

Even the camp appeared deserted and quiet. The only sign of life I found was in the NAAFI, when I nipped in for a couple of pints before retiring to my billet.

Later, I set to work polishing my kit in readiness for the morning and, when that was satisfactorily done, I plugged in the iron for my next big chore. It was no easy task pressing a thick heavy greatcoat, but it had to be done . . . and to perfection! While I waited for the iron to heat up, I busied myself by picking out the bits of hay which had lodged in the creases, which reminded me of the lovely Christmas Day I had spent with Katrinka.

The next day was still a holiday in the camp – except for those of us on guard duty.

The camp was quiet early that morning. I breakfasted, then changed into my best gear, ready to parade at 0900 hours. I would then remain on duty for 24 hours. The day would drag by, and the night would seem even longer. When the gates were closed at 2300 hours the feeling of solitude was almost total. There would be just one armed sentry outside the gate, and one unarmed sentry patrolling the inside. I was to find myself out there from one in the morning until three.

As I walked out of the small side-gate the retiring sentry handed me his rounds of ammunition. 'It's bloody freezing out here tonight,' he grumbled. 'I'm glad to be going in for a warm up, I can tell yer.' Then the gate clanged shut and I was on my own for the next two hours.

The cold was intense. I marched up and down in front of the main gates, stamping my feet to keep warm. My hob-nailed boots clattering over the cobbles was the only sound to be heard. The camp was in darkness now, except for the guardroom. Every now and then the moon would peep between the clouds and brighten up the whole area. Then the darkness would return and seem to weigh even heavier upon me. My gaze wandered across the way to our woodland, which seemed much friendlier now that I had explored it with Katrinka. I noticed a dim light in the far distance and wondered if it was the farmer, perhaps tending to a sick animal. Farmers would be the same the world over, I thought to myself. If they were needed they would be there. Then my thoughts turned to the hay barn. Oh, how I loved that girl! I expected she was tucked up in bed and fast asleep at that moment. More than likely she would be still wearing the watch I gave her; she was so pleased with it. My mind then travelled home. I thought about my family and wondered how their Christmas was faring. In her last letter, my mother had written to say that a neighbour of ours – an old lady named Sara Jane – was very ill. She was a kindly woman whom I had known all my life. I spoke softly to the dark night. 'Hang on, Sara Jane, I will be home on leave soon.' I would like to see her again. My hands were getting stiff and numb with the cold, so I placed my rifle between my knees in order to massage them and warm them up a little. I nearly lost my rifle when an owl suddenly hooted. I almost jumped out of my skin. Even so, it was nice to have its company for a short while, but it soon flew off and only served to make me feel more alone than ever. At long last I heard heavy boots marching outside the guardroom. They were changing the sentries over. I walked stiffly over to the gate, more than willing to hand over the five rounds of ammo. It was with a marked feeling of relief that I placed them in his hand and entered the warm guardroom. The first thing I did was to help myself to a mug of hot tea from the urn. The taste was ghastly – it had been stewing for hours – but at least it was hot. I certainly needed something to thaw me out. The rest of the guard were sleeping. Lying fully dressed on beds with no mattresses. No one was allowed to get too comfy. We had just ten seconds to get outside if we were called. And we had to be smartly dressed!

I sat beside the other sentry who had come in with me; he was almost sitting on the fire, he was so cold. The old heavy, black tortoise-type stove did its job well, and before long my body had returned to normality. I decided to lay down for a while and try to get some shut-eye. I unfastened the two small hooks on the top of my coat, but my chin started to chafe against the coarse material, so I ventured to undo a couple of buttons as well. Having made myself as comfortable as possible, I dozed off. My blissful sleep was soon shattered by a bellowed order: 'Stand to, the quarter guard!'

I leapt off my bed, my heart pounding. Everyone was scrambling to make themselves presentable for the turnout in ten-seconds. It was sheer pandemonium! One chap fell out of bed. Another tripped over his rifle. I couldn't get the hooks to do up on my coat at first, but mentally calming myself, I finally mastered it. I glanced around at the others. One was still having trouble with his buttons. The daft bloke had taken off his greatcoat altogether, so we all set to and gave him a helping hand. When the sentry called out, 'Guard turn out!' we just made it. We ran outside and stood rigidly to attention in two lines.

The Orderly Officer then inspected us. It was four o'clock in the morning! He gave one man a telling off for having his belt upside down, and threatened him with a charge. He never carried out the threat though. Maybe because it was Christmas.

The rest of the night passed uneventfully, and at 0900 hours the new guard came to relieve us. We then joined the rest of our platoon for the day's training. That particular day was to be map reading. I found it very hard to concentrate after my 24 hours of guard duty, but the army gave no time off. We just had to make the best of it. In the afternoon we had a religious hour with the camp padre. I'm afraid no one was very interested, and I for one, had a job to stay awake. He asked if anyone had any questions? No one spoke. There was an embarrassing silence. I don't know what made me do it, but I put my hand up. The padre, clearly pleased to have aroused some interest, coughed and said, 'Carry on, Private – what do you want to know?'

I gulped and said, 'Sir, if I wanted to get married here in Germany, could you do it for me?'

The room went deathly silent for a moment, followed by a buzz of whispered conversation.

Our corporal-in-charge barked, 'Quiet! The padre wishes to speak.'

The padre looked at me with eyebrows raised. 'It's Private . . ?'

'Rundle, sir,' I replied hesitantly.

'Mmm. Private Rundle, is it? I take it you are in love?'

A big laugh and cheer went up. Again the corporal had to quieten them.

'This lady friend of yours – is she German?' the padre asked.

A voice chirped up from the other side of the room, 'No sir, she's just 'ansome, sir.'

'Shut up, that man!' bellowed the corporal. 'The next one to interrupt will be put on a charge! Carry on, sir.' He nodded to the padre who gave another polite little cough before addressing me again:

'So she is not German, but she is 'ansome. I take it you have come to us from the DCLI, Rundle?'

'Yes, sir. The girl in question is Polish, sir.'

'I see, now we are getting somewhere.' He thought for a moment, then enquired, 'How in the blazes did you find a Polish girl in Gottingen? Don't tell me it was love at first sight!'

A loud roar went up from the chaps at that quip. My question had certainly woken them all up. The padre wanted to know if I was twenty-one yet.

'No, sir.'

'Then firstly, you must write to your parents for their consent. Then you will need the Commanding Officer's consent. If they all agree, then I would marry you! By the way, have you asked the girl yet?'

'No, sir, not yet!'

Another titter went round the room. The padre smiled. 'Then I suggest you had better ask her first.' He started to gather up his papers. 'If you want any more information on marriage, come to the Regimental Chapel and see me, Rundle.'

I thanked him, and with a slight bow to his congregation, he calmly walked out.

The corporal-in-charge quickly brought us to attention, then promptly dismissed everyone for the day. Except me!

'I would like a word with you, Rundle.' When all the din of the hobnailed boots had died away, he came over and sat beside me. 'Are you serious about this?'

'Yes,' I told him. 'I would go through hell and high water for my girl.'

'You will probably have to.' He looked thoughtful. 'I can't see the CO consenting to it, even if your parents are willing.'

'I will try my damnedest.'

'Well, good luck to you, my boy.' He seemed sympathetic to my cause, which heartened me to some degree.

That night, in the tavern with Katrinka, I told her about my public conversation with the padre. She listened in silence. When I had finished, I said, 'So I have to ask you. Katrinka, please will you marry me?'

The colour rose in her cheeks, and she gazed into the log fire for what seemed an eternity. When she faced me her eyes were glistening with tears. 'Do you mean what you say, Peter? You know nothing about me, or very little, do you?'

I took her hand. 'All I know is that I love you, and I want to be with you for the rest of my life. That's good enough for me.'

She was quiet for a moment, then she said, 'Also I am a Catholic. You are not.'

'Katrinka, there is only one God. I am sure he is looking down upon us now, and I know he would be happy if we were together.'

She withdrew her hand from mine and looked down at the table. 'I cannot marry you, my Peter.' Her voice was so soft I could hardly hear her. When she looked up, her lips were trembling. 'Not now, and perhaps never!'

I stared at her in disbelief.

'Cannot we go on the way we are, for the short time we have left together? When you return to your Cornwall, we will be parted for ever.' The tears were running down her cheeks, but she spoke the words clearly.

'Katrinka, is there something that you are keeping from me?' Gently, I questioned her. 'You aren't a nun, are you?'

She smiled then. 'Of course I am not a nun. You say very funny things.'

'Then why can't we marry?'

She gripped my hand. 'I love you very much. I also want to be with you, but I am unable to marry you. Please do not ask me now . . . some day, perhaps, you can know.'

I knew it was futile to carry on the conversation. I didn't feel too worried at that point, as no doubt it would be something trivial. But to Katrinka it could seem catastrophic. Maybe it was because she was so poor. Anyhow, I knew that I would win her round in the end. I wasn't going to give up that easily. I could see that, sadly, our conversation had destroyed Katrinka's jovial mood. I tried to slide gracefully on to other things; I couldn't bear to see her looking so unhappy. 'If we were in England now, we would have a cup of tea. In a time of crisis that's the thing to do. It always seems to do the trick. Oh how I miss my proper cup of tea.'

'Do you have tea always?' Katrinka asked.

'Yes, me 'ansome, we always do.' I talked to her about a few funny incidents which had happened to me in the past, and before long she was seemingly back to her normal smiling self. We enjoyed a frankfurter, then decided we wanted to be on our own, so we found ourselves out in the cold once again. I thought longingly of the farmer's hay shed, but it was dark, and much too far to walk that evening. We just wandered the streets, occasionally finding a suitable doorway to cuddle up in. Our options were sadly limited.

Chapter Ten

The next day I was attending a lecture, given by my platoon commander, when a knock came on the door. An orderly came in and handed the captain a note. He read the content, then scanned the class with his gaze until his eyes rested on me.

'Private Rundle, you and I are to report to the adjutant's office, right away!'

Everyone's eyes were fixed on me as I made my way to the door. It was a serious business if you were summoned to the high office. The adjutant was the person who ran the battalion. The captain instructed the sergeant to carry on in his absence, while he escorted me to the HQ. On the way he asked me if I had done anything unlawful.

'Not that I know of, sir.' I was beginning to feel nervous.

'It must be something important if they want me there as well,' he complained. 'By the way – that girl you're seeing – she isn't in the family way, is she, Rundle?'

'I don't think so, sir,' I stammered awkwardly.

'Well, she had better not be, or you will be in for the high-jump, my lad.'

As we marched through the HQ entrance I began to wonder if Katrinka had dropped something when I smuggled her into the camp, and someone had found it, whatever it might have been.

The captain rapped loudly on the adjutant's door.

'Enter,' shouted a brusque voice.

We entered together and both saluted the adjutant who was seated at his desk. He glared at me. 'Private Rundle?'

'Yes sir.' My voice trembled as I spoke. I had noticed that standing to the left of me was a redcap sergeant, and beside him stood a tall, stern-looking man dressed in a long, black leather coat and holding a black trilby hat in his hand. I wondered what they were both doing there.

The adjutant cleared his throat and addressed me. 'As you can see, Rundle, we have here a sergeant from the Military Police. With him stands an inspector from the German Immigration Department.' He studied them both before turning back to me. 'These two gentleman have brought me some very disturbing news, Rundle. It is so serious that your platoon commander has been asked to accompany you here to represent you if necessary. Do you understand?'

'Yes, sir,' I replied meekly, now seriously confused and worried.

His gaze reverted briefly to a document on his desk. 'You do realise that it is out of bounds for any British soldier to enter a displaced persons' camp?' His eyes left the paper and bore into mine. 'Well?'

'Yes, I do know that, sir.' My voice shook with consternation.

His eyes never left my face. 'Have you been inside that camp? These two gentlemen say they have proof that you have.'

My fear turned to anger. 'They can't have proof because I have never been in the camp . . . anyway why should I go into an out-of-bounds camp? – there is no need. I have a girlfriend in the town; there is no reason for me to go into such a place, sir.'

The man in the leather coat stepped forward. An image of the Gestapo flitted through my mind. 'Private Rundle.' He spoke in a smooth and icy voice. 'This so-called girlfriend of yours – is her name Katrinka Wazda?'

This took me aback. 'Yes, sir.'

'And did you know that she is Polish, and that she lives in the Displaced People of Europe camp?'

Wham! It was as if I had been hit in the face with a sledge hammer. My body seemed to freeze. Katrinka from the camp down the road? – No! Never! It must be some sort of ghastly mistake. I put my hand out to steady myself on the adjutant's desk. Vaguely, I heard a German voice saying, 'Did you know? Did you know?' It seemed very far off. The room seemed to blur. My eyes refused to focus. I just couldn't take it in. I heard my captain saying:

'I think we should let him sit down for a minute or two.'

I sat down and was given a glass of water. The military police sergeant started to fire more questions at me, but the adjutant intervened. 'Sergeant, this is my office. I am in command here. I will tell you when to resume questioning.'

My hands were shaking so much I had difficulty in drinking the water. My mind was racing back over the previous weeks. No wonder Katrinka wouldn't let me see her home. There was no way she was going to say goodnight outside the refugee camp; she would know that I wasn't allowed near the place. It all fitted into place now. So many little things she had said. What a fool I had been! My head was clearing a little now. I moved to get up, but the adjutant said in a fatherly tone, 'Stay seated, Rundle.' Then, more formally, 'Well, did you know this girl came from the camp?'

I looked him straight in the eye. 'I know it sounds foolish, sir, but I never had a clue.'

'Thank you, Rundle, that is what I hoped you would say.' Then, turning to the German inspector, he asked, 'And where is your proof, sir?'

Clearly annoyed, the German drew himself up to his full height. 'This soldier was seen walking towards the Displaced Persons' camp on Christmas Eve. He was accompanied by the girl, Katrinka Wazda. Later that same evening, he was seen walking outside the same camp and heading for the town of Gottingen.'

The adjutant turned back to me. 'Is this true, Rundle?'

'Yes, sir, we walked past the camp. It is difficult to know where to go when you are courting in a foreign land, sir.'

'Yes, I expect it is, soldier – do go on,' he said, with a flourish of his hand.

I cleared my throat. 'Maybe the gentlemen already know that on Christmas Day we went up through the woods just across the road from this camp. We spent an hour in the farmer's hay barn.'

A faint smile flickered across the adjutant's face as he turned to his two visitors and inquired if they did indeed know of our whereabouts on that holy day. The redcap sergeant coughed a little nervously.

'We were not on duty that day, sir – it being Christmas.'

The adjutant rose to his feet. 'No, I don't suppose you were. In fact, I do not think you have any proof whatsoever of Private

Rundle ever being in the refugee camp! We are therefore wasting our time. Good day, gentlemen.'

The inspector raised a protesting hand. 'I think this soldier should be banned from any more contact with this girl, forthwith.'

At this point my platoon captain stepped forward. 'I say, sir, surely that is not on! Private Rundle and his young lady have broken no rules – military or civilian!'

The adjutant added his support. 'Quite right, Captain!' Giving the other two an icy glare, he again bid them 'good day'.

The MP sergeant saluted, and the German inspector bowed stiffly and clicked his heels. They left the office together, both clearly displeased.

'Now look here, Rundle.' The adjutant was frowning. 'You can see that this is going to turn into a bloody great row if we aren't careful. Why don't you dump the girl and find yourself a nice young Fraulein?'

'I'm sorry, sir, I can't do that . . . I love her, sir. I will keep her even if I have to fight for the rest of my life for her.'

He sighed hopelessly. 'You might well have to if you continue to annoy the immigration people. Right, for the moment you may go. I'll have a word with your platoon commander.'

I saluted and was dismissed.

That evening I went into Gottingen but there was no Katrinka. I waited for over an hour, then slowly walked past the wireless shop, hoping to find her there, to no avail. I realised they must have been to see her at the camp. She had almost certainly been warned to stay away from me, and was probably doing as they ordered, more for my sake, I guessed, than for her own. Slowly, and with a heavy heart, I made my lonely way back to my camp. No sleep came to me that night.

The following evening I went down to the town and repeated the same routine. Still no Katrinka. I started to worry that she may have been moved to another camp. On the Saturday afternoon I had an idea. Providing she was still around, she might just visit the wireless shop to pay her rent. It was a slim chance, but it left me with a faint shred of hope. This time I didn't hang around, but headed straight for the shop. There was still clutter everywhere, but it was empty of people. I rang the bell and waited with rampant impatience. After what seemed ages, the proprietor sauntered out from the back room. I pointed to the big ledger which was open on the counter. 'Has Katrinka paid her rent today? Have you seen her?'

He leafed through the book, then shook his head. No, maybe she comes later.' He pointed to the chair in the shop. 'You wait if you wish.'

I smiled my thanks and made myself comfortable. I had a strong feeling that I was in for a long wait. Indeed, I was there for well over an hour. Each time the wireless man served a customer, he would glance over to me. I was beginning to feel self-conscious and in the way. I made up my mind: One more customer, then I would leave.

I was really beginning to lose hope, when the door opened and in she walked. My heart skipped a beat. She didn't notice me at first; she headed straight for the counter and rang the bell.

'Katrinka!'

She whirled round, her face a picture of sadness – then her expression was transformed by a dazzling smile. I swept her into my arms. 'Where have you been? I've been worried out of my mind about you.'

She looked down at the dusty floor. 'You know about me now, yes?'

'Yes – you come from one camp, and I come from another. What the Hell! – I love you! I don't know what all the fuss is about. Gently I lifted her chin and kissed her. It felt so right to be holding her again. Out of the corner of my eye I could see the German shopkeeper looking at us sadly. I said to him, 'You knew all the time, didn't you?'

With eyes downcast, he nodded.

I asked Katrinka what had happened.

'They have threatened to send me back to the Communist zone if I continue to see you,' she told me in a trembling voice.

'The bastards!' I felt so angry. 'We need to talk about this, Katrinka.'

The German proprietor coughed discreetly. 'I have to go out,' he said. 'Would you like to go into the back room? – there is a fire. I will be gone for about ten minutes.' Without waiting for a reply he locked the shop door and ushered us through to his workroom.

'You're very kind,' I said, as he slipped out of the back door.

'Peter, what can we do?' Katrinka spoke despairingly. 'Do you still want to be with me now you know my terrible secret?' She started to cry.

I held her close to me. 'I love you more than ever . . . it's not your fault that you are in such a place.'

'But what will become of us now? The immigration people or the army will part us for ever!'

I dabbed at her tears with my handkerchief. 'We must think hard; there must be a way out of this. We will find a way! I feel like running away together, but it would be hopeless. I have no civilian clothes and they would pick us up in no time. Besides, I just couldn't desert; it would bring shame on my family. It would kill them. My father was a proud soldier, decorated for his bravery in the Great War. No, that idea is definitely out!' We were too young to get married without permission. I simply did not know what to do.

Then Katrinka dropped another bombshell. 'It is rumoured in the camp that many of the people are to be shipped out – to somewhere in Poland.'

I knew then that we had to think of something quick! But the answers were slow to come.

All that night I tossed and turned in my bed. My body was tired but my brain was racing. I had to keep thinking, I had to!

In the morning I felt terrible, and I was still without a solution. Instinctively I started out for my breakfast, although I wasn't in the least bit hungry. At the bottom of the stairs I paused, then I found myself drawn towards the chapel. I took off my beret and went inside.

The padre was playing the piano. He glanced briefly in my direction, then continued on with his music. I sat with my head in my hands, listening to the sweet refrain echoing all around me. After a while I realised that I had been completely lost in the calming tones, and that for a few moments my mind had been free of worry. I felt better, as if a weight had been lifted from my shoulders. I couldn't explain it, other than I knew in my heart that one day Katrinka and I would be together.

I felt I needed some breakfast, suddenly I felt hungry. I ate my bacon and eggs with gusto. It was the best, and the most, that I had eaten for several days.

I passed John on my way back to the storeroom.

'Have you seen the company orders this morning, Pete?'

'Not yet.'

'They have us down for leave, next Monday week. Several have been selected from A and B Company, but we are the only two chosen from our platoon.'

I stopped in my tracks, shocked! 'Hell, they've moved quickly; they're making sure that I will be out of the way when they move Katrinka. When I get back, she will be gone!'

'I'm sorry, mate,' John said helplessly.

Back in my storeroom I threw my enamel mug and eating irons on to my bed in disgust. It seemed like the end of the road. I was really up against a brick wall now, and no mistake. A loud banging on the door made me jump. 'Come in, it's not locked,' I shouted.

John came bursting in. 'Listen!' he exclaimed. 'I've got an idea.'

'You have?' He was shaking with excitement. He said, 'In nine months' time, we will be out of the army, right?'

I nodded, wondering what was coming.

'Well, I don't mind giving up my leave this time, I will be more than happy to stay with Helga for the fortnight, in her flat. And you see, my dear boy, then you will be able to have my travel pass for Katrinka. Take her home dressed as a soldier; pass her off as me! All your troubles would be over. What do you think of that for genius?'

I looked at him in astonishment. 'What, on a troop train and troopship to England?'

'That's exactly what I mean,' he said, grinning like a Cheshire cat.

I thought about it. He was crazy. 'We would never get away with it.'

'You won't unless you try. Come on, man, it's your only chance, otherwise you're going to lose her.'

I desperately wanted to take the chance but it was absolute madness. 'But what if something goes wrong, John? You would be in as much trouble as me.'

He wouldn't be deterred. 'Look, nothing will go wrong. With all those troops on the move, have you ever seen anyone being asked for their pay book? – or for anything else, come to that? No, you haven't.'

'I don't know . . .' I was dithering.

'Where are your balls, man?'

'No, I'm not afraid to try it. It's you I'm worried about. This is not your problem, John.'

'Look,' he said firmly, 'if it wasn't for you I wouldn't be here. I could have been knifed to death that night in Minden. I owe you, Pete. I'd like to do this for you.'

'You're a true mate,' I told him. So we put our two heads together and started to work out a plan. We decided that firstly Katrinka would need a uniform. I knew where I could get hold of one. In the stores were two sets of army uniforms and kit. They originally belonged to two chaps from Liverpool who had deserted. I could borrow one set quite easily. Katrinka would have to smuggle it into her camp for alterations. It would have to look perfect; we wouldn't want any attention drawn to her. She would also have to cut her hair – short back and sides, army style. She would have to learn how to salute, and to recognise an army officer when she saw one. If she saluted the wrong ranks it would all be over! Apart from that, with so many troops travelling together, no one would take much notice of anyone else. They all just wanted to get home. John's scheme was looking good to me, after all. With a bit of luck we might win the day. John said, 'You had better warn her of the swearing she's bound to hear.' He smiled. 'Not to mention their saucy stories, and what they are planning for their womenfolk once they arrive home. By the way, have you and Katrinka ever? – you know what I mean?'

'Let's just say we know each other very well. Does that answer your question?'

'I thought so,' he smiled.

We thought it wise to run through the plan once more, in case there was something we had overlooked. John reminded me that she would need a case. 'No women's stuff in it mind – just shirts, socks and shaving gear. It wouldn't hurt to put in a couple of hundred duty-free fags, just in case Customs search her. It will look more like a bloke's belongings. Oh, and yes, she will need a pay book.'

I hadn't thought of that. My heart sank but John didn't give up hope.

'Perhaps there is someone in her camp who will forge one for her.'

I thought very carefully for a few minutes. 'No, Katrinka will carry your travel documents and that is all. Forging one of those is a very serious business, so no book fraud!' My mind raced on. 'All you will have to do is to bring your travel documents with you when you come to see me. When you leave, you will forget to take them with you. Have your shady fortnight with your German girlfriend, and then if you are found out it won't look so bad for you in the army's eyes.'

He looked somewhat relieved. 'I think that's a good idea.'

Getting the uniform out of the camp was the next problem. There was no way in which I could carry it past the guard; they would spot something of that size a mile off. After several futile suggestions, we came up with an answer. The hole in the fence would serve its purpose once again. I would wrap the uniform up in a package, wait for nightfall, then conceal it in the bushes, just on the inside. Once there, it could easily be retrieved from the outside. Katrinka could then take it back to her camp and hopefully get it altered to her size. We were feeling quite pleased with ourselves, at last we were getting somewhere.

After John had gone, the doubts started to creep in. I would be a criminal if caught. But if I didn't try, I would have to live with a broken heart. I needed to occupy my mind to stop it exploding. It would be a sensible idea to check on the deserters' uniforms – heaven knows what state they would be in. They were stuffed into two kitbags, and to my knowledge had been there for quite some time. It would do them good to have an airing. I emptied them onto the floor and picked out the smaller of the two uniforms. I found two fairly decent shirts, a belt and a beret, but no shoes or socks. The socks were no problem – she could have some of mine – but I would have to find a pair of shoes for her. Pants and vests, I had plenty enough of, so all in all things were looking up. I stuffed the unwanted items back into the kitbags, sharing them equally between the two, so as not to arouse suspicion. Everything was terribly creased, so I ironed it all. It took me ages to have it looking presentable, but finally it was done. I carefully folded the garments and packed them neatly in a waterproof bag. That done, I concealed the package in the back of my locker. Feeling pleased with myself for doing something positive, I left the camp in plenty of time to meet with Katrinka by the farmyard in the woods. It was pretty lonely up there, so I wanted to be there first. But she was there waiting, even though I had made good time. She looked cold, sad and worried as I took her hand. 'Come on, let's find our tree trunk,' I said, 'I have something very important to tell you.'

'Is it more bad news?' She looked uneasily at me.

'No, quite the opposite – at least, I hope you will think so, my darling.'

We found our special tree trunk and sat close together for warmth. 'What are the officials going to do with us now?' She was extremely nervous.

'Don't worry about them. No, I'm taking you back to Cornwall.'

Her face lit up like a shining beacon. 'Take me to your home? – but it is impossible!'

Brimming with excitement, I outlined John's plan to her. 'And so, Katrinka,' I concluded, 'you will travel with me dressed as a soldier, and your name will be John Osborne. What do you think of that?'

She looked at me in amazement. 'You must be crazy. We cannot do this thing . . . can we?'

Holding her tightly, I said, 'We must try. I can't live without you and there is no other way.'

She said nothing for a few moments and I was growing anxious. 'What do you say, Katrinka? Many more daring escapes than this have paid off for those who risked them. Please, please say yes. I am willing to stand up and be counted. Are you?'

Her cold, slender fingers tightened over mine. 'I do not understand when you say you have to stand to be counted, but I trust you, my Peter. I will come!'

I breathed a great sigh of relief. 'Oh Katrinka, I don't know what I would have done if you had said no. Without you, my life wouldn't be worth living!'

Excitedly, we went over the plan in some detail. We thought it best if the uniform was smuggled out the next evening. I told her to bring one of her bags to carry the parcel in, then she wouldn't look so noticeable when she returned to her camp. 'Can you get it altered to a professional standard?' I enquired with some concern. 'It has to be perfect.'

'I will do it myself,' she assured me. 'I have made the clothes I wear. I will make it good for the army.'

Now for the shoes. Passing her some money, I told her to buy a pair. 'They must look like mine,' I stressed. She smiled when I told her she would have to wear my pants and vests, and feigned a look of shocked horror. I had put off telling her about her hair for as long as was possible, but it had to be done. 'Short back and sides,' I told her. 'Just like mine. Is there anyone in the camp who will cut it for you?'

Her eyes were downcast. I could see she wasn't happy about it. 'Yes, my friend will cut my hair. Afterwards, in the camp, I will always wear my shawl.'

I nodded my satisfaction. 'Good.' Then came the difficult part. I had to teach her how to recognise the officers. But by then we were shivering with the cold, so we decided to walk while I endeavoured to impart the necessary information. 'Officers wear their badge of rank on their epaulettes,' I explained.

'What is epaulettes, Peter?'

'On their shoulders,' I said. 'These are the men you must salute.' The next thing was the salute itself. We stopped on the road and I stood in front of her. 'The simple way to remember it is: the longest way up – and the shortest way down. Like this.'

I demonstrated a few times, then told her it was her turn.

We had a lot of laughs, but in the end she had the hang of it. 'We will make you into a soldier yet,' I told her with a grin.

'What will your family say when you bring to your home a girl dressed as a soldier? And also with her hair like a man?' She looked decidedly worried.

I gave her a big cuddle. 'Don't you worry about that. They will love you as I do.' We stayed cuddled together, both locked in our own thoughts as we walked back through the woods. It crossed my mind that if Katrinka told her mates that she had relations somewhere up on the Baltic coast, anyone searching for her might assume that she had made her way to them. It could give us some extra time. 'Do you think that you could let it slip out that you would go straight there if ever you had the chance. Then, when the authorities discover you have gone, they might take several days searching for you up on that coast instead of the English Channel. Could you do that?'

'I think so.' She was slightly hesitant. 'It makes me feel very nervous. They will be searching for me, and not for you.'

I kissed her. 'We will make sure nothing goes wrong. I am sure we can get away with it. And before long we will be in England, eating fish and chips, and Cornish pasties.'

Her trusting little face looked up. 'I will have to learn how to cook these Cornwall dishes; there will be so much to learn. I am excited, and yet so worried.' We had nearly reached the town and it was quite dark. 'Please, Peter, can we enter the church for just a little time?'

She was virtually pleading with me. For a moment I didn't know what to say. I wanted to be with her more than anything, but I was afraid that someone would see us together. Then a thought suddenly struck me. If they had truly planned to part us when I took my leave, they wouldn't be worrying too much about us now. As long as I kept away from her camp they probably wouldn't bother us. 'Lead the way,' I told her, feeling a little more confident.

Katrinka pushed open the massive wooden door and we stepped inside. It was quite empty, apart from a few people sat in the far corner in hushed discussion with the priest. Katrinka led me down the aisle, until we were almost under the altar. We sat down and she took off her gloves and laid them on the seat beside her. She found my hand and guided me down to the kneeling position alongside her. Being a Methodist, and one who did not go to chapel very often, I was completely in her hands. She released my hand, then put her own hands together in prayer. I did likewise, while Katrinka prayed softly in her native tongue. I didn't understand a word of it, but I knew it was meant for both of us.

When she had finished she turned to me and began to whisper the *Lord's Prayer*. So then I was able to join in. We spoke the words together, very softly. I felt the bond between us grow stronger at that moment. I thought, God has put us together . . . we will make it! 'Sing *Ave Maria* for me,' I whispered.

A faint smile brushed her lips, then she started to sing in a sweet, hushed voice. The group in the corner turned to listen. One of the men promptly rose from his pew, crossed to the organ and began to play a soft accompaniment. The priest smiled and gesticulated for Katrinka to sing louder. Her beautiful voice filled the church, and as she sang, tears wetted her cheeks. She did indeed have the voice of an angel. As the organist played louder, Katrinka matched him, and I am sure that the people in that church felt just as I did, that if I lived to be a hundred, I would never again hear it sung so beautifully. When the dying notes echoed around the high ceiling, even the priest had tears in his eyes. He spoke to Katrinka in German, so I was none the wiser, but he studied me a long moment before returning to his flock in the corner. It made me feel very conspicuous. I quietly asked her what the priest had said.

'He asked me if I needed help, and would I wish to speak with him?'

'And what did you tell him?'

'Do not worry. I only say that we have what we came for.' She took my arm. 'Come, it is time for us to go.'

It was snowing again as we ventured back into the street. The air felt crisp and cold after the warmth of the church. We held each other tightly as we picked our way along the treacherous pavement. 'Thank you for singing, Katrinka, you sing so beautifully. I wish I could have heard your grandmother when she was in her prime. If she could teach you to sing like that, she must have been very good.'

'She was wonderful,' Katrinka replied. 'So wonderful!'

We had covered a fair distance, and the cold was beginning to take effect. Then Lady Luck stepped in for us, in the shape of a road menders' hut. It was only small, with a canvas front. I lifted the flap and peered inside. There were various tools and several lamps, and a very strong smell of paraffin. What really caught my eye was the welcome sight of two stools. 'Come on, Katrinka, at last a place to shelter and be alone.'

She tried to pull me back. 'We must not go inside. They may return!'

Gently but firmly tugging her in, I reassured her. 'No one will come at this time of night. The workmen won't be back until morning. We have lots of time.' I sat her on one of the stools and pulled down the canvas front. In spite of the surroundings and the obnoxious smell, it was heavenly. We snuggled up and made the most of it. When it was time to leave, we furtively slipped away into the night. Katrinka to her camp, and me to mine. Before I knew it, I was standing outside the guardroom door. My mind had been so busy on the way back, that I had no recollection of the journey. We had agreed that Katrinka would pick up the uniform the following night. That should give her plenty of time to make the alterations. I was now beginning to feel that what had seemed like a dream was becoming a reality. Feeling guilty, I opened the door and stepped into the guardroom. The Duty Corporal was sat at his desk. My heart went down to my boots when I noticed that the Provost Sergeant was in there with him. As always he had something to say. Looking up at the clock, he said, 'You have cut it very fine tonight, Private! Hurry up and be on your way.'

I needed no second telling. I signed in and scampered back to my block. As I neared the storeroom door, John suddenly emerged from the shadows. He made me jump.

'Well how did it go? What did she say?' He could hardly contain his impatience.

'Come inside and I'll tell you all about it.' I unlocked the door, switched on the light, and motioned for him to sit on my bed while I hung up my greatcoat. 'Do you want a piece of mother's Christmas cake. It's damned good.'

Nodding enthusiastically, his words tumbled out. 'Well, is it on?'

I handed him his cake. 'Yes, we are going to try it!'

John was delighted. 'You can make it, I know you can!'

As we enjoyed the cake we went through the list again. 'She will have to make sure the cap badge is gleaming on the day,' John said, busily stuffing his mouth with icing.

I said, 'I will carry her belt in my pocket, then I can adjust it to fit her waist. It will need bulling of course, but I can attend to that. It will be perfect for the great day,' I told him confidently.

'Great,' John said, all smiles as he left to return to his quarters.

I locked the door and sorted out a spare pair of vests and pants for Katrinka, along with a pair of socks. She had to look the same as us underneath, just in case any of her tunic buttons came undone. Every tiny detail had to be right, even down to the brand of soap. All the soldiers had the smell of 'Lifebuoy' on their person. I smelt the soap before wrapping it in paper – it still takes me back whenever I smell it today – then I put it in together with her underwear. I smiled to myself, these pants are going to have a revelation in the near future! And with that provocative thought, I went to bed.

The days seemed to fly by. On one hand I couldn't wait for my leave, but on the other I almost wished I had a bit longer, even though everything was going to plan. Katrinka had learnt her lessons well, and was turning out to be a pretty good soldier. There were times when I thought about what we were doing and I would be gripped by fear. My body would be covered in sweat. Then I would tell myself that it was the only way, or I might never see her again. Eventually I found myself with just two days to go. I was on my way to dinner when I again visited the chapel. The place was deserted. I sat on one of the seats and I prayed quietly for help. Before long, with my head still bowed, my prayer was forgotten as worrying thoughts plagued my mind. Was I plain crazy to even think about such a plan? I could even land up in the glasshouse. What would my parents think? I must get a grip on myself; we were going to be on that train! I felt a hand on my shoulder. It was the padre.

'Why it's Private Rundle, isn't it? You are looking a little down in the dumps. Don't tell me she has run away and left you.' Smiling at his own little joke, he motioned for me to remain seated as I made to rise, then he sat down beside me. 'You look as if you have a lot of worry on your shoulders, lad. Do you want to confide in me? I might be able to help in some way.' I shook my head, but he placed his hand on my shoulder and said, 'A trouble shared is a trouble halved. Come on, it can't be that bad.'

I looked at him in despair. 'It is, and worse.'

'Come now, start at the beginning,' he urged. 'Her Majesty has time to spare.'

So I told him all about Katrinka. How we met; our walks into the town; her singing in the church, and how we fell in love. I concluded by telling him of our problems with the military police and the immigration people – how I had been warned to stay away from her. I stopped there; the rest would have to remain secret, even though I felt like telling him the whole story.

He remained pensive for a while. It was as if he knew he hadn't heard the whole story. Then he asked me if I would join him in the *Lord's Prayer*. We prayed together, and at the end he added, '*May you guide this soldier on whatever course he takes. Amen.*'

'Thank you, father.'

As I rose to leave, the padre also rose and faced the altar. Without looking at me, he said quietly, 'It is unfortunate that I am unable to marry you, but like you I must obey army rules. I have a feeling you know already what you are going to do.' His voice remained kindly as he tried to read my thoughts, but there was no answer I could give him. When I bent to pick up my beret from the seat beside me, he said, 'Do not do anything foolish, and may God go with you.'

I came out of the chapel feeling much better. Just talking seemed to ease the pressure. I had a strong feeling that the padre had guessed that I was up to something, but I also felt that he was on my side. It left me with a warm feeling and I felt that what I was about to do was correct. I hurried on to the cookhouse; I would need all my strength. I really did feel like a new man.

e

Chapter Eleven

My next shock occurred during a very wet guard duty. The ice-cold rain was lashing down relentlessly as the corporal marched me outside at 2200 hours to relieve the sentry at the gate. It was certainly a night for ponchos. The retiring guard handed me the five rounds of ammunition before leaving me to brave the elements alone.

It was fairly quiet at first, apart from the odd car that came in or out. At 2300 hours the guard commander closed the big iron gates and then all was quiet for a while. Alone with my thoughts, my mind raced forward. The day after tomorrow we would be on the troop train heading for the Hook of Holland. I started to feel sick in the pit of my stomach. I felt like a cornered rat. I was in her Majesty's army, in a foreign land, and I had fallen in love with a Polish refugee. Why did things work out this way? – it wasn't fair. Why should this have happened to me? But it had, and now there was no turning back. I had to take this chance, perhaps our last. The rain had eased slightly so I ventured out into the middle of the dark road. The distant woodland looked black and ghostly; I turned my eyes towards the town. The dim street lights were twinkling and shimmering through the rain, and I wondered about Katrinka down there. Was she asleep? How was she feeling? Then I stiffened. Out of the corner of my eye I thought I saw something move in the shadows by the perimeter fence. I strained my eyes in the gloom . . . no, nothing there. It must be me, I was all jittery. Then I had doubts. Perhaps it was a soldier coming in late – no, he wouldn't walk through the main gate; he would go over the fence at the back of the camp. I scrutinised the fence again. I still wasn't sure. I slipped my hand into my pocket and carefully removed the five rounds of ammo. Easing them into the rifle's magazine, I slipped off the safety catch and drew back the bolt. My heart was thumping madly. Should I call out the guard, or merely challenge whoever was out there? The freezing rain was pelting down again, which made it very difficult to see clearly. 'Advance and be recognised,' I barked. My voice sounded strange.

Nothing, so I called again. This time there was movement. A shapeless figure emerged from the shadows. My fingers had stiffened with fright but I managed to control my mounting panic. Then a voice: 'Peter.' It was Katrinka's voice. I couldn't believe it.

'What the hell are you playing at? I could have shot you,' I gasped. 'I could have killed you!' My words were sharp, but I had been terrified.

She stood beside me, drenched through to the skin. 'Maybe it would have been better if you had, I am so mixed up inside of me. I do not think I can go through with the plan.' She started to cry. 'If we are caught, you will be imprisoned, and it will be because of me.'

'No,' I said, pulling her closer. I kissed her streaming wet face. 'I love you. I may as well shoot myself right now if you won't come with me.'

Katrinka lifted her face to mine. 'No, my darling, we will take our chances together,' she whispered between her tears. 'Please forgive me, I'm so sorry to make so much worry for you.'

I gave her a long, reassuring kiss, then told her to hurry back to her camp. We couldn't afford to jeopardise our plans now. Then she was gone and I was left alone in the black, unfriendly night.

The next morning, feeling rather worse for wear as I sat picking at my breakfast, Helga came by me with an armful of dirty dishes. Resting them on the end of my table, she whispered, 'How do you feel for tomorrow? OK?'

'I'm really scared,' I confessed.

'Don't worry. Tomorrow, all will be good.' She gave me a sympathetic smile, then retrieved her pile of crockery and sped back to the kitchens. I had forgotten that Helga knew of our plan. Hell, she played a big part in it.

Back at the mortar platoon it was work as usual. I had

difficulty in concentrating that morning, so I was delighted when John came down to the stores and told me he would be working alongside me for a while. We were to sort out the camouflage nets which were needed for the coming manoeuvres. 'How come they picked on you?' I asked him.

'Oh, I just happened to mention that they hadn't been checked since the last time we used them, so they sent me down to help you. I thought you might be glad of my company today.'

He was a real mate. I really did need his company, if only to reassure me again that I was doing the right thing. As we worked we spoke of nothing else but our impending arrangements. John had found out from the other company notice boards exactly how many would be travelling on our train. He reckoned there would be at least thirty-five in our party alone, which meant there would be two wagons to take us to the station. On this occasion, the more the merrier! When the bugle sounded for the end of the day's work, we couldn't believe where the time had gone. Our tongues had worked as hard as our hands, but I was feeling in a little better frame of mind by then. We had gone over our plan with a fine-tooth comb, and I felt pretty confident that we had covered everything. I gave John the case with Katrinka's spare underwear and soap, and we agreed to meet early the next day. Later, when I met Katrinka, I would go through the procedure with her.

After tea that evening, I dashed back to have a shower before meeting with Katrinka. The water was soothing, but my mind was racing. I must remember to tell her everything tonight, it was crucial that all our plans were perfect! Back in my room, I quickly undressed again and put the spare belt for Katrinka around my waist, next to my skin. I then donned my uniform with my own belt on the outside. It felt strange but didn't look too obvious. The shiny cap badge went into my pocket easily. I took a last look in the mirror, a deep breath, then off to the guardroom to book out. I encountered no problems booking-out, even though I felt my face reddening with guilt. As I walked toward the town, I realised this evening would be the last time that I would meet with Katrinka in Gottingen. When I returned from leave I was going to really miss her company. Still, it wouldn't be for long.

As usual she was there waiting for me. 'I am so afraid when I am not with you, my Peter.' She sounded nervous, which was understandable. I gave her a squeeze and told her that very soon we would be together for ever.

We walked in silence to the wireless shop. The rent was due, and I wanted to settle up my bill for the next two weeks. As I made to open the door, Katrinka gripped my arm. 'Do I say goodbye to them? They have been nice people to us.'

'I'm sorry,' I told her. 'We mustn't tell them, or anyone. If just one person spoke out of turn we would be caught before we were out of Germany.'

She nodded miserably. 'I suppose you are right!'

The door bell clanged loudly as we entered the shop. The proprietor's wife came bustling in from the back. She was looking hot and flustered and was jabbering something in German. She sounded distinctly cross. I asked Katrinka what all the fuss was about?

'She is very cross her husband is late. She says she has to do his work, and that his meal is no good any more.'

The woman was still babbling on as I paid her the rent. I hoped she had entered it in the ledger correctly. I didn't fancy having to pay twice. She passed me back my card and turned to go back to her duties. Katrinka looked at me, then turned to the fast disappearing back of the woman. Hell, I thought, she's going to say something. I quickly put my arm around her shoulders and led her to the door. As we went through, Katrinka called over her shoulder, 'Auf Weidersehen.' Her voice was tinged with sadness.

The wireless woman turned and studied us carefully before answering. 'Auf Weidersehen,' she said.

'I thought you were going to blow it in there, Katrinka!' I said, once we were safely outside.

Her eyes were shimmering with tears. 'Sometimes it is a sad thing to say goodbye – even to a German.'

I gave her a cuddle. 'Yes, I know how you feel. I like them myself. Anyway, I will see them when I get back off leave; I will still have my rent to pay. I will be able to send you news of them.'

She snuggled into me as we walked down the cobbled street. 'I feel a little better now, Peter. Thank you.'

I asked her if her friends in the camp still believed that she was keen to get to the Baltic coast.

'Yes, I tell them I have family in Bremerhaven, we talk about it sometimes.'

‘That’s good. When they discover you are missing, they are sure to ask questions. When they find out that I have gone home on leave, they will be sure to think you have gone to be with your family. I hope and pray that the German police will assume the same.’

We headed for the tavern. As we neared our sanctuary the warm light spilled out of the leaded windows to welcome us. Inside, the fire was blazing fiercely up the chimney. The people hugging the fireside seemed blissfully unperturbed by the volley of sparks being showered at them. Heads together, they were all earnestly chatting, and probably putting the world to rights. We found a seat in a dark corner. It wasn’t long before the landlord dressed in his long white apron, weaved his way through the tables to collect our order.

I held up two fingers and said, ‘Two beers please.’ He seemed to understand me, because he deftly turned and headed back to the bar.

Katrinka laughed. ‘Your German is perfect.’

It was lovely to hear her laugh, even though she was mocking me. The landlord soon returned and placed our two beers on the table before us, and Katrinka thanked him in his own tongue. You would not be able to thank him with finger language, would you, my Peter.’ She smiled at me over her glass.

‘You just wait until I get you back to Cornwall, my girl, then you’ll see who’s boss! Here, have a cigarette.’

‘I think I need one,’ she sighed, as she helped herself from the packet. We lit up and I watched the smoke curl lazily up to the ceiling, which was already blackened by a multitude of German smokers. I caught an old gentleman glancing longingly at our cigarettes above his German newspaper. Each time I took a draw he almost drooled, until I felt quite guilty at having this luxury. In the end I could stand it no longer and offered him one. ‘Danka, danka,’ he kept repeating all the way back to his chair.

With an impish smile, Katrinka said, ‘Would you like to look at his newspaper; he has finished with it now. He would be happy for you to have it.’

‘You are too kind, my darling, especially as you know I can’t read a bloody word of German.’

Katrinka chuckled softly and sipped her drink. It was lovely to see her so happy. This young woman had known nothing but trouble and strife. First it was the Germans and losing her parents in the war. Then communism, and now losing her beloved grandmother and ending up in a refugee camp. I must not be the one to let her down again. I cupped her face in my hands. 'People have always said the English are at their best when in a tight corner. That's why I can still joke, Katrinka.' I undid my breast pocket and took out my handkerchief with the cap badge wrapped carefully inside it. 'Put this on your beret just before you leave the camp. Try not to handle it too much because it's just been polished.'

She accepted it gingerly so as not to mar its shine, and placed it in her bag. I suddenly remembered the belt which was fastened next to my skin, and immediately became aware of how uncomfortable it was. With my mind so completely occupied, I hadn't even noticed the evident discomfort. It was time to go to the toilet and remove it. I soon found myself in the smallest toilet imaginable. With great difficulty, I managed to undo my belt and tunic, pull up my shirt and take off the spare belt. What a relief to get rid of that hard constricting band. I dressed as quickly as was possible in the confined space, then concealing the belt as best I could, headed back to Katrinka. I noticed she had company. It was the old chap who had enjoyed one of my cigarettes. He was very close to her, bent low with his face almost touching hers, appearing to be deep in conversation. As I neared our table, he glanced up and saw me coming. Without another word, he straightened up and shuffled back to his seat. 'What was that all about?' I brought my chair closer to hers. 'Were you talking about me?'

Katrinka nodded. 'I am sorry but yes, we were. The man was concerned for me. He say, "Is it wise to be with a British soldier?" I tell him very wise because I am Polish, not German!'

I gripped her hand. 'Good for you, my 'ansome . . . that's the way to tell 'em!'

She gave me a coy look. 'I am still your 'ansome?'

'Oh, Katrinka, yes. For ever and ever!' I felt like taking her in my arms and smothering her with kisses, but it wasn't the time to attract any unwanted attention to ourselves.

Under the cover of the table, I placed the belt on to her lap. 'You will have to be really careful with that one,' I explained. 'The blanco is easily marked. When you get back tonight, check it for marks. If there are any, spit on your hankie and gently rub them out. Just let it dry naturally and it should be OK.'

She felt in her bag and drew out her old scarf which she placed over the belt on her lap. The scarf was then folded over, and with the belt hidden inside was lovingly placed back into the confines of her bag. The tavern was now almost full, and very noisy. No one was taking any notice of us, so I thought it was time to discuss the next day's procedure. I managed to catch the inn-keeper's eye and he came across with two more beers for us. He picked up the empty glasses, wiped the table with a flourish of his damp cloth, and exchanged the dirty ashtray for a clean one at lightning speed before dashing back to serve his other impatient customers. I sat as close to Katrinka as was possible. The din around us was deafening, so there was no real worry that anyone would overhear us. 'Now my darling, we will go over tomorrow's plans,' I said. 'You must be at the station by a quarter-to-nine, no later! Carry the little case with your uniform inside, but first check that you have it all. If you forget anything, even one small item, you will not be able to board that train. And remember to always use the gents' toilets.'

She fidgeted uneasily in her chair but I carried straight on. 'When you get there, go straight into a cubicle, lock the door and change into the army uniform which you carry in your case. Make sure the beret is on properly, just as you see me wearing mine. Next, put all your discarded clothes into the now empty case. Remember, you are then a British soldier! All you have to do then, is to sit on the toilet and wait.' Katrinka was beginning to look very uncomfortable. 'John and I shouldn't be too long. He will be whistling *Ave Maria*, so as soon as you hear him, peep out just to make sure it is us! When you are sure, come out with the case. The three of us will talk together and in the meantime you will have swapped your case for the one which John will be carrying. He will dispose of your old clothes later.'

Katrinka looked as if she was about to say something, then changed her mind.

I carried on. 'Your new case will contain army underwear and everything else a soldier would normally carry. You and I will walk casually out of the toilets, whilst John will stay behind and hide in one until the coast is clear. When the train has pulled out of the station, he will make his way to Helga's place and enjoy fourteen days with her.' Katrinka managed a weak smile. I told her it would be best if we waited for the train a little apart from the others. 'Once we get on the train we will look for a compartment seating troops from Berlin. We'll be strangers to them, so they won't recognise us. And we won't talk any more than is strictly necessary. From then on we will take things as they come. Hopefully by then, you and Germany will be separated for ever,' I whispered as I snatched a quick kiss.

I could see that Katrinka was trying to be brave, but her voice trembled as she spoke. 'Peter, if we do not do it this way, I know we will be parted for ever. I could not bear that. Both the German and Communist police are ruthless people, we must pray we do not end up in their hands.' She turned away, fighting for composure. Then she faced me again. 'The British army I do not know about, but I think they would not be happy either, would they?'

'Katrinka my darling, look at me. If we tried to walk to Holland, then perhaps stow away on a boat, it would take too long. I am sure they would catch us. This way, within a couple of days, you will be safely home in Cornwall with me. We are going to do it. First we will boldly step on to the troop train, then the troopship. In other words, it will be first class all the way.'

We had finished our beers. The air had become thick with smoke, and my eyes and throat were stinging like mad. I took Katrinka's hand. 'Come on, I think it's time to go before I lose you in a cloud of smoke.'

Just ahead of us and wobbling unsteadily was the old man who had envied us our cigarettes. Someone else must have felt sorry for him because he now had another cigarette dangling from his lips. I had a feeling that his evenings in the tavern were quite profitable for him.

It was good to step outside. We both filled our lungs with the fresh cold air. We walked around for a bit until we came to a handy doorway.

As was usual, I stood with my back to the door and undid my greatcoat. Katrinka didn't need telling; she snuggled in close to me. As I put my arms around her and hugged her tightly, she looked into my eyes. 'This is the only place I feel I am safe,' she whispered, 'I would wish to stay like this for ever.' I bent to kiss her, but she turned her cheek and her voice shook as she spilled out her fears. 'If we are caught they will maybe shoot the both of us. They might say that we are spies.'

I could feel the wetness of her face. 'My darling, I am sure it will not come to that. But if anything should go wrong, at least our spirits will be together for eternity.'

We remained huddled in the doorway until we were numb with the cold, neither of us wanting to leave. But it was finally time to go. I moved to do up my coat. 'I think it's time we got back to camp, we have a big day tomorrow.'

'Please stay, just for a little while,' she pleaded, clinging to me for all she was worth.

'Just a few more minutes, my darling, and then we must go,' I said. I hated having to leave her. As we were walking back I asked her if she would like to visit her church once more. She nodded gratefully, so we slipped down a side alley and approached it from the rear. The entire building was in darkness, not a single light visible.

She looked dismayed. 'I cannot enter there tonight!'

Taking her arm, I led her to the big iron gates at the front of the church and pushed them open.

Katrinka held back. 'Where are we going? There is no one here.'

'It's all right,' I told her, 'I am just taking you to the door – that's as far as we can go tonight, but it will do.' She hesitated for a moment, then followed me until we reached the steps which led to the main doors. 'I think it will do the both of us some good to pray – you in your way, and me in mine,' I said. I took her hand and we sank to our knees and prayed together.

When we were back on the road again and had closed the gate quietly behind us, she gave me a kiss. 'Thank you, my Peter, I do feel better now.'

I was relieved to notice that her voice sounded firmer. I had been so worried that she might not be able to go through with our plan. If only I didn't have to leave her. But it was late and I did.

I stopped, as usual of late, a good hundred yards short of Katrinka's entrance door. Taking her in my arms, I whispered, 'I will see you in the morning, Private Osborne.' We clung to each other, both of us terrified by what we were about to do. Then, with the reluctance evident in her voice, Katrinka murmured that she had to go. I freed her from my arms, and she hurried away towards the camp gate. One last little wave and she was gone.

As I walked up the hill to my barracks my mind was in a turmoil. I had been telling that girl to be brave and strong all evening, and now here I was feeling as sick as a dog. I thought of my father in the First World War. He probably felt afraid each time he went over the top, but he went just the same. I must be brave. But those bastard redcaps, and the German that I had met in the Adjutant's office, wouldn't they just gloat if I was caught! You won't be, I told myself. Pull yourself together, man, and show them what a Cornishman can do.

The corporal greeted me as soon as I put my foot in the door. 'You're the last one in tonight, lad, just time enough to get smartly into bed before *lights out*. Hurry it up now.'

When I turned on the light in my storeroom, things somehow looked different . . . eerie and cold, yet nothing had changed. I realised it must have been how I was feeling. With a shiver I took off my greatcoat and tunic and hung them up, then I swiftly checked my case for the morning. Everything seemed to be in order, I would just need to put my shaving gear in when I had finished with it after breakfast. Shivering, I climbed into bed and pulled my knees up to my chin. The bed itself was shaking, my body just wouldn't keep still. I pretended to myself that it was the cold, but it was nerves of course. As the bugler sounded lights out, I reached for the broom handle which I kept by my bed to turn off the light and prodded the switch. I was in darkness and alone with my thoughts for company – they would probably keep me awake all night!

As the hours dragged slowly by, my mind raced from one part of the journey to another. Then I began to wonder what my parents and family would say. It was almost dawn when I eventually succumbed to a merciful oblivion.

Chapter Twelve

The next thing I knew was that the bugler was sounding *Wake up you lazy buggers!* or *Reveille*, to give it its rightful name. I lay there for a few minutes, wondering what Katrinka was doing, and how she was feeling. Please God, don't let her back out. The day we had planned for was here. I took stock of my own feelings. Surprisingly, I felt quite calm. It was probably due to my whole nervous system having gone numb with panic. I grabbed my towel and shaving gear and raced up to the washroom. Half of the basins were already in use. I selected one and put my towel between my knees to stop it from going on the floor. The water was lovely and hot. I began to lather my face, when suddenly another image appeared next to mine in the mirror. It was John, looking over my shoulder.

'Everything OK, Pete?'

I nodded in reply. 'See you on the truck later on.'

He gave me a wink and his face vanished from the shaving mirror. I managed to finish shaving without any nicks, then washed and combed my hair. At least I now looked normal on the outside. Back in my storeroom, I dressed into my best battle-dress and checked my case once more. Next I checked my money: thirty-one pounds, ten shillings. I felt quite rich, seeing that we earned just three pounds, seven-and-six a week. The bugler had now changed his tune, and was playing *Come to the cookhouse door boys*. So grabbing my eating irons and enamel mug, I sped off for breakfast. I forced myself to eat because I knew that it could be hours before my next meal. On my way back to the block I saw the padre coming towards me. Oh Hell, I thought – I would have preferred not to see him right at that moment. I saluted him, and as he returned the salute he smiled and said, 'Off on leave, lad?'

'Yes, sir.'

'Splendid – be sure to enjoy yourself.' His next remark completely unnerved me: 'Not taking the girlfriend with you then?'

'No, sir,' I spluttered, whereupon he chuckled shamelessly and went on his way.

My heart missed a beat. Why did he say that? Did he know? As I let myself into the stores and flopped down on the bed, I was trembling all over. Why did I ever drag Katrinka into this mess? I can't back out of it now . . . she will be on her way. What have I done? A booming voice cut in on my thoughts:

'All those going to the station will parade outside now!'

This was it, no going back now! I put on my beret and greatcoat, picked up my case, checked our travel warrants, and was out of the door in a flash. I passed my key into the office on the way out, and joined the others, all excitedly waiting for the wagons to take us to the station.

John sidled up to me, case in hand. 'Well this is it, Pete. Let's hope Katrinka will be down there waiting. Helga will be pretty sore with me if I have to go home after all.' I must have had worry written all over my face. 'Cheer up, mate,' he added, 'everything's going to turn out OK, you see if it don't.'

By this time the trucks were reversing back to us. As soon as they stopped we all piled in. Someone banged the tailboard to let the driver know we were ready, and we were off. Our perilous journey had begun.

It was only a short run to the station, then we were all piling out on to the platform. The station was really crowded. There were military personnel from other regiments, and scores of German civilians waiting for various trains. John walked close beside me as we hurried straight to the toilets. I had a sinking feeling that Katrinka would not be there. After much weaving and dodging we made it. There were a few men inside, but mainly civilians. John started to whistle *Ave Maria*. It was a good job that the whistling was down to him. My throat felt like sandpaper and I was shaking like a leaf. I couldn't have whistled a note if my life depended on it, which it more or less did! We started walking past the cubicles, John whistling away merrily. Nothing was happening. One of the doors opened slightly, then closed again. We looked at each other – it must be her! Then the door opened wider and out came a fat, middle-aged German, busily puffing away at a king-size cigar. My heart went down into my boots. She wasn't there!

John was whistling with all his might as he walked ahead of me. I stopped as I saw another door open; just another soldier. But was it? My breath caught in my throat – could it be? I was afraid to look. Yes! – it was Katrinka! I was elated.

With no show of emotion, Katrinka placed her case on the floor next to John's. His eyes scanned her from top to toe. The transformation was truly amazing. 'You look even smarter than us, old chap,' John said with a wry smile. Then, to me: 'No day dreaming now, Pete, it's time you were on the platform. Good luck.'

Katrinka picked up his case and followed me outside. We picked a spot away from the other military personnel. When I offered Katrinka a cigarette I saw that her hand was shaking. 'Peter, will I pass as a soldier? I almost did not come . . . I am still not sure if this is the right thing to do. My heart tells me yes, but I still think we're crazy.'

'You are perfect,' I whispered, 'and thank God you are here.' Our voices were drowned by the noise of a train pulling in. Not ours, worse luck. I couldn't wait to get away from here and to feel settled on our journey. Several people were getting off. Probably workers in the town. The Tannoy crackled out some messages in German.

'Brackwede and Dortmund,' Katrinka informed me. Nothing to do with us, so we smoked on. Then I saw an officer heading in our direction. I strove to control my instinctive panic. 'Quick, look the other way,' I told Katrinka, then, as he drew near, I saluted him. He returned the salute, after a fashion, and almost dropped his cane in the process.

About three paces past us, he half-turned and called back, 'I say, has the Dortmund train departed yet, soldier?'

'No sir,' I managed to reply. 'Any minute now though!'

'Jolly good,' he remarked in his cut-glass accent, and then thankfully continued on his way. Numerous trains were coming and going. As the loudspeakers continued to blurt out their, to me, unintelligible messages, I could see that Katrinka was growing ever more nervous. Where was our train? I glanced at my watch. It was running late. Then a message in English issued from the Tannoy: '*All military personnel bound for Holland be ready to board when the train arrives at Platform Two.*'

The platform was suddenly a scene of frantic activity as the waiting troops collected their gear together, some of them so heavily laden that they were probably changing units. I was thankful we had just the one case each to carry. At long last our train roared into the station. It was very long, pulled by two powerful diesel engines. As it ground to a halt, the doors were flung open wide and several people alighted. Then it was every man for himself. There was a lot of pushing and shoving as everyone tried to get on at the same time. It suited our purpose. No one was interested in anyone else. It was with a feeling of great relief that we finally stepped on to that train. I told Katrinka to follow me as I made my way to the back of the train, hopefully away from anyone I knew in the KSLI. The train was filling up fast. I was beginning to think we would never get a seat when an airman who was standing in a compartment doorway, beckoned to us. 'There's seats in here, mucker,' he informed us in a broad cockney accent. I thanked him and gratefully accepted his offer. We were lucky, there were only three airmen occupying it, so we had plenty of room, and no soldiers for the moment. I put my case up on the rack, then looked at Katrinka and raised my eyes to indicate that she had to put her own case up there. It would have looked most strange if I had attempted to help her. I was thankful her case was lighter than mine. Without hesitation, she slung it up into the rack before taking a seat next to the window. That was good. She would be able to look out of the window and keep herself to herself as much as possible.

We settled into our seats and I glanced across to the three airmen. They all looked as if they had been travelling for some time; their tunics were undone, and they had been reading. Two of them were typical 'Brylcreem boys' – far more refined than we infantrymen. The other one looked as if he could be a tough customer. He was sandy haired, with big bushy eyebrows. It was he who had invited us into the compartment. When I asked him how long they had been travelling, he gave a cheesed-off sigh. 'Since last night, mate – all the way from Berlin.' He stretched out his arms and legs. 'You see, they like us to travel through the Communist zone when it's dark. That's because we are forbidden to see what's going on. We did sneak a look, of course, but there was bugger-all to see. Nothing! I don't know what all the fuss is about.'

I told him that I had been there once before, with our running team, and how we all thought it was an awful place.

'Too bloody true it is, mate,' retorted our new-found friend. 'So you're a runner, are you?'

'Not really,' I explained. 'My brother was in the regiment before me and gained a reputation as a top cross-country runner. When I arrived on the scene they thought I must be in the same league and pounced on me. I couldn't match up to him, no way. I must have been a big disappointment to them. I prefer boxing – that's the sport for me.'

He moved to the edge of his seat and leaned closer. 'Ain't that funny?' he grinned, 'it's mine too. I'm the BAOR middleweight champ.'

I stuck out my hand. 'Pleased to meet you, champ.'

While we had been chatting, the train had left the station. I hadn't even noticed. It felt good to be speeding away from Germany. At least we had got this far, but I wouldn't rest until we were safely home. I glanced at Katrinka. Her face was very pale. How I wished I could take her in my arms and comfort her.

The champ came over and sat by me. He produced some snapshots of himself, taken in the ring. They looked impressive, I could see he knew his stuff. 'Would your mate like to see them?' he asked me. He looked at her, but she appeared to be sleeping. 'Perhaps another time,' he said, sounding disappointed. 'He looks very pale. Isn't he well?'

He couldn't know how his simple question had boosted my confidence. He really thought that she was a he! I told him that 'John' was on compassionate leave, that his mother had passed away.

'I'm sorry,' he whispered. 'No wonder he's so quiet.'

I hadn't taken any notice of our companions for some time. Their voices had droned obscurely through my snatches of sleep, but suddenly their words became very clear. They were chatting excitedly about what they would do once they were home. I gathered they were all from London, and what they were going to do when they arrived there was something else! There were words spoken in that compartment that even I would hesitate to utter. Whether Katrinka would know what they meant, I wasn't sure. I only knew that I felt extremely uncomfortable. I threw her a quick glance, but her eyes were still closed and her face was expressionless. The train was hurtling along at great speed through the West German countryside. There were many canals and towering pine trees, but the terrain was generally much flatter than in England. The airmen, having exhausted their long list of erotic intentions, decided to move to another compartment in order to play cards with some friends. They invited us along, but I politely declined their friendly offer.

The minute their backs were turned we both breathed a sigh of relief. Alone at last, I couldn't believe our luck.

'Peter, could you please give me a little hug,' Katrinka whispered. 'I feel so strange. I feel that this is not myself travelling on this train.'

My darling Katrinka, she looked so lost. 'You know we can't risk it,' I said quietly. 'It would take only one military person to see us, and we would be in big trouble. They would think we were queer, and queers aren't allowed in the army!'

She smiled a little at that. 'Oh, you mean homosexual?'

I nodded.

She looked at me knowingly. 'You are not that, my Peter.'

I thought it a good time to give her the travel documents, and explain their uses. She listened carefully as I went through each slip of paper. We would need to show them when we boarded the troopship, and then there were some for the civvy trains when we arrived in England. Next, I gave her ten pounds in cash. Her eyes grew as big as saucers. 'All this money, Peter! Why do you give me so much?'

Quietly I explained, 'If anything should happen and we get separated, you will have some money to get yourself to Cornwall.'

'I will not let that happen. I will keep close to you all the way, my Peter!'

I explained about the money. 'Each pound note is worth seven marks, so you must be careful not to lose any of them.'

She folded them carefully and tucked them into her tunic pocket. 'I will be most careful, but I hope that I will not have to use them.'

'There is one other thing,' I told her. 'If things do go wrong and they send you back to Poland, I must know where to find you. You came from somewhere on the Baltic coast. Where exactly?'

Her face fell. 'A place called Goleniiow. It is roughly eight kilometres from the port of Szczecin.'

I thought it wise to make a note. I would never be able to remember those names. Retrieving my case from the rack, I managed to find a pen and some notepaper. I handed them to Katrinka. 'You had better write it down for me.'

She scribbled down the names and handed back the paper, which I folded neatly and tucked into one of my socks. 'Now don't forget, Katrinka,' I said pointedly. 'If you do get deported, stay near to that port. I will get to you, no matter what it takes.'

'Yes, I will do this.' Her reply was subdued.

I lifted the lid of my case to shield my hand from view, then gently squeezed her fingers. How cold they were; if only I could comfort her.

The train was slowing down. I looked out of the window and saw that we were pulling into a station. The sign on the platform read Osnbruck, and there were several servicemen waiting to jump aboard. Immediately the corridor seemed to be full of boots and loud shouting. I quickly sat down as a chap poked his head in. 'Sorry, this one is full, mate – the others will be back in a minute.' He looked at me in frustration, but thankfully moved along the train. In a very short time the corridors had emptied and all was quiet. Our RAF companions had not yet returned.

Katrinka had not yet seen the contents of her case. I lifted it down from the rack and placed it on her lap. 'Go on, open it up and see what you are carrying.'

She smiled when she saw all the menswear. After sifting through the various layers, she took something out of her pocket and slid it under the clothes.

'What have you put in there?' I asked, as I lifted a garment to see. It was her new scarf and the watch which I had given her.

Her hand brushed mine. 'These are the only possessions I own, I could not leave them behind.'

I felt so sad for her. 'It's all right, Katrinka, if anyone should look inside, you can say they are presents for home.'

I replaced her case in the rack and settled down beside her. The swaying of the train finally made me feel drowsy. Before long, I noticed that she had dozed off, so closing my eyes, I hoped that I would soon join her. There was still some way to go.

Chapter Thirteen

We were rudely awakened by the airmen returning.

'Wakey, wakey. Time for lunch.' They shouted. 'We've had ours.' They seemed to be in high spirits so I assumed they had enjoyed their meals and hadn't done too badly at cards either. I didn't need a second telling, I suddenly realised my stomach had started to complain. Katrinka followed me post-haste as I headed for the buffet car.

After we had eaten we returned to our compartment to find that the airmen had removed their tunics. Katrinka would clearly have raised a few male eyebrows if she had followed suit, so I quietly suggested that she remove her tie and undo the top two buttons of her shirt. Which she did gladly. The train was still thundering through the German countryside carrying us nearer by the minute to Cornwall.

'I won't be sorry to get this trip over with,' Katrinka remarked in a far deeper voice than usual. Nobody paid her any attention so the lower tone was clearly convincing. She never ceased to amaze me. Then it was her turn to be amazed as three members of the Seaforth Highlanders, wearing kilts, leaned into our compartment. I doubt that Katrinka had ever seen men in skirts before. They were each brandishing a well depleted whisky bottle, so we hoped they would pass us by. But one of them lurched drunkenly inside and pushed the bottle up to the champ's lips. I breathed a sigh of relief. He had picked the right one as far as we were concerned. The champ was having none of it. He grabbed the Jock's wrist and lowered arm and bottle away from him. The drunk not caring for the stern look the champ gave him, rolled round to stand facing Katrinka. He wouldn't give up. I noticed the look of terror as the bottle moved towards her lips. I had to act quickly. Pushing the bottle away from her face, I said, 'I'll have a drink with you mate, he's feeling ill.' The neat spirit burned my throat as I gulped it down. He was ready with the bottle again. 'Have another buddy,' The bottle swung towards me, he didn't get very far. Our airmen friends had had enough. In a flash they were off their seats, grabbed the bewildered Jock and unceremoniously hustled him and his mates out of the compartment and chased them down the corridor. For a few moments we were left alone.

Katrinka was looking at me with some concern. My eyes were watering and my throat was still on fire. It was the first time I had tasted whisky.

'Who were those strange men?' Katrinka asked.

Half afraid to speak in case my vocal chords had reacted to the fire-water, I explained in a whisper, 'They are wearing kilts. The Scots who live in the north of my country sometimes wear them. They are also responsible for making the whisky which they are so fond of. The men we have just seen look just like the Highlanders, but really they are Canadians in a Scottish regiment.

Our friends soon came back grinning, and assured us that we had seen the last of them.

After another short nap, I sat up with a start and shivered. One of the airmen had the upper part of his body hanging out of the compartment window. I realised the train had stopped and I could hear excited chatter going on, inside and out. Katrinka was awake and looked like a frightened dormouse hiding in her corner.

'What's going on?' I asked the bloke at the window.

'We're at the border with Holland. There are chaps out here hitting the wheels with hammers.'

I got up to have a better look. 'It's only a safety procedure,' I said. 'If the wheel doesn't have the right tone when it is struck, it means there's a crack in it. Then it must be changed.'

'Damned ingenious,' he muttered as he carried on watching with renewed interest. While I was up, I took out a couple of cowboy books from my case. It would help to pass the time away. Just as I threw one over to Katrinka, someone shouted, 'Customs are on their way!'

This happened on every trip. As a rule they might search one case in every hundred. All the same, we didn't want any official getting too near to us. I leaned across Katrinka, pretending to look at something out of the window, and whispered to her, 'Read your book!' A few minutes passed, and sure enough there were two Dutch customs men peering in the doorway. One held up his hand in greeting, then off they went.

Without exception, every face in that compartment wore an expression of relief. One of the airmen gave a huge sigh. 'I'm glad they didn't pick on my case. It's half full of French letters – I helped myself from the stores.'

We all burst out laughing. Even Katrinka smiled. I wondered if she really knew what we were all laughing about. I was curious.

'What the Hell are you going to do with that many? Are you trying to corner the market, or something?'

'You might well laugh soldier, but don't forget you have to pay half-a-crown for three at home – and I have a lot of threes in this case.'

I suppose it made sense. The train had resumed its journey, now whisking us through Holland. It was strange to look out and see such a flat landscape, and so many canals and boats such a long way inland. As I was taking in the scenery Katrinka put down her book and left the compartment, presumably to visit the toilet. After she had gone my pal the boxer looked over to me with an exaggerated frown.

'That mucker of yours . . . is he a bit of a Nancy boy? Didn't laugh a lot over Mal's French letters did he?'

I took a deep breath. 'John a bit of a Nancy . . ? No he's OK, as tough as they come. The thing is, the death of his mother has really knocked him back.'

He looked sorry. 'Oh heck, I'd forgotten. That explains it then.' He seemed satisfied with that and we carried on chatting. After quite some time had passed Katrinka still hadn't returned. I started to worry. I made an excuse to visit the toilet and went in search of her. Towards the end of the carriage, opposite the toilet, I saw her wistfully gazing out of the window.

'I wondered where you were . . . are you all right?' She nodded with a smile as I joined her at the window.

'Just thinking. It is nice to be by myself . . . sometimes it is very difficult for me to act as a man.'

The train was slowing down. The daylight was fading but I could see that we were entering a station.

A few weary faces stared back at us as we chugged slowly by

the platform, but this train was not for them. Hopefully theirs would soon arrive.

Someone squeezed by us heading for the toilet.

'Peter?' She spoke in a whisper. 'Why did everyone laugh when the airman told of his stealing of the letters . . ? Did a French girl write them to someone . . ? How can he make money from them?'

She had caught me unawares. How was I supposed to explain this to my naive little Polish girl. At nineteen my experience with girls was almost nil. I swallowed hard.

'They are to stop girls from having babies.' The words gushed hurriedly from my mouth.

'So . . . these letters will do this?' She looked bewildered.

'Yes,' I replied. But I knew this wasn't good enough. I thought, hell, here goes, so checking that the coast was clear, I pointed to my flies, then held up my finger and pretended to put one on.

Katrinka frowned, then all of a sudden she laughed and her cheeks turned bright pink. She jabbered something in Polish, then she said to me, 'So that is what the English call them. Now I can see the funny story.'

It was now quite dark outside, so we opted to return to our compartment. As luck would have it, the airmen were just about to leave for a wash and brush up. With their towels around their necks, they followed each other out of the compartment and along the corridor. Katrinka then wanted to know about the rest of the journey, so I spelled out the details of the boat, the train and the London Underground stages as best I could. 'Don't worry,' I said, 'We'll take each step as it comes.'

She sat quietly for a few moments, deep in thought. Her hand moved as if to hold mine, then remembering where she was, she swiftly placed it back in her lap. 'I am not afraid of the journey, Peter, but what will it be like for me on the boat? Will the airmen travel with us? Will there be much space?'

I told her that we would be packed tightly together on the boat; about two hundred to a deck. For one night only we would sleep on bunks, about three-high. But nobody will know us, nor we them. We will keep ourselves to ourselves. 'Everything will be fine,' I said, seeking to reassure her.

Her little face turned to me with love and gratitude written all over it. Even with her hair cropped short and in manly clothes she was still a Polish beauty.

It was pitch black outside now. Our company had returned and were all sprawled out untidily on their seats. They looked as if they were completely fed up with travelling, and no wonder – they had been on the move for many hours. We thought it a good idea to leave them in peace while we went to freshen up. I could have laughed aloud when I noticed Katrinka take out her shaving kit, but she had the right idea. We went into the wash-up together. I left the door partly ajar; the army was very strict on that sort of thing. I ran some water and told Katrinka to wash her face first, then I would wash and use the same water to shave. Washing was no problem, but I had to be careful with my razor. What with the motion of the train, and Katrinka looking over my shoulder and making faces at me, I think it was the hardest shave I've ever had. It's certainly not easy shaving and laughing at the same time. Eventually I finished my task and drained the water from the basin, making sure to rinse it out in readiness for the next person – a lesson well-learnt from my mother. As I turned I pushed the door shut with my foot. Grabbing Katrinka in my arms, I kissed her. I had caught her by surprise, but in a flash her arms were around my neck. It was only a brief moment, but it was wonderful. We emerged from the wash-up just as some chaps were coming along with their towels, which was an even closer shave.

Katrinka whispered, 'That was good, I did not think we would touch each other until we were in your home.'

I gave her a sly wink. 'Ha, but I didn't know such an opportunity was in store for us, me 'ansome.'

She clenched her fist and gave me a playful thump on my back, whereupon I pretended to fall over. Her hand covered her mouth to suppress her giggles. After all the tension it was good to see her enjoying a light-hearted moment, no matter how brief it was.

Back once more in our seats, we felt refreshed and in good spirits. Blurred lights raced past our window, signalling our approach to the Hook of Holland. The airmen had started to move and were sorting out their gear. Katrinka and I thought we had better do the same. A voice bellowed along the empty corridor, 'Arriving in ten minutes! Get your gear ready and smarten yourselves up!' The owner of the voice, in the shape of a red-faced and moustached sergeant, suddenly filled the doorway.

'Come on, get your finger out! Hurry it up!'

I glanced at Katrinka to make sure she was presentable. I could see she had learnt her lessons well. We could hardly move for the luggage on the floor, but finally we were all ready and waiting. As the train started to slow down we all shook hands and wished one another good luck and a safe journey back. Just time for a few slaps on the back, and the train was at a standstill. Everyone grabbed their kit and joined the crowds now milling on the platform, from where we would make our way to the huge transit sheds. The lights dazzled us as we passed through the massive doors. The place was lit-up like day.

The noise was deafening. Clanging trays, people shouting orders, and perhaps a thousand conversations all at the same time. Katrinka's eyes were like saucers; she had never experienced anything like this before. We were swept along with the others, until we found ourselves at the end of the long queue. We each grabbed a tray; there was food to be had and we were hungry. As we slowly moved along, I had a good look around All the tables were dirty, and the floor was none too clean either. Most probably another trainload had just left. There was so little time between trains. Still, it didn't matter. Food was the main priority.

I happened to glance over my shoulder and saw two redcaps coming towards us. Even at a distance they gave off that air of smug authority. I nudged Katrinka, and her eyes followed mine. Under my breath, I told her to look towards the cooks. 'I will do all the talking if there's a need,' I whispered.

She promptly faced the counter. 'They bring back so many horrible memories. I fear they act the same way in all countries.' Her voice was full of contempt and bitterness.

'They're not all bad,' I told her, remembering when I was pleased of their intervention.

They were almost upon us. 'I'm going for the sausage and mash,' I said, speaking to Katrinka over her shoulder.

One of the redcaps turned his steely gaze on me. 'You had better hurry then, or you won't get nothing. The boat leaves in twenty minutes.' He looked to his mate as if to say, there that's told him. Then, looking pleased with themselves, they strode smartly past. We helped ourselves to food and drink which we managed to polish off between us before the Tannoy summoned us to the quayside.

As we came through to the dockside the huge ship loomed above us. There were three gangplanks going up to its decks, each with a long queue of troops waiting to board. My heart sank when I spotted more redcaps hovering around. They seemed to be casting their eyes over everyone who went up the gangway. I didn't mention them to Katrinka; she was nervous enough all ready.

We were almost at the gangplank and my heart was in my boots. I made sure Katrinka had her warrants ready. There was a sailor checking them as the men boarded, and he was going through them like greased lightning. We moved up the queue until there were just a couple of men ahead of us. The redcaps were really close to us now, too close for comfort. I felt sure they were watching me. I steeled myself to act normally, otherwise I could arouse their suspicion. With any luck it might not be me they were after. We moved forward, another step closer to them. My throat was dry and my heart was hammering fit to burst. Then suddenly the redcaps were looking past me towards the far end of the queue. There seemed to be some sort of commotion going on. In a couple of seconds they went hurrying by us. Their faces looked grim. Mine wore a look of relief. I raised my eyes skyward. Thank you, God!

Katrinka gave me a wan smile. She didn't say anything but I knew she must have been terrified. Everyone stopped what they were doing and watched the fracas. It suddenly dawned on me that the troublemakers were none other than our drunken friends whom we had bumped into on the train – the very merry Seaforth Highlanders. Apparently they had not yet curtailed their merry-making. I hadn't realised how glad I would be to see them again.

Now the coast was clear for a few moments and all I wanted to do was get safely on that boat. I tapped the shoulder of the bloke in front of Katrinka. 'Come on, mate, we don't want the ship to leave without us, do we?' Then we were moving forward once again.

A sailor took our warrants and we stepped on to the gangway. My heart was beating normally now, but the pressure was telling on me. I stole another rearward glance. The Seaforth Highlanders were still going at it hammer and tongs, but at least Katrinka and I were safe . . . for now.

As we stepped on to the deck a sailor ushered us to a steel

stairway which led to the decks below. We had to descend several flights to find our quarters on the lower deck. It was jam-packed with three-tiered sleeping bunks, and there were already hundreds of troops down there making themselves at home. I managed to find an empty unit and threw my case on the top bunk. Katrinka took the lower one. Then we both sat down on the middle one to get our breath back. It would have been nice to keep all three bunks for ourselves, but that was looking unlikely. The din was deafening as scores of men dashed about looking for a suitable berth. The bunks were filling up rapidly, and anyone who dithered would be shoved in anywhere by the ratings whose job it was to accommodate the troops. A nervous-looking soldier stopped and looked at my lonely case on the top bunk. Oh heck, goodbye privacy, I thought, but I could do no other than remove the case. 'Here you are, mate, the top one is free,' I said ruefully. He gave me a grateful smile as I moved my case to the middle bunk.

Leaving him to sort himself out, I sat on the bunk to talk with Katrinka. With all the racket going on around us, there was no fear of being overheard.

'I was so afraid to see those redcaps, I thought it was the end of my journey. It was so lucky for us that the men in skirts were there,' she said. She still looked really pale.

I assured her that we would be safe for our brief voyage across the North Sea. In the morning we would be in England, which wasn't too far off now.

We were enjoying our own company when our bed-mate popped his head out. 'Will it be rough going across? I'm not a very good sailor.' Without waiting for a reply, he chattered on and on about nothing in particular. I had the feeling that he felt nervous on his own and badly needed some company. My ears pricked up when he asked, 'What part of Germany are you coming from?'

I could feel Katrinka's eyes on me. 'Minden – do you know it?'

His reply was comforting. 'No, I have come from Hanover.' As he was speaking I noticed the insignia on his shoulder: *Pay Corps* – so he was an office chap. His voice was drowned out by the loudspeaker informing us that we were about to cast off, and that nobody was allowed on the upper deck. We felt the steady throb of the engines beneath our feet and realised the ship was under way. Five minutes later we were informed over the Tannoy that we were now authorised to use the upper deck if we so wished.

I slid off my bunk. 'John, I'm going up on deck for some fresh air and to watch the lights of the continent fading away. How about you?'

Katrinka nodded and was standing beside me in a flash. Our friend on the top bunk was cleaning his spectacles with a khaki handkerchief. He gave us a forlorn look as we started to move away. We didn't want his company, so I asked him if he would keep his eye on our cases, assuring him that we wouldn't be gone for long. Weaving our way through the rows of bunks, we made our way to the steel stairway. On the bulkhead was written, Deck 3A. 'Remember that,' I said, 'or we could quite easily get lost.'

Up on deck the wind was blowing a gale and it was freezing cold. I guided Katrinka to a sheltered spot behind a stack of life rafts. As we stood there in the darkness, watching the lights of Holland vanishing into the distance, I felt for her hand and gave it a quick squeeze. A passing sailor remarked, 'Looks as if we're in for a rough crossing tonight,' which did nothing to boost our morale. I gripped her hand once more and told her how much I loved her. She was shaking with the cold and we were getting showered with spray, so I suggested we had better return to the warmth of Deck 3A. On the way down we needed to use the toilets, which of course was always a trial of nerves for her. She hesitated before going in.

'Will it be the same as the one on the train?'

'No,' I told her, 'these will be much bigger, so keep your eyes off the men.'

She didn't smile this time. 'I find this so embarrassing, Peter, but I have no alternative, do I?'

Trying to sound cheerful, I said, 'I'm afraid not me 'ansome, but you have no need to worry. Everyone thinks you're a soldier, so just be brave.'

It wasn't a pretty sight in the toilets. There were a few men being sick in the urinals, so we hurried by them and into the cubicles. I spent a long time carefully washing my hands while I waited for her. I understood it took a considerable amount of effort to organise herself, dressed in army uniform. Afterwards, we easily found our way back and I thanked our bed-mate for watching our cases and offered to do the same for him, if he fancied going up on deck. He didn't need twice-telling; he was away like a rocket. By the pallor of his face we had returned just in time.

We lay on our bunks and tried to sleep. The day's happenings kept going round and round in my head. It seemed so much longer than only just this morning that John had changed places with Katrinka. My mind took me back to almost every minute of our journey on the train, and to the unforgettable moments of panic, but luck had been with us. We had made it this far.

I had noticed that several of the bunks were empty. Perhaps the absentee occupiers were up on deck, leaning over the ship's rail. I had a headache, but I was untroubled by seasickness. And I was more than relieved to find that Katrinka seemed to travel well – that certainly was another blessing.

There were a few groups of card-players. Where ever you are, or whatever the time, there would always be servicemen playing cards. I suppose it helped to while away their time, but I could never get that interested in it.

It was no good, I couldn't relax. I slid down from my bunk and stood up, so that I could talk to Katrinka. No sleep was coming to her either. Her eyes were wide open and her face looked pale in the ship's night-lights. 'How are you feeling, down here on your own?' I asked.

'Not good,' she whispered. 'The noise of the engines is intrusive – even when I cover my ears. I wish I could lay beside you.' She mouthed the words silently but I got the message.

Our bunk-mate was still conveniently missing, so I deemed it a good time to remind her of our schedule for the following day. I explained that we would arrive in Harwich at dawn, where we would disembark and pass through Customs. 'The customs officers aren't too bad,' I explained. 'With there being so many of us, they will search only the odd case. If they should pick on either of us it will be OK. We are not carrying anything illegal, so we have nothing to fear. If you're asked if you have anything to declare, just say no. The customs officer will then mark your case with a cross. If he should ask you to open your case, just do as he says. Remember that it will be early in the morning, and there are thousands of us passing through. They can't search everybody.'

She put her hand on my arm. 'These officers – will they think I am a man?' There was so much trepidation in her voice. I had to ease her fears.

'You couldn't be in a better place,' I told her. 'With so many men going through, they don't look at anyone in particular. It's just a formality. Stay calm and you'll be all right, I promise.'

She seemed to relax a little then. I was about to say more when she caught my eye and gave me a silencing nod. Our bunk-mate was returning.

I noticed how ill he was looking. 'Hell, mate, you look rough. It will do you good to lie down for a bit,' I said caringly.

He gave me a sickly grin, and with the slow movements of a geriatric, managed to climb into his bunk.

I looked down at Katrinka. 'Time for some kip, I reckon. Sleep well, John.'

She gave me a smile and snuggled down into her bunk, using her greatcoat as a blanket. I clambered into my own bunk and proceeded to do the same.

The continuous drone of the engines was still throbbing through my head until I eventually passed into a fitful slumber.

I awoke with a start. My mind had still been working, even though the rest of my body had been asleep. Katrinka's watch! I was wide awake and fully alert. It was plausible that she could be carrying it for a present, but I had no idea of its real worth. The chap who bought it for me told me it was a good one, but I was unaware of its true pedigree. If Customs should question Katrinka about it, she would be unable to give them a plausible answer. More than likely she would get into a state, then where would we be? The best thing all round would be for me to carry it through. It's sometimes the smallest missed detail that gives the game away. I quietly eased myself to the deck. The chap in the top bunk was sleeping soundly. My eyes wandered down to Katrinka. She was sleeping almost face down, and one slender arm had strayed out from under her coat. In her clenched hand I saw a little of her beloved rosary.

The deck was peaceful and quiet but I needed to visit the toilet. I went in my stockinged feet, so as not to disturb my fellow bunkers. As I tip-toed between the rows of sleeping men, I felt as if I was trespassing in a ghost ship. I shivered. The feeling was really strange.

It surprised me, when I entered the toilets, to find some signs of life. There was a bloke standing there with his head bent over a sink. I could tell from his pitiful groaning that things weren't exactly going well for him. 'Feeling poorly, mate?' I remarked feelingly.

He slowly turned and regarded me with his bloodshot eyes. I realised he was one of the merry Highlanders. With so many men on board it was an odd coincidence that we had again bumped into each other, though he showed no sign of recognising me. I should imagine that his mind had been a drunken blank for several hours.

'Buddy, I'm dying!' he moaned, as he turned back to the sink, his face a pallid shade of grey.

You soon will be, mate, I thought to myself, if you go on drinking like that.

Katrinka was awake when I got back to the bunk. I explained to her why it would be wiser for me to carry her watch through Customs, whereupon she quietly opened her case and handed it over to me for safe keeping. That was another potential risk taken care of, which left me feeling more confident about the morning. As neither of us was in the mood for any further sleep, I suggested we ventured on deck for a while.

Dawn was barely an hour away.

Chapter Fourteen

It was like another world up on deck. Very gloomy, and with a piercing cold wind. Even to breathe cruelly stung our throats. The decks were almost deserted, but we didn't mind that. I came across a spot under the bridge which gave us a little shelter and a good view. With some difficulty we managed to light up a cigarette each, but it was going to be a short smoke because the wind kept them blazing like a blacksmith's fire. The big ship was ploughing and swishing through the waves, carrying us ever nearer to home, and with the wind screaming to keep up, the noise was deafening. I had to shout into Katrinka's ear to make myself heard. 'By late afternoon we'll be in St Austell in Cornwall, enjoying a lovely plate of fish and chips,' I told her happily.

She shouted back, 'Perhaps I will not like these fish and chips.'

'Then you will have to try our pasties!' I laughed.

It wouldn't be long now. I felt in good spirits. I could just make out a scattering of lights on the distant horizon, and beckoned Katrinka to have a look. 'Those are the lights of England. We will soon be in Harwich and having our breakfast.'

Away to the east I saw the first rays of dawn, and as the darkness receded we could see the early mist rolling back like a blanket. Morning had broken.

We stood together, quietly gazing in wonderment, until the decks gradually came alive with men dashing around, busy with their different duties. A sudden clang of bells and the engines instantly became quieter, we were slowing down. The ship's Tannoy stirred us to action:

'*All personnel are to report below. We will be docking in thirty minutes.*'

We raced back down the stairways to our deck. The whole ship was alive now, a hive of frantic confusion. Unbelievably, some had actually overslept and were only now scurrying off to the washroom. Others still sat on their bunks, rubbing their eyes and wondering where the hell they were. Our friend from the top bunk had disappeared, probably gone for a wash. We sat together on the middle bunk, thankful we were ready as mayhem reigned around us.

Katrinka remarked about the men, 'They all look so young; not hard and fierce as I had imagined.'

'Most of these men are conscripts,' I explained, 'in for two years whether they like it or not. The majority of them will then return to their civilian jobs, just like I hope to do. They come from all walks of life. Some have really good jobs to go back to, whereas others come from poor homes. But we all have to do our National Service.'

The sound of the ship's engines changed to a mighty roar. It was so overpowering that our bodies trembled with the vibration of the ship.

Katrinka looked scared. 'What is happening?'

'I think we may be going backwards . . . don't worr . . .' My words were cut short as we felt a tremendous jolt which almost toppled us over, then silence. I looked at her frightened little face. 'Everything is fine. We have docked.'

We felt like hugging each other, but had to make do with a shared look of triumph instead. The chap from the top bunk came hurrying back, still looking pale and washed out. I felt quite sorry for him. He opened his mouth to speak, but the loudspeaker beat him to it.

'*Stand by ready for disembarkation. Listen for your deck number to be called.*'

The three of us stood together, waiting to be summoned. Our bunk-mate said he was sorry that he hadn't been more sociable, but travelling wasn't one of his strong points. I told him to think nothing of it. He wasn't to know we preferred the quiet type, especially on this journey

'*Deck 3A . . . Deck 3A – Proceed to disembark.*'

This was it. Katrinka was deathly pale. I knew the Customs men held a terrible fear for her, and I tried to reassure her as we shuffled along in the queue. 'There are thousands of us going through, and it's early in the morning – they'll all be half asleep. Everything is on our side. Stop worrying.'

We stood by the ship's rail, queuing for one of the gangways down to the wharf, and watched all the men being ushered into the Customs shed. The chap in front of me was heavily loaded down with kit. He was probably transferring to another unit. When we reached the top of the gangway I offered to carry some of his gear.

He looked at me with marked relief. 'Thanks, mate. I'm loaded up like a donkey here.'

We made it safely down, and I passed him back his kit as we entered the Customs & Excise shed. 'Over there,' I told Katrinka, having spotted a door at the far end, with a sign which read: '*Nothing to Declare*'.

This was certainly what we were looking for. The problem was the long counter which stood between us and a line of formidable-looking customs officers. Tired or otherwise, they weren't exactly welcoming us with open arms. I tried to give Katrinka a reassuring look. 'Right then, John, follow me.'

About three quarters of the way along the counter, and just when I thought we were safely through, an official held up his hand and pointed to the counter. We both placed our cases down in front of him.

He looked at Katrinka. 'Would you mind opening your case, soldier?'

She moved to open it. Her hands were shaking so much she couldn't do it. I watched her out of the corner of my eye. It seemed to take for ever. Come on, Katrinka, I silently prayed. She was still fumbling with the catch and the customs officer was beginning to look annoyed. She was in trouble; I had to do something to get his eyes off her. Without really thinking, I took Katrinka's watch out of my pocket and thrust it under his nose. 'I have this, sir, but I don't know its value,' I declared loudly.

He glared at me and bawled, 'You wait your turn, lad!'

'Sorry, sir.' I felt two inches tall, but it worked. When he returned his attention to Katrinka her case was open for his inspection. He quickly scanned the contents, turned the case round for her to fasten it, and then marked a cross in chalk. She was on her way.

His gaze shifted crossly back to me. 'What's all this about a watch?' He took it from me and studied it carefully. He turned it over in his hand, looked at the back, then passed it back to me. 'Who's it for?'

'My girlfriend, down in Cornwall, sir.'

By this time he had rifled through my case. He closed the lid and marked the cross. 'On your way, soldier!' he snapped, his eyes already fixed on the next unfortunate victim. With great relief, I made a hasty exit.

Katrinka was waiting for me outside. 'I thought I was going to faint in there,' she said, with the look of a worried rabbit.

'Never mind, we're through,' I said. 'Let's get some breakfast.' We followed the others into the breakfast shed.

It smelt good, and boy we were ready for it. The poor cooks looked hot and bothered, and no wonder with a boatload of starving men to cater for. Once again we joined the queue, and were swept along with all the other servicemen. Everyone seemed to be busy talking, no doubt happy and excited to be almost home. We filled our trays with bacon, eggs and toast, along with a mug of their infamous tea, and managed to find an empty table. We ate in silence. We were both really hungry, probably due to all that sea air and excitement!

I pushed back my empty plate. 'I really enjoyed that. How about you, mate?' I was relieved to see that Katrinka's colour was creeping back.

She swallowed her last mouthful of toast and managed a wry grin. 'Yes, it was good, but I am very uncomfortable. It is the uniform. My body, it itches all over. There is a soreness in places. My body that is covered by your underclothes is not affected. I wish that I could be covered all over with them.' Her face reflected her discomfort. I felt so sorry for her. But there was nothing we could do about it for the moment. Then I had an idea. My baby powder which I used for my feet – that would help to ease the chaffing a little. I retrieved it from my toilet bag and handed it to her.

'Here, try this. Slip it into your pocket and take it to the toilet with you. It's always worked for me.'

She accepted the tin gratefully. 'I hope so. I am glad that I am not a soldier for too long.'

We picked up our cases and went in search of the wash-ups.

'I hate to use the men's toilet each time, but I suppose I must?'

She sounded so miserable.

'Yes, you must,' I told her firmly. 'But this will be the last time. Once we are on the train, everything will be better for you.'

The place was packed. Men at the urinals, men at the basins, men in front of the mirrors. Men everywhere. Poor Katrinka, red faced, hurried through and straight into a cubicle. I took as long as I could in there. I knew she would be a while. It wasn't easy, undressing and dressing in a small space. I wondered if the next person to use her cubicle would notice the nice smell. Should make a pleasant change for him! I didn't have to wait for too long. Out she came, still rosy cheeked, but smiling.

'Feeling better?'

She passed me the tin. 'It is much better. It is good, and also it has a nice perfume.'

Most of the servicemen had started to move, heading for the railway station which was just a few yards from the docks. I told her that we had better get going. The train would leave the minute it was full. If we could get on this one, we would reach Paddington before lunchtime, then we would stand a good chance of being in St Austell by the evening. As we hurried on, I turned back to look at the huge transit sheds.

'Why are you looking? Is something the matter?' She was still on edge.

'No, nothing's wrong. I just wanted a last look. From here on, it's civilian travel all the way home!'

As we arrived on the platform the guard was shouting, 'Everyone aboard!' The Liverpool Street train was about to leave. We pushed our way through the seething throng and just made it as the whistle blew.

The train was jam-packed. We had to stand in the corridor with scores of others. Not that we minded; it was nice to be close. The locomotive gathered speed and we were soon scything our way through the English countryside. No one was taking any notice of us two ordinary soldiers. We spoke softly, enjoying our privacy. Katrinka asked me whether any other soldier had brought his girl home in this way before. I told her that I honestly didn't know. I had never heard of anyone doing it before. 'There is one thing I feel pretty sure about, though,' I said. 'I very much doubt that we are the first to fall in love. But bringing the girl home like this – well that's another matter all together. And if it wasn't for John, I would be travelling on my own now.'

Katrinka nodded, 'We will be in his debt for ever, won't we?'

'That's very true,' I agreed. 'But I have a strong feeling that he's not doing too badly for himself either.'

She knew what I meant and smiled.

Before we knew it we were pulling into Liverpool Street Station. A shrill squeak of brakes, one violent jerk, and the train shuddered to a halt. We all speedily piled out on to the platform. It was raining slightly, but it wasn't cold. The majority of the men were bound for the underground, so we followed suit.

It was an alien world down there for the likes of me, just a simple country boy. Soon our electric train came hissing and snaking along the track. As soon as it stopped, the automatic doors slid open and out poured a stream of people. They all seemed to vanish in a flash, then we found ourselves being swept inside by the tide of busy commuters. We were packed in like sardines; it was standing room only. I don't think they could have squeezed another person in if they tried. The doors slid shut and locked us securely in our prison carriage, and we started to move. I had just managed to get comfortable in my standing position, when the train stopped again. It had arrived at another station. A few got off, but it didn't relieve the cramped situation, because a few more jumped on. Never mind, it wasn't for long. We arrived at Paddington and followed the crowd up to the main station, where I looked at my watch in dismay.

It was well past eleven. The Cornish Riviera had left at ten-thirty. It meant that we would now have to catch the later, slower train to Cornwall.

The station was frantic with people bustling around all over the place, and the loudspeakers resounding out their instructions left, right and centre, only seemed to add to the chaos.

Katrinka looked lost and frightened. 'Do you know where we have to go, Peter?'

I told her that I wasn't sure, but I would find someone to help us. I feverishly looked around and spotted a porter trundling along with his laden trolley, oblivious to the people he was scattering in his wake. 'Can you help us, mate?' I asked. 'What time will the next train for Penzance be leaving? And from which platform?'

Without stopping or even looking at us, he flung out his arm and pointed the way. 'Platform four. Leaving eleven-forty-five.'

I couldn't even thank him, he had disappeared, swallowed up by the jostling crowd. But we both felt a little happier now. It wasn't too long to have to wait. By the time we had drunk a cup of coffee, the train would be due in.

We collected our coffee and a doughnut each, and sat at a dirty table. The coffee was barely drinkable, and Katrinka had never seen a doughnut before, but she enjoyed it. I was about to offer her a cigarette, when I noticed two army redcaps seated at another table. Katrinka had spotted them as well. The fear had returned to her eyes. 'What are they doing here?'

I told her I didn't have a clue, but thought it wise to go. We casually sauntered out to the platform. After a few more minutes I turned to check, but no one was following us. We could breathe easily again. I stopped at the station bookstall to buy a newspaper. Katrinka was happily scanning the magazines and about to pick one up, when I noticed that it was a woman's book. I froze for a moment. The assistant was watching and waiting for us to make up our minds. I picked up a motor cycle magazine and exchanged it for Katrinka's. 'You're having us on again, aren't you, John?' I laughed. It seemed to satisfy the sales girl. She took my money and moved on to serve the next customer.

Katrinka had moved on ahead of me. When I caught her up, she was almost in tears. 'I am so sorry. I really had forgotten!'

I assured her that no harm had been done, and that that was the first little slip she had made. I told her that I felt very proud of her because it took great courage to make a journey such as this.

It was time to make our way to platform four. When we were nearing the ticket collector's gate, we saw there was just a handful of people waiting to go through. It would be nice not to have to queue for a change. Then we noticed the two policemen with them. We stopped in our tracks and looked at each other in despair. We had to go through that gateway to catch our train.

I murmured to Katrinka, 'Just saunter on through. I'll stay between you and them, and if they stop us, leave all the talking to me.' We were nearly upon them and I had to think fast. 'If they ask us to go with them, you run like hell. I will try and delay them for as long as possible. Lose yourself in the crowds, then try and make your way to St Austell. The address is in your case.' She opened her mouth to speak but it was too late, just one other person in front of us.

As we passed over the tickets, I could feel the policemen's eyes burning into me. With a boldness I didn't feel, I stared straight back at them. Our eyes met for just a second; they looked right through me.

Our warrants had been checked, all in order. The collector duly handed them back and waved us through. So they weren't looking for us after all. I must be getting paranoid. It was good to see the train already in and waiting for us. I was beginning to feel the strain.

Chapter Fifteen

Once aboard the train, we began to relax a little. We walked along the corridor, glancing into each compartment, seeking the one that would suit us best. One looked promising – just a woman with two children. Then I thought again. Who knows what the children might ask us. Eventually we found what we were looking for. Empty except for an elderly couple at the far end; husband and wife, I imagined. We stashed away our gear and settled into our seats. The redcaps were still patrolling the platform. I was anxious for the train to pull out. Then the compartment door slid open and two nuns stepped inside. One was carrying a briefcase, while the other was struggling with a rather large suitcase. My offer to help with the heavier luggage was readily accepted, but it took most of my strength to lift it. It was even heavier than it looked. It made me wonder how on earth she managed to lug it around with her. I had always imagined nuns to be rather delicate creatures, which is clearly not always the case. The nuns gave me an appreciative smile and settled into the seats directly opposite ours. It was a good thing they didn't know what I was thinking, because they reminded me of the two boiled eggs mother used to give me for my breakfast.

The train was moving out. As Katrinka and I looked at each other, there was no need for words. I passed her my newspaper to read, while I glanced through the motor cycle magazine. As a keen motorcyclist, I was delighted to read about the new machines with rear springing. That should make for a more comfortable ride. If only I could afford one of the super new models now becoming available – oh well, one of these days perhaps. I suddenly became aware of someone speaking to us. It was the gent in the far corner, now brandishing a pipe and wanting to know if we minded.

His wife was looking at him with annoyance. 'Can't you wait until we get off at Exeter, Reg?' She screwed up her nose, and with a look of exasperation apologised to the nuns.

'Don't mind us,' came the quiet reply, 'but we can't speak for the soldiers.'

I said, 'We don't mind, John and me. We quite like the smell; reminds us of home.'

Reg happily took out an old well-worn tin of baccy, and we watched him lovingly rolling the leaves in the palm of his hand before stuffing them into the bowl of the pipe. It was quite an art, by the look of it. Out came the Swan Vestas matches, and Reg lit up. He took several long draws on the pipe to get it going. At one point he sucked so hard that the flame of the match completely disappeared into the pipe. Now the smoke was coming out of his mouth in great bursts . . . almost as if he was in competition with the engine that was carrying us home. Finally, he sat back in his seat, satisfaction written all over his kindly face. I asked him what sort of baccy he used.

'Digger Flake.' He spoke the name with reverence. 'Ever heard of it, soldier?'

'Yes, Reg – you don't mind if I call you Reg, do you?'

'Not at all, my boy,' he smiled, so I told him about my father, and how he also loved his pipe. Digger Flake was his favourite tobacco as well, so that particular aroma always reminded me of home. I asked Mrs Reg if she smoked?

Her eyes flickered across to the nuns. 'Only when I'm at home – then I may have a cigarette with my cup of tea.'

Reg gave me a sly wink. I think he knew better!

Katrinka had remained engrossed in the newspaper and was pretty bored with it by now, I suspected. 'Feel like stretching your legs for a bit, John?' I asked her, as I started for the corridor. She followed me out and we walked along to the end of the carriage. We had the place to ourselves for the moment. It was nice to be able to talk freely and without any pretence. I told her that I had been thinking about her name and was a little concerned about it.

'My name, I thought you liked my name?'

'Of course I do, my darling, it's a beautiful name. But the authorities will be searching for Katrinka Wazda. It could go on for years – they don't give up easily. Your surname will automatically change when we marry. If you choose a different first name as well, you will have a completely new identity. What do you think?'

She gave me one of her worried little frowns. 'I feel very frightened by all these changes, but I trust your judgement. I will do whatever you think is for the best.'

I noticed our train was pulling into a station. We were at Reading. Katrinka tugged excitedly at my sleeve and pointed to a large advertisement board. *Long live Elizabeth R* read the sign. 'Look,' she said. 'That will be my name. Will that be a good English name for me, my Peter?'

'Perfect,' I laughed. And one day soon you will also be Elizabeth R. Will you marry me at the first opportunity we get?'

Looking at me very seriously, she replied, 'I have been told that when an Englishman proposes to his lady and asks for her hand in marriage, he drops onto one knee.'

'I will, I will,' I answered truthfully, 'but it would look very strange – me going down on one knee and proposing to another soldier. What if anyone should see us? We would be arrested as homosexuals.'

Katrinka smiled and briefly touched my hand. 'Of course I will marry you, my Peter.'

The train was chugging its way out of the station, taking us ever nearer to home. We both felt a lot easier in our hearts and minds now that our journey was almost over. We just gazed contentedly through the window and watched the countryside speed by. The train was rapidly approaching Swindon when Katrinka suddenly whooped with delight. 'Look!' She was pointing to where the shape of a huge white horse had been carved out of the hillside. 'It is so white. Why is it there?'

I told her that its whiteness was due to the chalk in the ground. People believe, that many years ago, Celts had carved the horse, and were also responsible for the enormous earthworks above it. Her eyes grew wider as she listened, so I went on to tell her about another famous landmark. 'Legend has it that a very brave Saint called George slew a ferocious dragon on another hilltop in this area. It is known as *Dragon's Hill*.'

'I would like to visit it one day. There are so many different things to see . . . I am so happy, my Peter!'

I gave her a warning look. One of the nuns was coming along the corridor towards us. I sincerely hoped that she hadn't overheard snatches of our conversation. She gave us a gentle smile as she passed.

Katrinka whispered, 'I feel there is something strange about the nuns. Have you noticed how smooth their hands are? The nuns that I have known have rough hands; they have hard work to do. I do not know why I feel this way about them – it makes me feel ashamed to have these bad thoughts.'

It was odd, but I had wondered about them myself. They hadn't minded a bit when Reg lit up his pipe, nor when his wife admitted her cigarette-smoking habit. I had a strong feeling that they could have enjoyed one themselves. Katrinka broke into my thoughts:

'Do you think they are in disguise, and are really looking for us?'

'I don't think anyone's going to go to those lengths to find us,' I laughed. 'At least, I hope not!'

Katrinka said, 'Will the Cornwall police come to your home to seek me out?'

'I've thought of that,' I said, 'and if they do, you won't be there.'

She looked at me, puzzled. 'What do you mean?'

'Don't worry, you won't be too far away. My married sister lives just a few doors down from us. I will ask her if you can stay there for a while. You will like her, she's a good sort. I know I can rely on her.' Things were gradually falling into place; our worries were gradually diminishing. We decided it was time to return to the compartment.

Reg and his wife were asleep in their corner. He still had his pipe in his mouth, loathe to part with his comforting friend. One of the nuns was reading our newspaper, and she glanced up, embarrassed, as we returned to our seats. 'I hope you didn't mind,' she said, offering it back to me.

I assured her that she and her colleague were most welcome to borrow it, and Katrinka and I settled back in our seats to try and catch up on our sleep.

Our afternoon nap proved all too brief. The ticket inspector suddenly appeared and demanded to see our tickets. Katrinka must have been in a deep slumber, she didn't waken until I moved to get my ticket. Then she jerked bolt upright!

'What is it? What do you want?' There was terror written all over her face as she looked up at the man.

'He just wants to check our railway passes – that's all, John,' I said quickly.

She somehow regained her composure and passed her ticket to the inspector. I could feel her body shaking. It was awful; I couldn't even give her hand a comforting squeeze.

Some time later, I noticed Katrinka had her eyes closed, so I nipped out to the toilet. On the way back I met one of the nuns. As we were about to pass each other she laid her hand on my arm. 'Is your friend a Catholic? I thought I glimpsed a rosary in his hand.'

I nodded. 'I believe he is.'

'Just one other thing' – she looked me straight in the eye – 'I believe your friend is not a he . . . I believe *he* is a girl, dressed in a soldier's uniform.'

I was dumbstruck. I felt the colour draining from my face. My heart was pounding. Then the words came tumbling out; I didn't know what I was saying. 'That's funny, we thought that you two were impostors!' I put my hand to my mouth in total disbelief; what had I said!

The nun remained impassive. 'And why do you think this of us?'

I had difficulty in speaking; my throat felt constricted. 'I, er John, thought your hands looked too smooth.' It sounded ridiculous after I said it, which of course it was. But it was too late to withdraw it.

But she merely gave me a gracious smile. 'Maybe we do our work in the convent office. But we will keep it our secret, shall we? We will forget we had this conversation.' She surprised me by putting out her hand for us to shake on it. She started to walk away, then stopped and looked back. 'What is her real name?'

'Katrinka.' My voice sounded hollow.

'Would that be Russian or Hungarian, I wonder?'

'Polish – she is my sweetheart.' My voice was barely audible.

She gave me an angelic smile and moved on her way. I stayed rooted to the spot, struggling to regain some semblance of composure. I quickly decided not to tell Katrinka about it. She had enough to worry about. And so did I.

After passing through several more stations our travelling companions alighted at Plymouth, and we then had the joyful privilege of having the compartment to ourselves. It was a great relief to see the back of the nuns, notwithstanding their kindness. It was strange how they guessed about Katrinka. Thank goodness other people weren't so observant.

As we slowly pulled out of the busy Plymouth station, I was just able to make out the shimmering waters of the River Tamar. As we drew closer I pointed out to Katrinka the bridge we would soon be going over. 'See there, Katrinka, when we reach the other side of that bridge we will be in Cornwall.'

Her face positively glowed. 'At last. I cannot believe that we have travelled from Gottingen to Cornwall without being found out. I truly did not expect the plan to work.'

The train slowed to a crawl as it passed over the bridge. Underneath us the water glistened and rippled with a myriad of small boats and brightly-coloured sails bobbing in a gentle swell, as if dancing to the rhythm of the waves. Katrinka looked down in wonderment. 'It is so beautiful. I am so happy.' And so was I.

Our new-found privacy was all too brief. The compartment door slid open and two mischievous boys came bursting in, followed by a harassed young woman who was vainly trying to get them to sit and behave. I sensed trouble. If you are doing something shady, children can be your worst enemy. They have the knack of asking awkward questions at the wrong time. These two were on the attack right away. The elder of the two wanted to know where we had come from.

I explained that we had come all the way from Germany, then I asked him where he had come from? He stood looking at me with his mop of ginger hair standing on end, and with a rather large gap in his front teeth. His look told me he thought I was stupid.

'That's my auntie Violet,' he said. 'We've been staying with her for a week. Mum has been in hospital, but she's meeting us today and we're going home.' He sounded relieved as he gave the other boy a poke and turned his attention to Katrinka. 'You don't look very tough!'

Here we go, I thought. It's time for some tactical answers. 'That's where you're wrong, sonny,' I said, swiftly speaking up for her. 'He is an expert in unarmed combat, and *Su-sing*.'

His eyes widened and he looked at Katrinka with renewed respect. 'What's '*Su-sing*? – I've never heard of that before.'

I tapped my finger on the side of my nose. 'It's very hush hush.'

He stood there for a moment, carefully weighing us up, then decided it was much more fun tormenting his brother.

The train slowed. We were almost at our destination. We collected our gear, donned our greatcoats and waited at the door, eager to step out on to home ground.

As the train ground to a stop, I opened the carriage door and was almost knocked off my feet by the two rascals hurrying out to meet with their mother. She was standing there waiting for them, and judging by all the hugs and kisses they were nothing but little angels in her eyes. We walked along the platform together, and gave our final passes to the ticket collector. There were no police or redcaps waiting for us.

WE HAD MADE IT!

I just wanted to drop my case and hug and kiss my girl, but we were still soldiers so it was out of the question. But it didn't stop me from looking into the most beautiful eyes in the world and reading all the love and gratitude in them.

I was a very happy man.

Chapter Sixteen

The bus terminus was adjacent to the railway station. It was handy for us, as we needed to catch a bus to my home village of Penwithick, which is a couple of miles out of town. It was now about six in the evening and quite dark, except for the street lights which shone brilliantly down on to the wet road. Thank goodness it had stopped raining for the moment. There were several buses parked in the station. Little queues of people huddled together under cover while they waited, and uniformed drivers and conductors silently checked their vehicles and routes. I intercepted one of the conductors as he came striding our way. 'Ah, just the man, could you tell me the time of the next bus for Penwithick?'

Tucking his clipboard and tickets under his arm, he pulled out a rather splendid pocket watch from his inside pocket. 'I'm afraid you have just missed one,' he told me. 'The next one leaves in an hour's time. I should pop down to the town for a pint while you're waiting, if I were you.'

We were both feeling hungry, since it was several hours since we had eaten anything substantial, so I suggested to Katrinka that we have some fish and chips.

She laughed. 'Fish and chips, yes – I think I am ready to try them.'

Luckily, we were able to leave our cases with one of the bus drivers. After extracting a promise of six-pennyworth when we returned, he kindly locked them away in the depot. Katrinka wanted to know what he had meant by 'six-pennyworth'. I explained that he wanted us to bring him back some chips.

'Do all English people do this?' she asked. 'Is he a friend of yours?

'No,' I said, 'but one good turn deserves another.' She had started to learn our English ways.

We were soon in the high street but most of the shops were either closed or closing. But it was heaven for me just to be walking on familiar ground; even the shops looked like old friends. As we came to the end of the street, I stopped to look in the window of a jeweller's. A silver cross and chain caught my eye. Straining to see the price tag, I was just able to read *seventeen shillings and nine-pence*. Yes, I could just about afford that.

When I tried the shop door, to my surprise it opened. Katrinka, mystified, followed me inside. The jeweller was busy covering his valuable stock with red velvet cloths. I was lucky to have caught him before he locked up.

He looked up as we entered. 'Good evening, can I help you in any way?' I asked if I could look at the silver cross and chain on display in the window.

'Of course, sir.' He carefully eased the necklace from its cluttered location in the window and gently laid it on the counter in front of me.

'Very nice,' I said, after a cursory examination, 'I'll take it.'

'Is it for your girlfriend?' he asked, as he slipped the necklace into a suitable box.

I assured him that it was and handed him a one-pound note. He counted the two and threepence change into my hand, and we left him to cover up the rest of his treasures for the night. I tucked the little box into my coat pocket and we headed for the fish and chip shop. If I didn't know where it was, I would have easily found it. The smell was wafting through the cold night air; absolutely delicious! We stepped into its steamy interior and climbed the uncarpeted staircase to a small, first-floor restaurant with room for only half a dozen tables – all with green tiled surfaces – and an assortment of odd chairs. The place was empty except for two mature ladies sipping tea at a corner table while awaiting their meal.

When we sat down Katrinka wanted to know what was in the bottle on the table.

'This,' I said, picking it up with unbridled affection, 'is one of the most important ingredients for our fish and chips – vinegar! My mouth is watering already, just thinking about it.'

The sound of heavy footsteps on the stairs heralded the appearance of Ron, the red-faced proprietor. Wearing a long, once white but now grease-stained apron, he was carrying two large plates of fish, chips and peas, which looked hot and delicious. He bustled over to the two women and proudly placed the food in front of them. 'There you are Doris. You and Mabel will be able to face the cold when you have finished that lot.'

He came over to us. 'Why it's young Pete Rundle, isn't it?' So you're in the army now, boy. Make a man of you, they will, and that's for sure.' He lifted up his pad and pencil which was suspended on a piece of string and tied around his ample waist. 'Now what will you have?'

I ordered fish, chips and peas, and two mugs of tea. 'No sugar,' I told him, whereupon he acknowledged my order with a nod and dashed back down the stairs to tend to his frying. Everything was timed to perfection.

The women in the corner were busy tucking into their feast, oblivious to anyone or anything, other than the next delicious forkful. I took out the box with the necklace and handed it to Katrinka. 'That's for you to wear when we get home; I had to buy it for you. I feel someone has been watching over us on our journey home.'

She opened the box and looked inside. For a moment she didn't speak. Then, in a voice choked with emotion, she whispered, 'It is beautiful . . . I will treasure it for ever.' She fingered the chain lovingly, then, as if she were handling the crown jewels, she carefully placed the necklace back in the box, then into her pocket.

Ron suddenly popped up with our plates of golden masterpieces. Trundling behind him was his assistant, a young woman bearing our steaming mugs of tea. 'Mind you don't spill any, Muriel,' he scolded. He dropped down our plates on to the tiled top with a loud clatter. 'That will be three shillings and eight-pence,' he informed us.

When I passed over five bob, he lifted his apron and produced my change from his trouser pocket. Muriel, in the meantime, had been giving us the glad-eye. I wasn't sure which one of us she fancied most. If only she knew!

As they moved back towards the stairway, Ron said, 'I hope you enjoy your meal.' It surprised me to hear Katrinka reply,

'Merci, Monsieur.'

Ron stopped in his tracks and drew himself up to his full height. He was clearly delighted. 'Muriel, that's French, that is,' he said, and almost pushed the poor girl down the stairs in his excitement. Exercising his new importance, he ordered Muriel to attend to the customers who were waiting below.

Katrinka watched me carefully as I liberally sprinkled on the condiments, then hesitantly followed suit. I waited expectantly as Katrinka had her first taste of fish and chips. She was tucking in, seeming to enjoy them. I asked her if she liked it.

She slowly cleared her mouth. ' 'Ansome . . . truly 'ansome,' she laughed.

It didn't take us long to finish our food. Katrinka had decided that tea wasn't so bad after all, not a bit like the army liquid we had been forced to drink. I checked the time; we didn't want to miss our bus. It might mean we would have to walk the two miles home, and I didn't relish the thought. We said goodbye to Ron and Muriel, and feeling much better, made our way back to the bus station. There were already a handful of people waiting for the Penwithick bus. Katrinka had started to worry about the next stage of our journey. 'I am afraid your parents will not approve of me. They may wish for you to marry an English girl. Will I fit in, in your family? Please do not leave my side, Peter. I am afraid.' The words tumbled from her lips.

I reassured her the best I could. I knew in my heart that everything would be all right, but it was only natural she would be feeling anxious.

The bus arrived dead on time. As we clambered aboard, the conductor told us to put our cases on the seats beside us. There weren't many passengers at that time of night. A buzz from the bell and we were off. Most of our fellow travellers had opted to sit towards the front of the bus. We favoured the back, nearer the door. It was hard work lugging those cases around.

I could see Katrinka was still looking a little agitated. 'Peter,' she said, frowning, 'perhaps your parents will say that they will want no part in what we are doing. I will be homeless in a foreign land. I will be a criminal. I will be put into prison.'

'My darling,' I whispered, 'whatever happens from now on, there are two of us. I will never leave you, except to finish my army service. Everything is going to be perfect, just you see. And any problems we do have, we will face together.'

The old Bristol bus was slowly labouring up a steep hill. Outside we would be surrounded by the Cornish clay mountains, hiding from us now under the thick black cover of night. The bus had started to pick up speed once more, when I motioned to the conductor that we would be getting off at the next stop. He gave the bell a couple of jabs and after a few seconds the bus started to slow down. We stood by the door and duly waited until the bus stopped. 'Home, Katrinka, this is where I live,' I announced joyfully as the bus pulled away. 'This is my village. This is Penwithick.' I pointed to a brightly-lit house opposite. 'That's my home.'

We crossed the deserted road and walked along the path around to the back door. I stopped briefly to kiss her. 'This is the happiest moment of my life,' I told her. 'Don't worry, they will all love you.' I tapped on the door and went inside, a nervous Katrinka almost treading on my heels. We tip-toed through the kitchen and into the living room. My mother was busy mending socks. Dad was sitting in his favourite armchair, reading one of his favourite cowboy books. And my brother Joe, who was still living at home, was seated at the table, the whole top of which was littered with the remains of an old clock which, knowing him, he would be intent on making as good as new.

'Anyone home?' I said. They all looked up, startled.

'Peter!' My mother dropped her sewing and rushed over to me. She flung her arms around my neck and nearly squeezed the life out of me. 'You've lost weight; they aren't feeding you properly. But it's so lovely to have you back.' She eventually released me, and turned towards Katrinka. 'I see you've brought a mate back with you?' This was nothing new to her, as Jack had brought home several of his mates to stay. In fact, two of them had married my two sisters. Mother liked her little joke: 'I hope you have told him that I have no more daughters.' She offered Katrinka her hand. 'Pleased to meet you,' she smiled. Then she paused. Still clasping her hand and looking her straight in the eye, she suddenly took her in her arms and hugged her. 'It's Katrinka, isn't it?'

Pale faced and trembling, Katrinka nodded.

My mother once again took her into her arms. 'Welcome home, me 'ansome,' she said, in a voice brimming with emotion.

Time seemed to stand still as my father and brother looked on in amazement. My own relief was almost overwhelming.

When they broke apart, Katrinka was crying. 'I am sorry, I have held my tears back for so long. It has been a terrifying journey for both of us.'

My brother decided to make some tea. He shot off into the kitchen to put the kettle on, but was back in the living room in a flash, determined not to miss anything.

Next, it was my father's turn to speak. He was clearly annoyed. 'What made you do such a thing? Do you know what would have happened to you both if you were caught? In fact, I don't know how you have got this far.'

Katrinka was looking very concerned. I said, 'Dad, did you always do what you were told in the First World War? From all the tales you have told us, I should think not. Anyway, I had no choice. If I didn't bring her home with me, the Germans would have sent her back behind the Iron Curtain in no time at all. I couldn't let that happen. There was no other way. We love each other!'

He thought about that for a moment or two. Then he went over to Katrinka, took her hand, and told her she was very welcome.

We sat close to the fire, drinking our comforting tea. Everything else was forgotten as we related the whole story to my family They sat and listened without interrupting until we had finished. Then my mother took over. Now then, Joe, you run down to Winnie's. Tell her what has happened, and ask her to sort out some of her clothes for Katrinka. There isn't too much difference in their sizes – anyway, it will have to do for the time being. That uniform must be torture for the poor girl!'

Joe was already at the door when mother said, 'It will be best if she sleeps down there as well. Then if the army or anyone should come looking for her . . . well, then she won't be here, will she?'

My sister, Win, lived with her husband and two young daughters just a few doors down the road.

It wasn't long before Joe returned with Winnie in tow. 'What sort of army are you in, boy?' she said at once. 'Them letting you bring a foreign girl all the way back from Germany.'

Katrinka didn't know what to make of her at first. I told her not to worry, my sister called everyone from outside Cornwall a foreigner. Win asked Katrinka to go back to her house where they could sort out something for her to wear.

Katrinka looked at me with fear in her eyes. She was in a strange country, with strange people, and afraid to leave my side. I put my arm around her. 'It's all right, I will come with you.'

We left the warmth of the fireside with promises that we would be right back. The minute we stepped inside my sister's house she hauled Katrinka off upstairs to her bedroom, leaving me below with her husband and children. After a while I heard them giggling and even laughing heartily. It was music to my ears to hear her so happy. Eventually Katrinka was paraded for our inspection. She took my breath away. She was looking lovelier than ever. I had only seen her dressed in rags before. She was wearing a knee-length skirt, a green jumper, and a pair of brown, medium-heeled shoes. Even with her army haircut, she looked stunning. I will not forget that moment for as long as I live.

Win was quite outspoken. 'Fancy dressing the girl up in army underpants. It's a wonder she made it at all? She gave Katrinka a playful pat on her bottom. Now off you go, before mother sends Joe down to look for you. In the meantime, I'll get your bed ready.'

That night we all sat cosily by the fireside and talked almost non-stop until the early hours. Joe kept sneaking sly glances at Katrinka, which left me thinking that he would have liked to have been in my shoes. My parents had told us that Katrinka was welcome to stay with them until I had completed my National Service, and that they would enquire about a visa for her. Everything seemed perfect. I was so happy, I was fit to burst.

I walked Katrinka down to my sister's home, where we were able to kiss and cuddle in the porch before going inside. It was wonderful to have her as a girl again.

Win was wondering what to do about the army uniform, until I explained that it belonged to a deserter and I had to take it back. 'I hope he doesn't get back before I do,' I laughed. 'That might take a bit of explaining.'

Katrinka was looking pretty done in by the time Win took her up to her room. It had been a long and frightening day for her, for both of us. We decided it would be wise for me to sleep on the sofa for what remained of the night, just in case she awoke and was afraid. I had a restless night, but Katrinka slept soundly until well after dawn.

Chapter Seventeen

On that first morning of my leave I insured my motorbike. Now that we had our own means of transport, I was able to whisk Katrinka into St Austell to shop for some new clothes. She was so excited by it all. She insisted on my approval before buying anything, which wasn't a problem for me because I thought she looked lovely in everything she tried on.

Afterwards we rode out to the countryside and walked together across the heather clad moors, and around some of the old clay-workings. She was overawed by Carn Grey, a massive rock the size of a house, which stands starkly alone on the edge of the moor. We climbed the rough path to the top, from where we could see for miles. The scenery was breathtaking. We could see the shimmering blue waters of St Austell Bay, and the busy docks at Par. It was like being on top of the world. We felt as if no one else existed; we were alone and together. I knew that Carn Grey had played host to multitudes of courting couples over the years, and we were no exception. Thereafter we spent several moonlit evenings amid its craggy cracks and crevices, cuddling up and planning our future together. But sadly the time slipped swiftly by and it was suddenly the eve of my departure for Germany. Those two weeks had been some of the happiest times of my life. I loved my Cornwall, but looking at it through Katrinka's eyes, I loved it even more.

Katrinka wanted to spend our last evening together up on Carn Grey. 'I feel it is our rock. I will never go there without you,' she told me in a voice tinged with sadness.

I knew how she felt. She had warmed to my family, and them to her. But all she wanted was to be with me. It was hard for both of us, but there was no escaping our existing situation. We stood there, arms wrapped tightly round each other, and watched the twinkling lights of the boats waiting to enter Par docks. I asked her how she felt about us now – me a Methodist and she a Catholic. I knew that neither of us really wanted to change our faith.

She kissed me. 'I feel good about us,' she said. 'We both know there is only one God. We will leave the situation as it stands. Agreed?'

I gave her a hug and we rarely broached the subject again.

As we strolled back to the village, I knew of course that I didn't want to go back to Germany; my life was here. But I had to go. My parents were most supportive. Dad had already spoken to our local MP about Katrinka, and it had been decided that she would move back to my parents' house, making use of my bedroom while I was away. The time would soon pass, and I now had a future to look forward to. It was only sensible to look on the bright side of things.

We arrived home to find that an old mate of mine had called to see me. Albert and I had grown up together. When I was called up to go into the army, he had joined the merchant navy. I introduced him to Katrinka, and after talking for a while, he asked her if she came from Poland.

The colour drained from her face. She gave me a frantic look, and I knew then that I had to confide in my friend. Taking Katrinka's hand, I said, 'It's all right, I could trust Albert with my life.' Then I related the whole story to him.

He was impressed. 'Phew!' he gasped, 'and I thought I was the tough one.' He gave us his word that he wouldn't tell a soul our secret. Not even my own mother,' he added. Then, to Katrinka: 'So where exactly are you from?'

'Szezecin – it is a port on the Baltic coast. Do you know of it, Albert?'

'Er, yes, I think I do. There's a sort of inland waterway to reach it, isn't there?'

'Yes . . . yes I think you are right. I was quite young when I left there.'

Albert said, 'You'll be a lot better off here, Katrinka. I've never found any of those Communist countries very pleasant. On the few occasions I've been ashore with my mates, the people seemed to be watching us all the time. We couldn't wait to set sail again. Well, best of luck, anyway. I have to get back now, but I'll run you to the station in the morning, Pete, if you like?'

'Smashing. Thanks, Albert,' I said, pleased of his offer as we waved him off.

Katrinka and I stayed in front of the fire until its dying embers had crumpled into dust. My parents had long since gone to bed. I took her in my arms and kissed her beautiful lips. But her heart was still troubled, and the tears rolled down her cheeks and wetted my face. I had no choice but to leave her in the morning. By doing things the right way, we had a chance of pulling it off. If I deserted so I could stay with her, our happiness was sure to be short-lived. They would pick me up in no time at all. No, I mustn't even think about it. I kissed her again and savoured the moment.

A little later I counted out all the money I had left. It amounted to a grand total of twenty-six pounds, three shillings and fourpence. I had withdrawn my Post Office savings, so I was otherwise penniless. I kept four pounds for myself and gave Katrinka the rest. She protested strongly, but I insisted. 'I'll have my pay when I get back,' I told her. 'Each week I will send some money home to you. You can give mother two pounds, ten shillings a week for your food and keep. My family will take care of you while I'm away, and we can write to each other every day. It won't be forever. We must just think of the future, my darling.' We cuddled up on the sofa, and that is where my father found us in the morning.

He had to be at work by 5.00am. It was a hard life working in the clay pits. But it was a job, and thousands of Cornish men were glad of it.

'Have you two been down here all night?' he wanted to know.

I nodded, wondering what was coming next.

All he said was, 'You should have kept the fire going – it must have been cold without any blankets.'

While dad was having his breakfast, I cleared away the spent ashes from the grate and relit the fire. He didn't hang about. Before I had a chance to wash my dirty hands, he was standing beside me in his overalls and clay-lagged boots. He tapped his pocket to make sure his pipe and baccy were there, picked up his crib-bag, and rested an arm on my shoulder. 'Don't worry,' he said, 'we will do all we can to help Katrinka. Finish your army service in the proper manner, son, and all will be well.' He gave my arm a tight squeeze, and then he was gone. I hadn't even thanked him; there was no time to clear the lump from my throat.

Before long, a sleepy-eyed Joe appeared. 'You're up early!' He looked surprised to see me there. Then he opened the living room door and spotted Katrinka still asleep on the sofa. He pulled the door to and glanced at me accusingly. 'You've been down here all night, haven't you?'

I gave a sheepish grin and poured him a mug of tea. He scoffed his breakfast in two minutes flat, grabbed his crib-bag, and with his mouth still half-full, said, 'Good luck, Pete . . . we'll look after her.' Then he, too, was gone, swallowed by the early morning darkness. Although he was running late, he had made sure of his breakfast. He needed it. I knew that he would fill at least four thirteen ton railway trucks with clay before he came back home again – and all with just a long-handled shovel. Mother had probably packed a large pasty in his crib-bag to help keep his strength up as the day wore on.

Katrinka soon joined me in the kitchen. She was very quiet as she helped me clear the table. I could see she was close to tears, but there was nothing I could say or do to make her feel better. I was more than grateful when my mother put in a timely appearance. She at least was pleased to find that her daily chore of lighting the fire had been taken care of, and she insisted on cooking us both a good fried breakfast, refusing to take no for an answer. 'You have a long journey ahead of you, Pete, so you must start the day off right, my boy.'

'Why does your mother not eat?' Katrinka asked, as our bacon and eggs were put in front of us.

I explained that she was upset because I had to leave. She was the same when Jack used to go away. Katrinka looked down at her plate, not at all sure of her own appetite for food at that precise moment. 'Don't worry!' – I tried to sound cheerful – 'You'll both be OK after a while.' But neither of them spoke as we ate in silence. I managed to do justice to my breakfast, but Katrinka had only nibbled at hers. It would be better for everyone when I had gone. After a day or two we would be able to concentrate rather more on the future. Time would soon pass, or so I hoped.

It seems strange to say this, but I was glad to hear Albert's motorbike revving up outside. The morning had dragged by, and yet there hadn't been time to do anything of real value. I had felt like a fish out of water. When Albert sounded his horn, I grabbed my case – which now contained the spare uniform worn by Katrinka, as well as a few of my own essentials – and hastily donned my greatcoat. As I gave my mother a hug, she whispered, 'Don't worry about anything.'

Then I turned to Katrinka. Her eyes were brimming with tears as we hugged each other tightly, both aware that this memory would have to last a long time. I tried to maintain an even tone. 'I love you, Katrinka. I'll write every day.'

'I love you too, Peter.'

Albert sounded his horn again. Time was racing by. I simply ran – it was the only way. One more look at Katrinka's tear-stained face and I knew I would be finished. I leapt on the back of Albert's motorcycle and balanced the case precariously on my knee. One quick wave at the two pale faces at the window and we were off in a cloud of exhaust smoke.

Germany beckoned, and I had to go.

Chapter Eighteen

The journey back proved relatively straightforward, much different to the hair-raising trip over. Back in the Gottingen barracks I was able to assure John that everything had gone according to plan, notwithstanding a few major scares along the way. 'How was it for you?' I asked.

With a grin stretching from ear to ear, he said, 'Marvellous. I spent the entire fortnight imprisoned in Helga's flat and enjoyed every single minute of it.'

All in all, we had both done very well.

The next few months passed very slowly. I rarely left the camp, except for my weekly visits to the wireless man. I told him that Katrinka had gone away, and that she wished to be remembered to him and his wife. I had a letter from her nearly every day, which made life a little more bearable, but I missed her terribly and couldn't wait for us to be together again. She seemed to be settling down to her new life very well, and had even landed a part-time job, thanks to Win. The café where my sister worked as a waitress had found themselves temporarily short-staffed, so Katrinka was filling the gap. It sounded as if she really enjoyed it, and the money came in handy and gave her an element of independence. My mother also wrote to me from time to time. Each of her letters mentioned the difficulty they were experiencing in obtaining immigration papers for Katrinka, but she always added that they all still lived in hope.

Sometimes I would go up to the Regimental Chapel. It was the only place where I could sit quietly and feel as if Katrinka was there beside me. Now and again the padre would come and sit with me. One day he said, 'I think your problems are far from over. Am I right, soldier?'

He didn't press me further when I replied: 'It's just that I have to be patient for a little longer yet.'

Time went by, and I was now down to my last month of service. On one particular afternoon I was playing football for the platoon when I was summoned once again to the Commanding Officer's office. I felt apprehensive as I wondered why. I hadn't done anything wrong to my knowledge. I had to wait outside until I was called, and could hear several raised voices from behind the closed door. What the blazes was this all about?

I was soon to find out. The CO glared at me as I entered his office. I became aware of others in the room. Then my blood turned cold as I realised that it was my old adversaries – the German policeman and the redcap. My own platoon commander was also present. I stood to attention as the CO addressed me.

'Private Rundle, you have met these gentlemen before in this office.'

'Yes, sir?'

'They inform me that you have contrived in some way to take the refugee, Katrinka Wazda, to your home in Cornwall. Is this true?'

Out of the blue, a bombshell. My heart skipped a beat, I felt sick to the pit of my stomach. He was glaring at me, waiting for an answer. My mouth opened to speak. I couldn't. It had to be a nightmare!

His raging voice bellowed out, 'Well soldier?'

I could only nod, and hang my head in shame. The CO sat as if carved in stone, but his eyes burned into me. After what seemed a silent lifetime beneath his gaze, he turned and addressed the two policemen. 'You may go. You have your evidence. I will deal with Private Rundle concerning his part in this sad matter.'

His voice sounded flat. I felt ashamed that I had let the army down, and what would happen now? My platoon commander made to escort the two men out, but the German wanted a last word with me.

'You have been foolish. She will be sent back to Poland.' His face exuded evil as he turned and left the office.

There followed a heavy silence as the CO studied a file that I presumed was mine. My platoon commander was standing rigidly to attention, his eyes staring straight ahead, yet boring into me. My mind had finally grasped the true situation. Boy, was I in trouble! How was I going to explain this away? I couldn't bring John's name into it. I had thought that after all this time we were home and dry. Why should this happen now?

The CO's voice jolted me back to earth. 'Rundle, you have been very stupid! How on earth did you think you would get away with such a plan?'

'I love her, sir.' There was nothing more to say.

He rose from his desk and walked to the window. His back was towards me but I could tell he was deep in thought. The silence weighed so heavily on my mind that I couldn't begin to untangle any of my problems. The only thing to do was to keep quiet about the whole affair. At least John wouldn't be implicated; I couldn't let him suffer for my wrong-doings.

The CO returned to his desk. 'You have a good record, Rundle. And you will soon be demobbed. I feel you will have punishment enough when this girl is deported. Therefore I propose to take no further action against you. I can only say to you, that in the future you will look before you leap, otherwise you could find yourself in very hot water indeed.' Then he dismissed me with a wave of his hand.

So I was safe; the army didn't want to know. It was an incident which they would rather not remember. My whole body suddenly felt like jelly, I was in shock! I can't remember walking out of that office. A tiny part of me felt relief, but it did nothing to allay my fears of what would happen to Katrinka. My Katrinka, they would take her away. I couldn't bear it. I could imagine how she would feel; she would be terrified. If only I could get home. I had only a few more weeks to do. Why couldn't it have waited until then? Another thing to think about was my parents. How would they be feeling. What trouble have I brought to them? I walked back to the football pitch in despair.

The game had just ended and the players were walking off, heading for the showers. I met John and told him what had happened.

He was as upset as I. 'What will you do, mate? I never expected this to happen. I thought you were home and dry.'

'So did I, mate. It's her I'm worried about. I must think of something. I can't lose her now.'

John was speechless for once, but I could read in his eyes what he was thinking. Hopeless!

The next day I received a letter from my mother. Katrinka had gone! My family were all devastated. They, like me, had grown to love her. There weren't many details in the letter. I would learn the facts when I arrived home after being demobbed. But I was sorry for my parents, who felt as if somehow they were to blame. But I knew they couldn't have prevented what had happened. It was entirely out of their hands at that point. I couldn't wait to get home, to be able to talk to them.

Chapter Nineteen

When the day finally arrived for me to leave the army I still hadn't come up with a solution, even though Katrinka was never out of my thoughts. Over those last few weeks I had performed my duties like a robot. But no one, except perhaps John, realised that I wasn't really there. I felt sad to be leaving some of my mates – we had lived closely together for the past two years – but the longing to be home to hear if there was any news of Katrinka outweighed the sadness of leaving. I had arranged to meet John in our local pub on our first Saturday home. He was almost as anxious as me regarding any news of Katrinka. Having a few minutes to spare before the trucks came to carry us to the station, I visited the chapel for the last time. I felt I couldn't leave without saying goodbye to the padre.

He came over to greet me as soon as I walked in. 'So you are leaving us, Private Rundle. I can see you are still very troubled, but you will soon be home with your family and friends around you; at least your problem will be shared.' He shook my hand warmly. 'God go with you, my son. I am sure there will be a solution for you.'

I couldn't answer, my heart was in my mouth. I squeezed his hand and hurried out to the truck that would begin my journey home.

My trip home seemed long and tedious, and to make matters worse, at the end of the journey we had to go to Bodmin Barracks to be officially demobbed. Finally, after three days, all the paperwork had been completed, and I found myself on the National bus, heading for my own village.

My mother had seen the bus and was waiting at the door. I

could see that she was close to tears. 'I am so sorry,' she said, 'if only there was something we could have done . . .' Her arms drew me close as she tried to give me strength.

'I don't blame you; you have been wonderful to her,' I whispered, my own voice breaking with emotion. 'I know there was nothing more that you or anyone could have done.'

I followed her into the warm kitchen and she related the full story to me over a cup of tea. She and Katrinka had been in the house on their own. My father and brother were at work. They had been busy that day, cooking and cleaning. They had just sat down for a welcome cup of tea when a loud banging on the door made my mother leap out of her chair. She hurried to the door, wondering with some concern whether it was trouble for her men at the clay works.

When she opened the door, two policemen and several other men pushed past her into the kitchen. 'They literally grabbed Katrinka,' mother told me, adding, 'It was then I realised they were from the immigration department.'

She paused at that point, unable for the moment to carry on. I could see the pain both she and Katrinka had suffered and it made me angry. Katrinka was doing no harm here.

Regaining her composure, my mother carried on with the story. I could hardly bear to hear it, but I had to know. She said, 'They just took her away, with nothing but the clothes she stood in. I will never forget her face . . . she was so frightened. She was screaming and trying to get away from them. I could hear her cries, even when they were forcing her into the car. A policeman stayed with me, so I wouldn't follow her, I suppose. He stayed until she had gone, then he left. As I closed the door behind him he told me coldly that she would be deported.' My mother started to cry, and I cried with her. We both felt so helpless.

I took her hand. 'All will be well in the end, I will see to that. I will find her if it takes me the rest of my life!'

The next few weeks were terrible. I was broken-hearted; it was as if Katrinka had vanished into thin air. There was nothing to give us any fresh hope. But life had to go on. I managed to get a job in the clay works down at Par. The work was really hard, shovelling clay into huge trucks, just like my father and brother were doing. The sweat poured off me in the stifling heat, but even with all the hard grafting, Katrinka was never far from my mind.

When I came home after my day's shift, I would just mope around. I spoke very little, my mind was too busy with all the thoughts churning around in there. Every time I felt there was a breakthrough, I would come up against another brick wall. The trouble was, she could be anywhere. They could have even sent her to Siberia. It was useless! I think all my family and friends were getting concerned for me. I was coaxed into playing football for the village team. I didn't want to – my heart wasn't in it – but I felt I was letting my parents down if I didn't have a go. I knew what they were thinking. If I could get myself more involved in everyday things, it would help me to forget. Only I knew, of course, that I could never forget her!

As the weeks dragged by I was still heavy-hearted and no nearer to a solution. Then one day when I arrived home from work, my mother handed me a letter. It had been delivered with the morning mail and bore a Liverpool postmark. I was slightly curious as I had no connections with that part of the country. I slit open the envelope to find two neatly folded pieces of notepaper. When I read the first few words I very nearly passed out. It began: *My dearest Peter*. My eyes quickly dropped to the bottom of the page. It was signed K.x. It was from Katrinka!

My mother was staring at me. 'Is everything all right? Who is it from? What is it?'

I couldn't answer her, I had to read on. My heart ached to see the familiar writing, and to hold in my hand the paper that she had been holding. The letter was brief:

> *I have only a few moments. I am at Gdansk Ship building. Just a few days in Germany before I was handed back to the Communists. Life is unbearable without you. I pray you receive this note, which I place in the hands of a British sailor. All my love always.*

As if in a daze I passed the note to my mother. Then I unfolded the second slip of paper. It was from the sailor who had posted it for Katrinka. He had written that he had met Katrinka at the docks in Gdansk. She had asked him if he would post the note she had written, when he arrived back in England. I read on:

> *I felt so sorry for her, I can still picture her eyes; they*

reminded me of a hunted animal. The note was thrust into my hand, also there was a small scrap of card inside, which told me your address. I could do no more than send this to you as soon as I reached Liverpool.

My regards, a British sailor.

I would be eternally grateful to this unknown friend of ours. My mother was hugging me and crying at the same time. This time though, they were tears of joy. At least she was alive. I fetched down the world atlas and spread it out on the table. She would be somewhere up on the Baltic coast of Poland, surrounded by the Communist states. I traced my finger along the route. From England, across the North Sea to Holland, then to West Germany. Here my finger stopped at the border with East Germany, and my heart sank as I realised there was an entire hostile country between me and Poland. It could be a million miles away. In other words, there wasn't a hope in hell of slipping in and sneaking her out.

I looked despairingly at my mother. She put her arms around my shoulders. 'How could they do this to a young girl? Isn't there anything that can be done?'

Angrily, I closed the atlas. 'I don't know . . . but surely there must be someone who knows how we can get her out – and sooner or later I will find him!'

But time passed, and winter gave way to spring, still with no further progress. I had not received any more news of or from Katrinka, and as yet I was still working entirely in the dark. We were continually making great plans, which at the beginning gave me some hope but, as always, my spirits would sag when inevitably a drawback would follow the bright idea. There were times when I felt defeated and would think to myself, what's the point of carrying on? It's hopeless! Then I would hear her call my name, and I knew she needed me. My resolve would then be stronger than ever.

One morning, while at work loading bags of clay on to railway trucks at Par docks, my old pal Albert dropped by. His ship was in the harbour, unloading steam coal for the clay driers. He had heard of Katrinka's fate and wanted to know what the situation was at the present time. I jumped down off the lorry and told him of the note that I had received from her. I explained how she was working in a shipyard in Gdansk, and how I was desperately looking for a way of bringing her back.

He pondered for a moment. 'Gdansk . . . yes, I know of it. It's up on the Baltic – I've been there a few times.' He was silent for a moment, deep in thought, then he said, 'I wonder . . . can you cook, Pete?'

What a silly question, I thought, but he proceeded to tell me what was on his mind.

'The thing is, Pete, our cook has to go into hospital for a major operation. The Captain thinks he will be away for the best part of twelve months. He's upset about it because he's one of the best cooks around. D'you reckon you could stand in for him? It could be a way of getting you to Gdansk.'

My heart skipped a beat. This could be what I had been waiting for. Then another thought crossed my mind; it was the usual drawback – there was always one. I couldn't cook! Once again my spirits dropped to below zero. With utter dejection I gave Albert my answer. 'I'm no chef, mate, I wouldn't know where to begin.'

His face fell momentarily, then immediately brightened as another plan formed in his mind. 'Your mother is a good cook, can't she teach you the basics? You've a couple of weeks to learn, and we don't eat any fancy dishes on board – just plain wholesome food. I think that even I could do that. Go on, what do you say?'

The idea was tempting. My spirits started to soar. Perhaps I could do it. I must! I had to try! 'You're on,' I said.

Albert's face was beaming as he eagerly outlined the course of events. 'When we've finished unloading the coal, we have to reload the boat with clay for Sweden. With any luck, we should be docked back here at Par in a fortnight's time. That's when you will have to join us. Don't forget, learn all you can. Don't let me down or else the Captain will be after me . . . he loves his belly. I know you can do it if you try.'

The lorry driver who I was supposed to be working with was getting impatient. 'Tell your Captain that you have found him a cook,' I shouted to Albert as I leapt back on to the lorry.

He was grinning as he waved. 'See you soon . . . Happy cooking!'

When I told my parents about my plan, my poor mother almost

fainted. 'You expect me to teach you all I know about cooking in five minutes?' she exclaimed.

'Two weeks,' I pointed out.

'I have been cooking for you lot all my life,' she gasped, 'and you think you can learn all that in just a fortnight!'

'No, Mum, just enough to get me by. It's for Katrinka,' I reminded her.

She mellowed. 'I know, my dear,' she said. 'We can only try.'

Chapter Twenty

During the following two weeks I spent every spare minute I had in the kitchen. Mother was a strict teacher, and I wasn't allowed a minute's peace. Apart from being taught the bare basics of Cornish cooking, I learnt how to decipher recipes from her well-worn cookbook, and how to cover-up in case things hadn't turned out as well as they should have done. At least my pasties and under-roast were enjoyed by all the family; even Joe complimented me by saying that I should have tried my hand at cooking earlier. I was feeling quite confident, but as the day drew nearer to my maritime appointment the doubts began to surface. It was all very well, here with my mother to help me out, but cooking for half a dozen hungry men was another matter altogether. I felt sick every time I thought about it. But it had to be done if I wanted Katrinka back.

Dawn broke on the day of my departure into the merchant navy, and I hadn't slept a wink. I put some working clothes into my case, and wore my grey flannels and sports jacket. My mother fussing around me as usual, suggested I take an old duffel-coat which belonged to my father. 'You will be glad of that when you're out on the cold sea,' she insisted.

I was saved from carrying various other unwanted warm items by a loud knock on the door, followed by a cheery, 'Ready, me hearty?'

It was Albert. Was I glad to see him. He assured me that I was now employed as cook, and that the Captain was pleased to have a Cornishman at work in his galley: 'Will he do, Mrs R?' Albert looked expectantly at my mother.

'I think he will do splendidly,' she asserted proudly. 'He has his heart and soul in this venture.'

We said our goodbyes. 'Look after him, Albert, he's not used to the sea,' came mother's parting remark. She tucked the dog-eared recipe book well down into my pocket. 'You will need it more than me. Remember all I have taught you, use your common sense, and you'll get through, my son.'

I kissed her goodbye, and stifling an urge to take her with me, hurried outside to my makeshift taxi. Albert was now the proud owner of an old Bedford van that had seen better days. 'You can't go by looks, old man,' he said defiantly, 'she hasn't let me down yet!'

The short journey to the docks took me past the clay works where I had been employed. The tall chimney stacks were billowing out great plumes of grey smoke from the fires and dryers below. I imagined the terrific heat inside and the gallons of sweat that poured from the men who slaved there. Today I would be absent, but somebody else would already have taken my place. It was a job, and it was the industry of Cornwall. In spite of the back-breaking toil, these men were proud to be part of such a big industry. They worked for themselves and for their beloved Cornwall.

Albert parked his van on some wasteland, and we walked through the dockyard gates and on to the jetty. There were four coasters lined up. One was unloading coal, while the other three were taking china clay aboard. Albert paused alongside one of the clay carriers – an imposing black hulk of a ship bearing the name *ALSOVEAR*.

'This is it,' he shouted above the din.

Clutching my case in a sweaty hand, and with my recipe book safely in my pocket, I followed him up the gangway to the deck. Without preamble, he led me up a steel ladder to the wheel-house to meet the Captain. 'This is Pete Rundle, Cap'n, the replacement cook.'

The Captain had his back to us. He was wearing the biggest pair of gumboots that I have ever seen. He was bent low over a table, seemingly studying a rather large chart. As he turned to face us, he straightened up to his full height. If ever I had felt small and insecure, it was now. He towered above me like a giant. His massive frame was covered by a thick, navy, polo-necked sweater, and faded denim jeans. His face was wrapped in a coarse, greyish-red beard which matched to perfection the stiff, wiry coils that covered his head. His voice matched his appearance, loud and gruff – he certainly gave the impression of being a very tough nut indeed. An uneasy thought flickered across my mind – What have I let myself in for? I wasn't to know, then, that he was to prove one of the fairest men I have ever met.

He extended a huge, rough hand. 'I'm Captain Garrity of the *Alsovear*, and what I say goes around here! Remember that, and you won't go far wrong, lad. I'm an Irishman, and proud of it – and you, laddie, are Cornish, I believe?'

'Yes, sir, a cousin Jack,' I replied.

'A cousin Jack, eh?' A gold tooth winked at me as the Captain's lips parted in a friendly smile. 'That's good, that it is. And I'm Captain, not sir to ye boy. You can cook, I hope?'

I swallowed hard and secretly crossed my fingers. 'Yes, Cap'n.'

He looked at his watch. 'We'll be in need of a meal at six. If you need supplies, fetch them from the chandler on the other side of the wharf. Don't go over fifteen pounds. Just sign for the goods and bring me back a copy of the bill.' He regarded me for a moment, his eyes swiftly sweeping from top to toe. Then with the interview complete, he turned back to his chart.

Albert touched my arm. 'Right then, mate, first I'll show you to your cabin.'

I took a deep breath. Now I had to prove my worth.

The cabin was quite small, and I found that I would be sharing it with two other deck-hands. I just had time to drop off my case as Albert was in a hurry. 'The galley next, Pete.' I hurried after him. I didn't want to lose him, I would be lost around these new surroundings.

The galley was much smaller than I expected, but compact. I noticed a coal-fired range for the cooking, and all the surfaces were edged with bars to prevent the utensils from sliding off when the ship pitched and rolled. Albert paused in the doorway. 'Have a good look round, Pete, and don't forget to make a list for the chandler. You'll need to stock up for at least two weeks. See you at six. Oh, and by the way, we all sit and eat together here – the Cap'n likes to make sure we don't eat better than him.' He left me with a cheeky grin and went below to his engines.

Left to my own devices, I looked around the unfamiliar room

and felt utterly lost and alone. At least my predecessor was clean. The galley was spotless. Willing my body to move, I started to get to know my new environment. Some of the things I recognised; others I certainly didn't. No doubt I would learn as I went along.

Eventually I worked out what stocks I would need, and accompanied by Jess, one of the deck-hands, I went across to the chandler. I knew my way there. Many is the time that I used to shop for sweets and cigarettes when working on the docks.

I handed my shopping list to the chandler.

'Name of boat?' he enquired.

'The *Alsovear.*' – the name sounded strange on my tongue.

'Where's Charlie?' The question was directed at me, but Jess, who had been wandering idly round the store, piped up, 'He had to go into hospital. Anything else you want to know?'

'No, no,' the chandler said, and busied himself by gathering my groceries together. I made a mental note. Jess looked small and harmless, but I would do my best to keep on the right side of him in future.

Back in the galley I glanced at the time. Just three hours before the crew would be expecting a meal. I studied the shining black range. First things first, I needed to get the fire going. Then, while it warmed up, I would plan what to cook for the evening meal. Lighting the fire was easy; it had been one of my duties at home. Next, I checked the food cupboard. My eyes were drawn to a large tin of ham. That's it, I decided, ham, mashed spuds, and beans in tomato sauce. I would mash the potato with a big blob of butter to make it creamy. Now for the desert – stewed apple and custard – I could just about manage that! The kettle started to sing and I was beginning to feel more at home. After filling some mugs with the scalding tea, I ventured out to find the rest of the crew.

They were scattered all over, but after locating all of them I was left with one mug standing on the tray. It was for the Captain.

Entering the wheel-house, I handed him his tea, which by now had lost its piping hot steam and looked rather flat.

He took a large gulp and rubbed his hand over his damp whiskers. 'Is there a reason for oneself to be served last?'

I felt pretty silly. 'In the army, the troops were always fed first, Captain. I thought it would be the same here.'

He grinned. 'Sounds as good an answer as any to me. Carry on as you've started, laddie.'

Somewhat relieved, I returned to my galley for my own much needed mug of tea. I would be like my mother now; always last to eat. And if there wasn't enough to go around, then I would probably have to go without, just like her.

By ten-to-six everything was going nicely. Albert was the first at the table. 'What have you got for us? I'm absolutely starving,' he said. 'You don't have to wait until we are all here. Dish out the grub as we come in. When we're at sea, some will be on duty all round the clock. It's a bit different here than in the army, Pete!'

As the men came in, I served them the food I had prepared. They seemed to be enjoying it, judging by the speed with which it vanished from their plates. I didn't have time to feel nervous, but it was gratifying not to have any leftovers. They pulled my leg a little from time to time, but it was all light-hearted banter, and before I knew it they had finished and were back at work, battening down the holds and putting tarpaulins across the top to make them weatherproof.

The Captain was the last to leave. He enjoyed a pipe of tobacco before he made his move. As he was leaving he said, 'That was good. I think you'll do.'

I felt a whole lot better when he said that. It gave me the confidence that I so badly needed. I made everything shipshape in the galley, then went out on deck to watch the men struggling with the heavy planks of timber they were using to batten down the holds. I've never minded manual labour, so I helped them prepare for the voyage. When all the holds had been secured, I was told to get back to my galley. We would soon be casting off.

My galley suddenly came alive with a cacophony of sounds from the metal utensils that surrounded me. The engines had started. Albert would be standing by, waiting for the command to set the ship in motion. The muffled vibrations raced from my feet, through my body, and mingled with my already jangling nerve-ends, until I seemed to be shaking uncontrollably from head to foot. Deliberately I switched my thoughts to Katrinka. This trip would take us to Kotka in Finland – we were loaded with clay for the paper mills there. I suppose it would have been too much to hope for, that my first journey would take me to Poland. Never mind, at least I was on the right track, I would go there and find her one day. My trembling gradually subsided and I looked out of my open porthole to watch all the activity. The engines were now revving at a steadier pace, and our ship was easing out of its berth. We were at sea.

We sailed past the massive open-sided timber sheds as we headed for the harbour entrance. How different they looked when viewed from the water. A crewman popped his head round the door. 'Get the kettle boiling, cook, we all want a mug of tea. And one for the pilot before he goes back.'

While I waited for the water to boil, I returned my gaze to the porthole. The ship was already slicing through the water at great speed, and the receding docks looked almost insignificant as they dwindled into the distance. The spitting and frizzing of the kettle boiling over brought me back to reality. I finished the brew.

The mugs of tea which I had diligently filled to the brim in the galley were sadly only half-full by the time they reached the thirsty crew. Going up and down the ladders, and swaying with the ship had taken its toll. Happily, there were no snide comments about my sloppy service. I expect the crew had realised by then that I was a mere greenhorn, and no doubt were hoping to see a rapid improvement as the voyage progressed. I was determined not to disappoint them.

Before I turned in that night I planned my menu for the next day. Although I was dog-tired I experienced some difficulty in getting to sleep. My body ached all over, and no matter what position I lay in, I simply couldn't get comfortable. I thought it a good time to study the old cookery book; I realised I still had a lot to learn. I read it until my eyelids grew heavy and closed, and I slept.

I woke some hours later and sat bolt upright, staring at my unfamiliar surroundings. For a second nothing registered, except for the pounding beat against my rib-cage. Then realisation dawned. I was in a cabin at sea! My cabin mates were whispering and scuttling around on tip-toe.

'Sorry to wake you, Pete, we're just changing the watch.' Danny – a prematurely balding bloke with a quiet disposition – was feverishly undressing, his stint over and done with for the night. His partner – Scouse to his friends, which I hoped now included me – was just about ready to go on duty. He was roughly the same height as me, but much thinner, and his hair wasn't so black as mine. I was wide awake now, and knew that it would be

h

impossible to get back to sleep.

'Do you want some company up there, Scouse?' I asked.

His expression mirrored his amazement that anyone would choose to spend their night hours up in the wheel-house. He nevertheless seemed pleased by my unexpected offer. 'You'll need to get a move on,' he said.

It was cold on the bridge, coming as I did from a nice warm bunk, and I felt slightly disorientated in the unfamiliar surroundings. The moon was casting an eerie glow across the vast expanse of ocean. I wondered if I was dreaming for a moment or two. It was so unreal. To my left, I could just make out tiny pinpricks of light, and I asked Scouse what they were?

'That's the lights of Dover. Soon we will leave the English coast and later follow the Dutch coast up to Denmark. We will sail around Denmark and then on to the Baltic Sea. Are you feeling homesick?'

'No, but if it gets any rougher I could well be seasick.'

He gave me a playful slap on the back. 'It will get rougher, I can promise you that, but you'll get used to it.'

I watched with interest all the varied tasks Scouse had to tackle. He worked diligently and quietly. For a while he was oblivious to my presence, his concentration directed wholly to the job in hand. When he was satisfied that nothing more could be done for the moment, he relaxed and asked me if I had ever been to Liverpool? That he loved his town was quite evident, as the next twenty minutes were filled with an idyllic monologue of his birthplace. 'If ever we dock there I'll show you around,' he promised.

He moved to resume his duties, and I felt it was time to go back to my cabin.

'There's no town like it anywhere in the world!' His proud words followed me out of the wheel-house.

I was greeted by Danny's snores as I crept back into my cabin. I tried to make as little noise as possible, but my teeth were chattering like castanets; it certainly was cold up on deck. I managed to get warm again, but couldn't sleep for fear of over-sleeping. I had to be in my galley by six. Breakfast was at seven. Bacon and eggs – I reckoned I could cope with that.

Chapter Twenty-one

My confidence was growing with each hour that passed. The knowledge that my mother had instilled in me in such a short time was truly amazing. I was lucky in that I really enjoyed my newly acquired skills, and that probably helped me a great deal in mastering what I had always previously considered to be 'a woman's job'.

Scouse – a born seaman – was always willing to answer any of my maritime queries. And he would often volunteer helpful and useful information which, in my very green state, made my path a whole lot smoother. I considered myself most fortunate to have him as a shipmate.

'We've just rounded the northern tip of Denmark, Pete,' he told me one bright, cold morning when I handed him his mug of tea in the wheel-house. 'We now follow the Swedish coast along to Finland, and to the port of Kotka.'

After following the route Scouse had described, we eventually entered Finnish waters where I heard the loud clanking of the anchor chain, followed by a gigantic splash as the anchor plunged into the sea. We then had to wait for a local pilot to come aboard and guide us into the harbour.

My thoughts returned to Katrinka. I wondered where she was and what she was doing at that moment. How surprised she would be if she could see me now. If only I could let her know. What a situation to be in! Most courting couples could at least write to each other to soothe their aching hearts. My only hope was the *Alsovear*. The thought crossed my mind that some day I would be forced to tell the Captain of my plans, but as yet I would remain silent. I had no specific plans anyway. I was just living from day to day, taking each one as it came.

We waited patiently for the best part of three hours before the pilot came and took us into the harbour. It looked a very industrious place and I couldn't wait to set foot on dry land once more. So armed with my shopping list, I stepped ashore and weaved my way through the web of busy dockers in search of the chandler. I was conscious of each step I took. The ground below my feet was as hard as iron. I must still be wearing my sea-legs, I thought with a smile. I hadn't been at sea for that long – it just shows how quickly the body adapts to different conditions.

I found the chandler, and my wobbly sea-legs were soon forgotten as I selected some fresh red beef for an under-roast. I had already tried out mother's old faithful standby on the men, and they had all without exception wolfed down their meal amid grunts of pleasure and appreciative smacking of lips. It was so easy to make – potatoes, meat and onions straight into the oven in one dish, and cooked slowly. What a treat! My reputation went sky high; they even took to calling me chef when the mood grabbed them.

In the evening my shipmates decided to go ashore for a couple of hours. I caught up with all of my duties and went along with them. The few people we saw appeared friendly, but hardly anyone spoke English. In the cafés it was either vodka or coffee. I had never tasted vodka before and thought it wise to stick with coffee. Before returning to the ship I managed to buy a couple of small bottles of beer. The labels were not very informative, but after tasting it I knew that I wouldn't be getting drunk on that stuff.

Next morning the Captain informed us we were being loaded with timber that afternoon, and we were bound for Plymouth. My heart sank. No Poland this trip. I told myself I had to be patient; my day would come.

It was several more weeks before my prayers were answered. At long last the *Alsovear* was berthing at Gdansk in Poland. Now that I was there, I couldn't believe it. I didn't know what to do with myself. I was really close to her now, I could feel it. The daylight hours had passed slowly, although everyone was kept busy and there wasn't a moment to spare. Albert had agreed to go ashore with me after I had cleared up from the evening meal. I really needed his company on this mission. I succeeded in cooking a presentable dinner, even though my mind wasn't on it, and I was grateful to pick up plates that were empty and to receive some satisfying comments. I imagine the crew must have marvelled at the speed with which I delivered and collected the dishes that evening. They probably thought I was anxious to get ashore, desperate for a bit of skirt. How right they would have been, but not in the way they thought.

I couldn't eat anything myself. Albert came in as I was untying my apron. 'All ready, mate? Don't forget to bring some cigarettes – they'll get you anything out here. You might be able to swap them for some information.'

We headed straight for the shipbuilding yard. This was my goal, my first and main hope of finding her. Albert was struggling to keep up with me. I couldn't get there fast enough.

To my utter dismay, we arrived to find the shipyard gates locked. I looked at Albert with panic in my eyes. 'I must get in,' I said. 'I know she's in there, I can feel it!'

My foot was already on the bottom of the steel gate as I started to climb over, but Albert regarded me sadly and pointed a finger upward. The gates and the wall were both topped with evil-looking steel spikes and skin-tearing barbed wire.

Shaking with rage, I gripped the ice-cold bars of the gate. I felt so angry and cheated. To be this close, and yet to feel a million miles away. It was wickedly unfair!

I remained there for a while, peering through the bars, willing her to be there. I didn't want to leave. If Albert hadn't insisted we move on, I think I would have stayed there all night.

'Come on, mate.' He started to walk away. 'There's nothing for us here. Let's start on the cafés – maybe we'll learn something there.'

Despondently, I trailed after him through the drab streets. Ruins from the war were scattered everywhere, which did nothing to lift my heavy spirits. We found our first café and went inside.

I felt in my pocket to make sure the cigarettes were handy. Katrinka's photograph lay alongside them. Please, God, let someone recognise her. We have only tonight. I must have news of her!

When the waitress came over with her little notepad, I ordered two coffees.

'You American?' she quietly asked.

I shook my head. 'No, English.'

'English seamen?'

'Good guess,' I thought, then she enlightened me.

'Seamen are the only foreign people to visit here.' Her voice sounded wistful.

Placing the cigarettes on the table where the girl could see them, I showed her Katrinka's photo. She looked longingly at the cigarettes, then scrutinised the picture.

'Have you seen this girl anywhere around?' I placed the packet of cigarettes in her hand and whispered, 'She's Catholic.'

With the cigarettes imprisoned safely in her pocket, she studied the photo more intensely. I was beginning to feel a faint flutter of hope, when she dropped the photo on to the table. 'We are all Catholic, sir. I am sorry, I have not seen this woman.' But as she moved away, she lowered her head close to mine and whispered, 'I will look out for her.'

Albert paid for the coffee and tried to cheer me up. 'I think you could have scored with that waitress; she was looking at you with eyes of love. Bit of all right too, if you ask me.'

I smiled. She was nice but I wasn't interested. My heart had already been taken.

We did the rounds of all the cafés we could find, but it was the same old story wherever we went. No one recognised my Katrinka. It was with a heavy heart that I made my way back to the ship. If only I had one more day . . . surely someone must have seen her. I had felt so sure that I would get some good news. My only hope now was that we would return to Poland soon and I could then try again. I was more desperate than ever . . . So near yet so far. It was galling.

The days turned into weeks; the weeks became months. I was beginning to wonder whether I would ever get to visit Poland again. I was really getting used to life at sea now and enjoying it. My cooking was coming quite naturally, and if it wasn't for the heartache over Katrinka, life would have been near perfect.

Nearing the end of summer, we found ourselves in Liverpool. Scouse was like a cat with two tails. He had been wound up all day, and at dinner that evening he couldn't stop talking. After a few well-meaning gibes from his mates, he said, 'Come out with me tonight and see for yourselves. I'll show you all what a terrific place Merseyside can be. You don't know what you're missing!'

His excitement must have rubbed off on all of us, because even the Captain opted to come along.

I must say I have never seen such a place for night-life. It seemed that the whole of Liverpool was out on the booze. We visited a few crowded pubs, just spending a short while in each, as Scouse would be eager for us to be moving along. He wanted us to see everything there was to offer.

Our next stop was a lively fairground. The noise was deafening. Loud popular music blended with piercing shrieks as boys and girls braved the perilous fairground rides. I could even smell the excitement; a mixture of fear and diesel fumes filled my nostrils. We wandered idly along until a small crowd caught my attention. As we drew closer, I saw that the source of attraction was a boxing tent. Five boxers were lined up on a raised platform as an announcer used a megaphone to ask for challengers to take on his boys. We stopped to listen and my interest grew. 'Stay three rounds and earn yourself an easy ten pounds!' came the call as his eyes swept over his audience. 'Knock out one of my boys and I'll double it to twenty!' He looked pleased with himself, as if he was doing everyone a big favour.

I was tempted. Twenty pounds was a fortnight's wages for me. One of the boxers looked like a welterweight – just my size. I wrestled with my thoughts as I studied him more closely. He had dark curly hair, a broken nose, and looked pretty tough. Still, he must have fought a few times already this evening, so he had probably tired a little by now. Before I could stop myself, my hand shot up in the air.

The announcer pounced on me quicker than a cat with a mouse. He wasn't giving me any chance to change my mind. With a look that said I had just made his day, he raised his megaphone to his lips. 'What's your weight, son?'

'Welter.' My voice sounded puny after the megaphone.

He motioned for the boxer that I had picked to step forward. 'Ladies and gentlemen, we have our first welterweight challenger.' He looked back to me. 'Where are you from, lad?'

'Cornwall,' I shouted, trying to outdo the voice machine.

'And what's your job?'

'I'm cook on the *Alsovear*.' I told him, to cheers from my mates.

'Good! Make way for the cook, all you good people. I can see you're all in for a treat!'

The Captain was looking at me aghast. 'I hope you know what

you're doing,' he said, 'he's as tough as they come!'

'I'll be all right.' My voice sounded less than convincing, even to my own ears, but all eyes were upon me now, eagerly anticipating a blood bath by the looks of things.

Almost before I knew it, I found myself standing in front of the tent, beside my opponent. I knew that the spectators wanted their pound of flesh. The announcer placed his megaphone on the floor and stood between us. Then he took my arm and raised it high. 'Ladies and gentlemen, a Cornish janner who thinks he can knock out O'Driscoll, the Irish Champ!'

An excited buzz rose from the crowd, but my friends were starting to look worried, no doubt thinking how they were going to manage without their cook. I followed O'Driscoll past a little cubicle, where a peroxide blonde with thick bright red lips waited to collect the entrance fees. The tent inside appeared to be quite spacious. The ring stood in the centre, with two boxers already inside the ropes, energetically warming up. By their relatively puny bodies, I presumed they were featherweights. I followed meekly along to the back of the tent, where a curtain gave privacy to undress. It was already occupied by a foxy-looking bloke who promptly thrust a pair of long red shorts and oversized boxing boots into my hands. 'Get them on,' he said. He sounded bored with the whole thing, as if he would rather be somewhere else.

As I fumbled with my clothes, I was suddenly aware of a high-pitched babble of voices from the other side of the curtain. I realised the show was about to start and the eager crowd had been allowed inside. Mr Foxy handed me a pair of gloves.

I squeezed my hands into them and he laced them up without a word. Meanwhile, O'Driscoll, who was already prepared, made the most of his time by flexing his impressive muscles and smiling at me with a cocky grin. He didn't look one bit tired!

As I waited for my turn, I tried to calm myself mentally. I hadn't consumed too much beer – about four half-pints in two hours – so that shouldn't be a problem. I could hear the other bout in progress, and the roar of the crowd. I consoled myself by thinking that I'd soon be twenty pounds better off if I played my cards right.

'Eight . . . nine . . . ten!' My confidence plummeted as the ref gleefully pronounced the challenging featherweight out for the count. I didn't have time to run, I was being led out to the ring and everyone was shouting for me. After the last bout all the spectators wanted was for me to get one back. They wanted a result!

I climbed the three steps and ducked through the ropes. The second pointed me to my corner. The Irishman was already in his, and staring at me with a look that said, *I'm going to kill you, you stupid little Cornish cook!*

A roar erupted from the crowd as we were introduced and called to the centre of the ring. The ref gave the usual pep talk, told us he was boss, then sent us back to our corners from where we would come out fighting on hearing the bell.

The bell sounded. My mind, with a rash bravery that my body didn't entirely agree with, sent me bounding in to take the fight to my rival. Very soon we were in some hard and heavy skirmishes. He was a typical fairground fighter, experienced and with rules made up as he went along. He used his wooden head on me at every opportunity. I tried to box as I had been taught, to stay out of trouble until I saw my chance. I knew I had to knock him out. But three rounds would soon go by! Spurred on by these thoughts, I launched a vicious attack, and had him back on the ropes as the bell sounded the end of round one.

I sat panting on my stool. So far, so good. I was still in one piece and ready for round two. But before the sound of the bell had died away, O'Driscoll had charged across the ring and caught me a hefty right hook on the chin. I was still in the act of rising from my stool. The tent almost lifted off the ground with the loud boos of the crowd, but the ref, who clearly wasn't on my side, appeared not to notice.

My stunned disbelief soon gave way to blazing anger. The crowd howled in excitement as I went for him. This time there was no quarter asked or given. His rigid head caught me on the bridge of my nose and sparks of pain flashed across my forehead. I felt little tickles of warm blood running down over my mouth, but I fought back. The crowd were going mad, and their support gave me the strength I so badly needed. I managed to get a good clean uppercut to his chin which stopped him in his tracks. Before he had the chance to recover, I caught him again with a left swing to the side of the head. He went down on one knee. The frenzy of the crowd almost drowned out the bell for the end of the round. That was over quick, too quick! Even the bloody timekeeper was on his side.

I must have looked a sorry sight, hunched up in my corner. But I wasn't finished yet. I really wanted that twenty pounds. I looked around the sea of faces and caught sight of my mates. They were smiling now, and giving me the thumbs-up sign, which gave me an extra urge to win. I glanced across at my rival. He did look tired now. But to give him his due, he had probably fought several rounds already this evening, and he was still man enough for me!

Clang! I was on my feet again. Faster this time. We met in the centre of the ring and immediately exchanged a flurry of stinging blows. As I moved away from him, my foot slipped on the canvas and I landed on my knees. O'Driscoll couldn't miss a chance like that; he slammed me on the side of my head and I was sent sprawling to the floor.

I was still conscious, even though the angry boos of the crowd seemed a little fuzzy. Through the din, I recognised the measured counting of the ref. I had to get up! I took a deep breath and struggled to my feet, just in time. I hung there for a precious few seconds, then I attacked. My strength surged back as it dawned on me the dirty trick he had played. I belted him around the ring and enjoyed it. His face showed utter surprise, and his body and arms seemed to have given up on him. Then the dreaded bell sounded. The knock out which I so badly wanted had eluded me. I had to settle for ten pounds instead of twenty.

While I was changing, my rival came across and shook my hand. He said, 'You should turn professional, mate.'

'No thanks,' I replied through stiffening lips. 'I have another mission which is much more important to me at this moment in time.'

My mates were waiting for me when I came out of the boxing tent. They slapped me on the back and congratulated me for putting on a fine show. The Captain looked as if he had enjoyed the entertainment. 'I think we have a dark horse here, lads. That was one of Ireland's best. If it had been a ten rounder with proper rules, I think our laddie here would have beaten him!' Praise indeed coming from him.

I felt great, even though my face was stinging all over, and my vision wasn't all that it should be. One of my eyes had started to puff up – I was going to have a real shiner by the morning.

On the way back to the docks I was treated to a pint of beer and some fish and chips. I felt it was the finest food I had ever tasted.

Chapter Twenty-two

The next morning the ship was being loaded with house coal bound for Par in Cornwall. We were hoping to make the evening tide. At breakfast the Captain was in a jovial mood. His night on the town had done him a power of good. For several days now, I had been considering whether to tell him my story. I was becoming increasingly worried that my spell as substitute cook might end before the ship berthed in Poland again. My time was fast running out. The Captain might be able to help if he knew the full story. It was a gamble, but I was desperate and I didn't know where else to turn.

I busied myself gathering up the dirty breakfast plates while he sat enjoying his pipe. 'Could I have a private word later, Cap'n?'

He nodded, puffing furiously at his pipe. 'Want to become a boxer, do you, me lad? Want to give up the sea job, eh?'

'Not it's not that,' I stammered.

He knocked out his pipe and rose to leave. 'Come and see me in my cabin in . . .' he paused to study his watch – 'In say half-an-hour. And by the way, I'd put some steak over that eye if I were you.'

I returned his wry grin. 'Thank you, Cap'n.'

Some twenty-five minutes later, having finished the washing-up, I made my way to his cabin. I had a million fluttering butterflies in my stomach and hardly knew where to begin. It was with marked apprehension that I tapped on his door.

'Go in, lad!' I almost jumped out of my skin as his booming voice reverberated in my ear. I was early and had got there just before him. He was standing right behind me. I was still trembling as I opened the door and went in.

He pointed to a seat and reached for a bottle of whiskey and two glasses. He filled both glasses to the brim and handed one to me.

I extended a shaky hand. 'I'm not used to drinking Scotch, Cap'n.'

'This is Irish, boyo,' he said, 'the best there is. Good for the soul! Try it – you look as though you need it.' He took a large, satisfying gulp, licked his whiskers dry, then proceeded to fire up his pipe.

I gingerly sipped at mine. I found it hard to drink; my throat felt as if it was being squeezed by an invisible hand. But the effect it was having on the rest of me felt good. My knees were no longer knocking together quite so drastically, and I could now hold my glass without slopping the precious liquid.

Settling back in his chair, the Captain studied me through a haze of thick blue tobacco smoke. 'Where did you learn to fight, laddie?'

'A retired Cornish champion taught me all I know,' I told him.

'Why do you work for us, when you could earn so much more in the ring?'

I met and held his steady gaze. My moment of truth had arrived. I related the whole story, without a single interruption from him. His face remained expressionless throughout the entire episode. It was a great relief to have got it off my chest. Now I was ready to face the music.

He refilled his glass and studied the amber liquid as if seeing it for the first time. His eyes never wavered from the glass as he finally spoke. 'You do realise that you're dealing with a Communist country here?' he said. 'And let's just suppose you do find this girl. What exactly would you plan to do about it?'

'Well, Cap'n, I haven't really thought that far ahead. First I have to find her, then . . .' I swallowed hard. 'I was hoping that you might be able to help me.'

He placed his glass on the table. 'You are a young idiot,' he said, but his harsh reply was tempered by the look of concern he gave me.

'I love her, Captain. I managed to get her out of Germany. I can't give up on her now.'

'I'm sure you do, my boy.'

I gave a hapless shrug. 'I suppose you'll be looking for a new cook now that you know my story.' I rose to leave, convinced that I had wasted my time.

'Sit down, boy,' he snapped, 'we haven't finished yet. Who else knows of your plans?'

'Just Albert, Cap'n. Nobody else.'

He smiled knowingly. 'I see now why he was so anxious for you to get the job as cook. I did wonder why he was so keen. Well you haven't lost your job, lad. Hell, I love your grub too much for that.' He rose from his seat. 'Tell no one else on board, but keep me informed.' He scratched his beard thoughtfully. 'I don't know how I will be able to help you. We will see. I only hope this Katrinka is worth all this trouble.' He walked with me to the door. 'By the way, what's for lunch?'

'Irish stew, of course!' I replied with a cheeky grin.

'On your way, you young monkey, I've wasted enough time as it is.'

My steps were a little unsteady as I walked out of the cabin. The strong whiskey had settled in my knees, but I was feeling happier now. At least I still had my job, and the Captain seemed fairly sympathetic to me. I felt that if it was in his power to sail to Poland, then he would, even though he must have considered me more than a little crazy. But I had to be patient.

Time passed, we were into winter now. My time as a sea-cook was speedily running out, and I was no further forward with my quest. We had called in at several ports on the Polish Baltic coast but, as always, I came away with a heavy heart. No Katrinka. It was as if she had vanished off the face of the earth. I was beginning to lose all hope of ever finding her. Although the Captain never mentioned my plight, I think he realised how I must be feeling, as one day when we were docked in Charlestown harbour in St Austell bay, he gave me permission to have the day off to visit my family. I was delighted, it would be lovely to see them again. And it was.

We sat talking for ages. My mother was eager to learn how my cooking skills had progressed and how I had fared at sea. Sadly I related the details of my fruitless search for Katrinka. 'If only I could have some little sign of her, it would give me hope,' I said, unable to hide my anguish.

My mother walked over to the mantlepiece and picked up an envelope which rested against a family photo. 'Here,' she smiled,

'I almost forgot. This arrived for you yesterday morning. I wondered whether I should have opened it for you. I didn't expect to see you so soon. It's fate you should turn up today.'

I knew that writing! My hands trembled as I tore the envelope open and hurriedly read the short note. She had been moved to a place called Gdynia – no wonder I couldn't find her. But she was all right, thank God. She wrote that sometime in the near future she would be returning to Gdansk, probably back to her old job in the shipbuilding yard. She went on to say that her duties were forever changing, and that she had a strong feeling that the authorities were making it difficult for anyone to keep track of her whereabouts. She felt she was under constant surveillance. The note ended with the words, *I love you for all time, my Peter . . . K.*

Underneath was scribbled: *To send this to you, I rely on and trust an English sailor once again.*

I again had cause to feel gratitude to an unknown sailor. If only he knew how important this was.

I ate a large pasty for my tea. It was a real treat to sample mother's cooking again, and to be waited on, and to have my hopes raised in such a wonderful way. And all on the same day.

After tea my brother Joe took me back to Charlestown on his motorbike. We said our goodbyes on the quayside and I headed straight for the Captain's cabin; I was anxious for him to read my letter from Katrinka.

I bumped into Albert on the way, and swiftly filled him in with the latest news. He laid his arm on my shoulder. 'Let's hope we will be sailing that way soon hey, Pete.' He looked so happy; anyone would have thought it was his girlfriend.

The next morning we were on our way to Sweden with a cargo of clay. It looked as if we were in for a rough trip. Scouse informed me we were sailing into a force eight gale. I must admit I felt scared. He made matters worse by telling me that the *Alsovear* was a liberty boat, and that it was welded together, rather than riveted. I asked him if that made any difference to the ship.

'Hell, yes,' he said. 'The traditionally-made riveted ship can give a little when the going gets rough, whereas the Liberty boats have been known to split in two in a hurricane! You can thank the Yanks for the *Alsovear* – it's just one of many they gave us during the war. The German U-boats sunk so many of ours, we couldn't have done without them. We were grateful at the time. But now!' He shrugged his shoulders. 'Who knows?'

I was beginning to regret becoming a seaman. Albert must have noticed my ashen face. 'Don't take any notice of him, Pete, he's just winding you up. He wouldn't sail on her if she wasn't safe.' I hoped he was right.

As we drew deeper into winter, it seemed we were sailing in darkness most of the time. The ship had called at Gdansk on one occasion, and the good Captain gave me more time to search. But I had no luck; it was hopeless. Albert fared better than me. He managed to date the waitress we had spoken to during our first visit. I was pleased for him; I always knew he fancied her. But he told me after his date that she was still unable to shed any light on Katrinka's whereabouts. It came as no surprise to me. In fact I was beginning to wonder if I would ever set eyes on her beautiful face again.

Some time later we again docked in Charlestown harbour, this time for a stay of three days because the ship needed a new winch and several minor repairs. Although displeased by this period of enforced idleness, the Captain kindly allowed me to spend this time at home.

That first evening at home was spent chatting with my family, and I was saddened to learn that a long-standing neighbour, Phyllis, had died. Joe told me how upset her husband had been, and how he had taken a part-time gardening job to help take his mind off things. Apparently, he was employed by a well-to-do chap who lived in an imposing house on the outskirts of the village. I had passed it many a time, and imagined the gardens to be as spectacular as the house, although they were hidden from view by a high boundary wall. Suddenly, Joe leapt to his feet.

'Pete! I've got it!'

'What?' I was bemused.

'The chap who lives in the big house,' Joe said excitedly. 'I've heard it said that he used to be with MI5. He probably knows about these Iron Curtain countries. Why not have a chat with him? It's worth a try.'

I nodded. It was a good idea if the rumour was true. 'I'll sleep on it,' I said.

The next morning, after a night of tossing and turning, I found myself on the gravel driveway leading up to the big house. I had been right about the gardens; they were magnificent. I paused nervously at the front door, wondering if I was doing the right thing. Even if the rumours of his involvement with MI5 were true, he was unlikely to be interested in my problem. He would probably have me thrown out.

My hand remained poised over the grotesque, grinning-devil door-knocker. I felt almost afraid to touch it, in case it snapped its mouth shut, and crushed my fingers in its fiendish jaws. Before I could make up my mind whether I wanted to run or risk it, the door opened.

'What do you want?' A woman, whom I knew only by sight, having seen her in the village, was waiting for a reply.

'I would like to speak to the master of the house, if it's convenient.'

I moved back a step, feeling uncomfortable as her beady little eyes bored into mine as if she was trying to read my thoughts.

She gave a haughty sniff. 'What is the nature of your business? He's a very busy man.'

'It's a personal matter.'

Her thin, pinafore-sheathed body turned away. Then she stopped and looked back. Begrudgingly, she invited me to step inside. She led me into a spacious hall and disappeared.

The walls were covered with large oil paintings, mostly of steam trains. Huge decorative pots full of lush green leaves were spaced along the length and breadth of this imposing foyer, interspersed with carved wooden figures representing many different cultures. The carvings were rather sinister. Everywhere I looked, wooden eyes were boring into me, watching my every move. I was really quite glad when the sour-faced woman returned. At least her cross expression was human.

'He will see you,' she said, 'providing you're not selling anything or begging for charity.'

I shook my head to assure her that neither of those exemptions applied, and meekly followed her to the far end of the hall. She pointed to a door and left me to my fate. I gave it a gentle tap and was immediately invited inside by a well-cultured but brusque voice. I stepped into a bright but cluttered room. The scent of hundreds of books and writing materials reminded me of my classroom at school. The master of the house – a military looking man with a shock of dark wavy hair and a waxed moustache –

was seated at a solid antique desk, its surface hidden by a motley collection of books and papers. The desk stood in the deep well of a large bay window which gave a panoramic view of the neatly-tended grounds. The wall on my right was covered from end to end with shelves of tightly packed books, and on the wall opposite a fire crackled cosily in an impressive marble grate. As the man rose with his hand outstretched to greet me, I wove my way between plush leather armchairs, carefully avoiding an ivory chess-set displayed on a small table which twinned with his desk. 'Charles Dawson,' he introduced himself, as we shook hands. His black eyes twinkled shrewdly underneath his thick bushy eyebrows. 'And you, sir, are?'

'Peter Rundle, sir.' My voice sounded feeble against the noisy crackle of the wood in the grate.

'You may sit if you wish.' He indicated a chair on my side of the desk.

I accepted his offer gladly as my legs were beginning to feel as if they belonged to someone else.

He studied me for a moment, then said, 'I take it you know my housekeeper Mrs Truscott, but what is your business with me?'

I found myself tongue-tied for a moment or two; my mouth had dried up.

'Come along man, do state your business!' He was a busy man, and fast losing patience with me.

After running my tongue over my parched lips, and swallowing hard to moisten my throat, the words came gushing out: 'Local rumour has it, sir, that you once worked for MI5.'

'I suppose I have Mrs Truscott to thank for delivering that information?' He spoke her name with annoyance. 'Has she imparted any other juicy tit-bits concerning my personal affairs?' He glared at me angrily, waiting for an answer.

'Mrs Truscott has told me nothing, sir. I know her only by sight. Although I live in the village, I have been away at sea for quite some time.'

'Royal Navy?'

'The merchant service, sir.'

'I see. And what bearing does this have on your visit?'

'Only that I need your help when I next visit the Iron Curtain countries, sir.'

'In what way?' Now he was intrigued.

'My sweetheart is being held in a displaced person's camp, namely in Gdynia and Gdansk. I have to get her out.'

I waited to see if his expression registered interest. He bent forwards and pushed something on the side of his desk. He watched me intently as a voice wafted out from its hiding place under the litter bin. It was my voice! He was recording our conversation!

His hand moved to turn it off. 'Lesson number one,' he said, 'never go into a strange place and talk of such things. It could easily get you killed.'

I felt rather stupid.

He pondered while I sat and waited to be thrown out. Then he said, 'Yes, it is true that I have been employed by MI5. And now you may tell me your story, from the beginning.'

Starting at Gottingen in Germany, I related everything that had happened. From time to time he would interrupt to ask questions and jot down items in a notebook. Eventually I came to the present time and convinced him of my desperate determination to find Katrinka.

He pushed back his seat and regarded me gravely. 'You are dealing with ruthless people,' he told me. 'If they get to know what you are after, they could put you into prison for the rest of your life – you might end up in Siberia, or worse. Is this girl really worth all this trouble?'

I stood up and faced him across the desk. 'As you can see, sir, I must love her to be here today. If only you knew her, you would understand what I feel. I have to find her. I need your help!'

His expression softened as he motioned me to sit down. He then extracted a fat folder from one of the desk drawers. He remained silent while he searched through the wad of papers, then, with a look of triumph, he extracted a single sheet and placed it down before him. His eyes scanned the text. 'Are you familiar with the Café Poznon? It's quite close to the docks in Gdansk.'

I told him that I was.

Next door to the café, there is a tobacconist shop, yes?' He waited for my nod of awareness. 'Go into the shop and buy something; ask for a man named Jerzy. Tell him that Seagull has sent you. Give him a good bottle of Scotch whisky, then ask him if he can help you to find your Katrinka. If anyone can help you it will be this man. That is all the help I can offer at this time.' His eyes delved into mine. 'If you had any sense you will go no further. But I can see that you are determined to pursue this matter to the bitter end. Remember, keep everything in your head; never have anything of importance written down. Have you got that?'

'Yes, sir, and thank you. I greatly appreciate your help and advice.' He shook my hand warmly and wished me luck. Mrs Truscott saw me out.

As I walked back along the crunchy gravel path I felt drained. But with more optimism than I had had for weeks.

The next day I caught a bus into town and bought a bottle of the finest malt. If it brought me the luck I was praying for, then on my return I would buy another just like it for my friend at the big house.

My next voyage on the *Alsovear* was to Bremerhaven in northern Germany with a cargo of rations for the BOAR. From there we travelled to Hamburg and took aboard machine tools bound for Plymouth. And it was during this return voyage that we encountered a severe storm in the North Sea. It was the roughest conditions I had ever known. I had trouble just trying to remain on my feet. The ship was rolling and pitching wildly, and the pots and pans in the galley were sent crashing all over the place. I had never in all my life felt so scared.

I remember Scouse poking his head round the galley door. 'Don't try taking tea to the men, you'll be washed away,' he warned. 'Keep it on the go and we'll come here for it.'

'What about the ship being a Liberty boat?' I called fearfully, but he was gone and I was left talking to a puddle of water.

It lasted for hours. I was convinced that the ship would split in two. It was a relief when the seamen came in at odd intervals for their tea. At least I learnt we were still in one piece. After one particularly loud roar, and a mighty surge which left me not knowing whether I was on my head or my heels, the Cap'n burst in. 'Get your oilskins, quick as you can! Some of the cargo has broken loose. We must secure it, and I need all hands on deck.' He shouted back to me on his way out: 'Make sure you are holding the rail at all times, or you will be blown overboard.'

I hastily donned my heavy-weather gear, and with great trepidation followed him down to the hold. The wind swirled around me as I clutched the rail for dear life. It threatened to pull my arm from its socket. I couldn't see a thing, my eyes were stinging like mad from the spray, and my eardrums were fit to burst with the booming roar of the wind and waves. I offered up a silent prayer as I was directed down into the hold. Conditions weren't a lot better down there. Although we were out of the storm, we weren't out of danger. One of the large lathes had broken loose and was smashing into the side of the hold. Much more of that and we would be in deep trouble.

'Do what I tell you and nothing else!' shouted the Captain, his voice barely audible above the roar of the storm. 'We don't want our cook killing himself down here, do we?'

He had no need to worry, I was too scared to do anything else but obey orders.

After a terrific struggle, we managed to secure a rope around the wayward machine tool, and then waited for the surge of the ship to lurch it back to its original position. Once it was in place, we swiftly made it fast to its neighbour. No sooner was that done, than there came another loud crash from further up in the hold. It turned out to be another broken rope. I followed the crew between the precarious machines, terrified with each step that another one would break loose and crush us. But eventually the job was done and we were all safe and sound. All of the ropes had been checked and the Captain was satisfied. The relief was overwhelming.

Back in the warm womb of my galley, I shed my oilskins. I was just as wet on the inside as on the outside. I think I had been sweating more with fear than with exertion. My fears really only disappeared when I noted the dawn creeping up on the far horizon. I had survived my first severe storm at sea, but after that grim episode I realised that seafaring was not the life for me.

It was to be three more frustrating weeks before I found myself in Poland again. I had spoken to Albert about my visit with Charles Dawson but, as yet, hadn't confided in the Captain. Albert had work to do on the engines while we were in dock, so I went alone to the Café Poznon. Tucking the bottle of whisky out of sight inside my jacket, and full of nervous optimism, I made my way down the gangway to the jetty. Once again part of me felt like turning back as I walked through the dock gates. Would this man Jerzy be there? Would he help me? I was completely on my own and I dreaded to think of the serious trouble I could land up in. Then I would imagine what life would be like if I lost her – I had to go on, there was no other way.

I had no difficulty in finding the Café Poznon. I think I knew virtually every café in the area by then. I rounded a corner and there at the end of the street stood the two shops. I stood looking at them with a mixture of trepidation and excitement. I thought it best to have a drink in the café first of all; I badly needed a few minutes to calm my shredded nerves.

My hand was shaking as I lit a cigarette. I stubbed it out before it was halfway through. I couldn't rest easy; I had to get into the shop next door. I felt in my pocket for Katrinka's photograph although I knew it was safely there. The whisky was still hiding underneath my coat. I was ready.

After paying the waitress for my untouched coffee, I made a bee-line for the tobacconist's next door. I paused outside and took a deep breath. Then with a boldness I didn't feel, I opened the door and strode in.

Although the lovely aroma of Continental tobacco filled the air, the shop itself looked rather bare. It followed the pattern of most of the shops over there. None seemed to be very prosperous. A loud bell above the door announced my arrival and a mature, wiry-looking man came out of a back room to serve me. His sandy hair tumbled over his forehead like an overgrown schoolboy's, and he was sporting a droopy moustache which had turned bright ginger from its contact with the smoke of countless cigars.

I took the bull by the horns. 'I would like to buy some cigarettes, and do you know of a man named Jerzy?' With my confidence mounting by the minute, I gushed on. 'My name is Peter Rundle, from the ship *Alsovear* which is lying in the docks. I am a friend of Seagull.'

'Seagull!'

I knew instantly I was face to face with the man who could help me.

'Is he well?' he asked.

I nodded.

He stared wistfully into space as if remembering past fond times, then he spoke. 'Yes, I am Jerzy.' His expression grew serious. 'Now, straight to the point – what do you want?'

As I opened my mouth to reply, the doorbell chimed and in came a customer. Jerzy quickly pushed a box of cigars in front of me, spoke in Polish to his client, and sold him a packet of cigarettes.

When we were again on our own, I showed him the photograph of Katrinka. I told him how I had been desperately trying to find her, and how I was certain that she was now in this area.

He pushed the photo back to me. 'I have not seen this girl.'

He didn't want to know. My spirits fell, then I remembered the whisky. I reached inside my coat, placed the bottle on the counter, and slowly peeled back the wrapping.

His eyes caressed the bottle. 'You certainly have been talking with the Seagull,' he said, as his hand quickly clasped the bottle. 'Come this way.'

I followed him into a back room where a woman was busy sewing. She appeared quite a bit younger than the tobacconist but I assumed she was his wife. When he spoke to her in Polish, she glanced at me briefly, then scurried out to the shop, taking her sewing with her. 'I have asked her to look after the shop while we speak,' he explained, as he motioned for me to be seated. He rested the whisky on the table and examined the bottle intently. 'A single malt!' An appreciative whistle escaped from his lips. While he was so occupied, I glanced around the room. It had a stove in the centre, the likes of which I have never seen before. The exterior was decorated in a lavish ornate design, and it looked as if it was fuelled by dusty black coal. Apart from the table and chairs, and just one freestanding cupboard, the room was very bare. Another doorway led to what I presumed to be the kitchen.

Jerzy placed his bottle in the cupboard, pulled a chair over opposite to me, and asked me about my quest, whereupon I related my well-rehearsed story.

When I had done, he pondered for a few moments. 'Even if you do find her, the authorities will send her back again,' he pointed out.

I told him that I was aware of that possibility, but that there would be no official involvement in my plan. 'If we have to keep on the move, then so be it,' I said.

'When is your ship due back here again?'

'Not for another four or five weeks, maybe longer.'

He looked at me kindly. 'We will try to find her for you, but it won't be easy. When you call again I should have some news of her whereabouts, provided of course that she is in this area.'

Grateful of his promised cooperation, I expressed my thanks and shook his hand. At last I felt as if I was getting somewhere. Smiling for the first time, he said, 'If I do locate her for you, will it be worth another bottle of malt?'

'That's the least you may expect, my friend. You have given me hope.'

'Now you must leave,' he said. 'I will sell you a packet of cigarettes. When you step outside, take one and light it. If anyone is watching they will assume that you are just another smoker who cannot wait until he gets home to enjoy his cigarette. We cannot afford to arouse any kind of unwanted interest in your visit here. Is that clear?'

'Of course, Jerzy.'

After thanking him again, I made my way back to the ship in high spirits. The men would have a good meal tonight. I felt like celebrating!

Chapter Twenty-three

A further five weeks passed, still with no return to Poland scheduled for the *Alsovear*. Then the ship needed some engine repairs and we found ourselves in dry dock at Falmouth for a while. It was while we were there that the ship's permanent cook came to see the Captain. He asked me how I had fared.

'Getting by,' I confided, 'but only just.'

He looked relieved. 'I'm hoping to get back in a month's time,' he told me. 'Will you find another ship, or have you had enough of life in the galley?'

I felt sick. Just one more month to find Katrinka. My heart was in my boots as I told him that I had made no definite plans. 'I'll make up my mind when you return,' I added.

'Best of luck, mate,' he said, as he left knowing that his old job was secure. I was left shattered.

Two days later we sailed up the coast to Fowey where we loaded china clay for Finland. I knew this could be my last trip on the *Alsovear*, and I prayed with all my heart that the return voyage would include a stopover at Poland. Everything was now riding on Jerzy. In anticipation of a positive outcome I had a bottle of malt stowed away in my cabin. I could only hope and pray that I would be needing it.

That night, while charging through a choppy sea off the coast of Holland, I made a jug of cocoa and took some round for everyone before I turned in for the night. The Captain was in the wheel-house, overseeing the watch. Gratefully accepting his steaming mug, he said, 'Pete, the cook reckons he will be back on duty very shortly. I'm really sorry you haven't had any luck finding your girl.' He took a large swig of cocoa. 'Maybe you should forget her – it's pretty hopeless, you know.'

'I will never forget her, Cap'n. With God's help someday I will find her.'

He polished off his nightcap and handed me the empty mug. 'I will give you a good reference – you deserve it. You might want to go to sea again, you never know.'

I thanked him and moved to go.

'By the way, show him how to make your under-roast. A fine feast to be sure, especially with the brown sauce.'

'I will,' I promised.

I collected the rest of the empty mugs and took them back to the galley to wash them. Like my mother used to say, 'Who wants to face a sink full of dirty dishes first thing in the morning?' Then, another day over, I stretched out on my bunk and stared at the ceiling, I couldn't sleep. Would I have one last chance in Poland? I would be a broken man if I was denied that. The *Alsovear* was my only ticket to Gdansk. The Communists would not even permit anyone to have a holiday there. In the end, I resorted to an old army trick and held my pillow in my arms, imagining it to be Katrinka. That way I finally slept.

The weather was very cold now. The warmest place was down with Albert in the engine room. We would often sit down there when time allowed, and reminisce of our younger days in Cornwall. Scouse and his mates joined us whenever the opportunity arose, just for a warm up.

When we eventually docked at Kotka in Finland, the Captain went ashore to the shipping office for his orders. I gave the galley a spring-clean, just to keep myself busy until he returned. This was it; I would soon know what my fate would be.

After what seemed an eternity, I heard voices outside the door. Then the door opened to reveal the Captain standing there, grinning like a Cheshire cat.

'Anyone here for Poland?' he asked.

My heart missed a beat – no, several beats!

'Yes, Pete,' he said, 'that's right, we're going to Poland.'

I had to sit down. It was an omen; I was meant to find her, I just knew it!

* * * *

j

Snow was beginning to fall as we sailed into Gdansk. I made pasties for the men, which I would leave in the oven when I went ashore. They could help themselves when they were ready for them. By the time the *Alsovear* had docked the snow was coming down thick and fast. I dressed in my warmest outdoor garments and was placing a woolly hat on my head when Albert came into the galley.

'I've come to wish you luck, Pete.'

I pulled the hat down over my ears. 'Thanks, mate, I think I'm going to need a lot of that.'

Albert sat down and beckoned me closer. In low tones, he said, 'I've been thinking, you will need stores from the chandler today, won't you?'

I nodded, wondering what was coming next.

He said, 'If they have found Katrinka, you will bring her back to the ship, yes?' Once again I nodded in agreement.

'If you leave your shopping order as you go out,' he went on, 'and tell them to pack it into two boxes to be picked up later. Then, if Katrinka should be with you, no one will take any notice of two seamen carrying supplies back on board, will they?'

'Albert, you are a genius! I hadn't thought that far ahead. I haven't dared to.' He looked really pleased to have made a worthwhile contribution as I left the warm comfort of the ship to face the harsh Polish climate.

I stopped off at the chandler's and gave him my orders. I felt good. The weather was on my side. The snow was obscuring even the objects which were nearest to me. It suited me to be invisible. I willed it to snow like hell all day long. Turning up my collar and tugging my hat firmly down on my head, I hurried on my way.

I met with very few people, and except for an odd tram jingling by, there was hardly any traffic. Under my coat was hidden another bottle of whisky. I hoped that the news awaiting me would be worth it.

The tobacconist shop looked chillingly desolate with the snow settling into its crevices and piling on to its ledges. I glanced about me before opening the door. No one was venturing out today with the visibility down to just a few yards. The harsh tone of the bell made me jump as I slipped inside. The place was empty of customers, but Jerzy soon appeared from his room at the back. 'Ah, so the Englishman from the *Alsovear* has returned.

This way, please.'

I followed him into the small room which served as a kitchen. 'Any news?' I couldn't contain myself.

He eyed me critically. 'Do not be so impatient – these things take time.'

'You have nothing for me then?'

'I did not say that.' He sat down on a tall wooden stool and gestured for me to pull out the remaining one for myself. I remembered the whisky and placed it on the table beside him, hoping it would help to loosen his tongue. 'We are satisfied you are who you say you are,' he said, as his eyes lovingly swept over the bottle. 'You understand that we had to check you out?'

'Yes, get to the point!' I felt like shaking him.

He said, 'Katrinka is a very elusive young woman – she trusts no one. We suspect that someone in high authority, in the secret police maybe, has other plans for her.'

I listened with growing dread, but they must have located her to know all of this.

'We have discovered that she has changed her place of worship,' Jerzy continued, 'maybe to avoid this person.' He shrugged his shoulders as if to say he wasn't sure; that it was very complicated. He must have noticed my look of despair because he swiftly added, 'But she is here, in Gdansk. Perhaps if you visit her church, you may have some favourable news. But be careful of the priests you may meet. Some are for us and others will be against us.' He told me how to find the church.

I thanked him profusely and rose to go, eager to make the most of this fresh information. He placed his hand on my arm. 'We have been very careful while making our enquiries. You must watch your step; you are playing a dangerous game. Good luck, my friend.'

He led me back to the shop and opened the door for me. I nodded my appreciation, then hurried outside. I turned to say goodbye, but he was gone, the door already closed behind him.

I raced along the icy streets, stumbling and sliding in my urgency to reach the church. There it was! Jerzy had directed me well. Kicking the snow off my boots, I ventured inside. I swiftly took in the unfamiliar surroundings. There were probably a dozen people seated in the pews.

Selecting a pew near the back, I sat and crossed myself, then bowed my head just as Katrinka would have done. I wanted to blend in. I let my gaze wander around the holy building. It was magnificent, but my interest was centred more on a priest who suddenly emerged from a doorway near the font. Someone coughed and took my attention. When I looked back for the priest he had gone. In that split-second he must have exited through the same doorway. Just my luck, I thought with annoyance. I became aware of movement quite close by. Risking a sideward glance, I saw an old woman in a shapeless black dress and head-scarf kneeling to scrub the floor. She was working her way towards me, feet first. Then I noticed a lone woman two rows in front of me as she stood up and crossed herself, before stepping out into the freshly-scrubbed aisle. She was coming my way. I had to start somewhere, so I withdrew Katrinka's photograph from my pocket. The woman slowed as she side-stepped past the old woman and her bucket, which gave me time to intercept her as she drew level.

'Have you seen this girl?' I whispered, thrusting the picture in front of her.

She looked at me, startled, then glanced briefly at the photograph. Amid a torrent of Polish, she brushed past me and hurried away.

'Can I be of any help to you?' The quiet voice from behind me made me start. I had no idea anyone was there. I turned to face a kindly looking priest. I was aware of the photograph still lying in my hand – he must have seen it. His English was good; I decided to trust him.

'I believe this woman worships here. Do you know her?'

He studied the photograph for a moment. 'May I ask why you want to know?'

This was awkward; I tried the truth: 'I have come a long way to see this girl. Do you know of her whereabouts, please? It is of great importance to me.'

He smiled, and I felt better as he said, 'I think I do. Please be seated . . . I will make some enquiries.'

I sat down, feeling very excited, and praying that I had done the right thing. The priest, after covering his shoulders with a long, black cape, passed from sight into the doorway near the font. The old cleaning woman was now beside me. She wrung out her cloth as she glanced over her shoulder. Then, to my utter dismay, she whispered, 'Do not put your trust in the priest. He has gone to inform on you!'

'You're sure?' I gasped.

Then she really did astound me. 'The girl you seek works at the café in the market,' she said, 'just two streets away.' She pointed with her scrubbing brush. 'Hurry!' she hissed as she furiously scrubbed the well-trodden floor.

For a second I froze. Who to believe? Without really thinking I was out of the church in a flash. My second sense had taken over. I knew I was in danger! It was still snowing hard as I belted up the street.

It took me about ten minutes to find the café, and by then I was winded and sweating gallons in spite of the cold. Time was running out, so I went inside without any plans of what I was going to say or do. I had the sense to find a secluded seat at the back of the café, where I sat and immediately started to scan the faces of the waitresses who were hovering about. Katrinka was not among them. Behind the counter a young woman was making coffee, and two other women were busy washing dishes, but no Katrinka. My heart sank. I had been sold down the river.

When one of the waitresses sauntered over to me, I ordered a coffee. Wondering what to do next, I watched the two women gossiping as they attacked the mound of dirty dishes. I fingered Katrinka's photograph. Should I ask them? Could I trust them?

Then I saw her!

Yes! – my Katrinka, coming in through a door behind the counter. My heart was turning cartwheels. Her lovely face looked so sad, I felt like running across to her and sweeping her into my arms. But I had to restrain myself; I had to be careful.

The waitress brought my coffee. Katrinka still hadn't noticed me. I had to think quickly. With a flick of my hand I sent my coffee cup crashing to the floor. Everyone turned to look at me, as did Katrinka. Her face suddenly glowed with recognition. She grabbed a cloth and followed another waitress who was already on her way to clean up the mess. While the other girl concentrated on mopping the floor, Katrinka wiped the spills of coffee from the table. As she leaned across me I whispered, 'Outside, quickly!'

I paid my bill with trembling fingers, and once outside, walked a few paces along the road to where I could shelter in a doorway. I closed my eyes and took a deep breath. When I opened them my girl was standing before me. We flung our arms around each other and kissed and kissed. Our faces were wet with snow and tears. Between sobs of happiness, she said, 'I thought we were parted for ever. How did you get here? How did you find me? Did you get my letters? It is so dangerous for you!'

'Later,' I said, taking her by the hand, 'I will tell you everything later. My ship is in the docks. We must hurry!'

Katrinka took out the scarf I had given her in Germany and quickly covered her hair. She no longer looked like a boy. Her hair had grown considerably; she looked truly beautiful. We began to run. I told her about the priest and the cleaner at the church. Panting with exertion, Katrinka said, 'The old woman is my friend. Thank goodness she overheard you.'

We slowed our pace for a moment to catch our breath. Katrinka was crying again. 'Peter, a terrible thing has happened. A man from the secret police wants me to go and live with him. If I refuse he will make sure that I am sent to the labour camps in northern Russia.' A pitiful sob escaped her lips. 'I would rather kill myself!'

I gave her hand a squeeze. 'It looks as if I have arrived in the nick of time. Don't worry, I am with you now.'

It was growing dark. I glanced at my watch; it was almost four o'clock. So far so good, no one was tailing us. We were approaching the extensive railway sidings close to the docks. We slowed our pace again as we walked by the wide opening of the goods-yard. The loud hissing of a steam locomotive blotted out the sounds of our heavy gasps as it shunted a line of wagons. Now that it had stopped snowing for the moment, I could see that the wagons were carrying heavy tractors, no doubt brought in by ship for a delivery somewhere in Poland. A little further along we were sheltered somewhat by the railway's boundary wall. Across the road from us was nothing but dark, open wasteland. We kept within the shadow of the wall as we hurried on, our feet barely touching the ground. A car cruised slowly past us. I assumed that driving conditions must be pretty treacherous by now. It travelled on just a few yards further, then it stopped and the driver got out. He was tall and wore a long black overcoat. I couldn't see his face clearly. He started walking towards us. I felt Katrinka stiffen; she gripped my hand in terror. 'It is him! – the man I told you about!'

There was no place to run, we stopped dead in our tracks. He was upon us before we had time to think. Angrily he glared at Katrinka. Then he spoke menacingly in his Polish tongue. She just stared at him, absolutely terrified.

I didn't understand one word he was saying, but when he pointed to his car, all became clear. Katrinka was transfixed, her body rigid with fear. He turned to me. I watched as his right hand moved to the top of his coat.

Katrinka suddenly jerked back to life. 'Gun!' she screamed.

I hit him with every ounce of power I possessed. My fist smashed into the side of his jaw. His knees buckled and he went down hard. His head hit the stone wall with a sickening crack. He was out like a light.

Katrinka looked at me, petrified. 'Now they will kill both of us!'

Chapter Twenty-four

My first instinct was to swiftly glance around. We were alone, thank God – nobody had seen us. Now what to do? My mind worked overtime; I knew I had to act, and quickly. Kneeling on the snow-packed ground, I checked his pulse. He was alive. I felt in his pockets for his keys. No luck! – they must be in his car. Now what to do with him? Should we leave him there and run? The sound of shunting from the railway sidings gave me an idea. If I could get him in one of those tractor laden wagons, he could go along with them for the ride. With any luck, a long one!

Katrinka hadn't said a word. She just watched me, her face frozen in shock. As I placed my hands underneath his armpits, I heard her terrified gasp.

'Try not to worry,' I told her. 'He's not dead. He's just going for a ride.'

He was no lightweight. My knees almost buckled under me as I hauled him up and over my shoulder. I took a deep breath and willed my wooden legs to move. The few yards back to the entrance of the sidings seemed like miles. I was worried that the train might have left. What would I do with him then? His long legs hung down in front of me and impeded my every step. At last I turned into the sidings. The train was still there and there was nobody about. I crossed to the nearest wagon and dumped him aboard. He landed with a thud beside a tractor, his head pillowed on the thick cord which held the machine captive. Not a moment too soon. The train jerked and started to move. He was in for a surprise when he woke up. Many miles away, I hoped. I hurried back to Katrinka.

'Are you sure he isn't dead?' She hadn't moved from the spot.

I assured her that he wasn't, then grabbed her arm. 'Come on, I want those car keys.'

They were still in the dashboard. I whipped them out, locked the door, and raced across the road. I flung them as far as I could into the snowy wasteland. I felt that anything that bought us a little more time was well worth doing. Katrinka still looked badly shaken. I kept my arm tight around her waist as we hurried on towards the docks. 'We're almost there,' I said, by way of encouragement.

Soon we were within a few yards of the dockyard gates, but I couldn't risk being stopped and questioned. I had to find another way in! Our sheltering wall had now given way to a wire fence. Inside were scores of trucks loaded with coal. If we could get in there the trucks would provide cover and we would be on board ship in no time. I studied the fence. At first it seemed that there was no way in which we could squeeze our bodies through the small gaps in the wire. Then, just as I was giving up hope, I found a weak spot. A couple of the stout wires were broken at the bottom, not noticeable until I gave them a yank. I held up the wire while Katrinka wriggled through on her belly. She did the same for me. It was a hard struggle – I was much bigger than her – but after much pulling and pushing, I made it through. Luck was with us. We brushed ourselves down and slipped silently between the waiting trucks. To my delight it had started to snow heavily again. We emerged almost directly opposite the chandler's building. On our way over, I quickly explained why there were two boxes of groceries waiting for us. I told her to wait outside until I passed one of them out to her. She would have been far too conspicuous inside.

It all went according to plan. Three or four minutes later we found ourselves approaching the *Alsovear*'s gangplank.

'Is this your ship?' Katrinka looked at it in wonderment.

'It is. Up you go – I'll be right behind you.'

It was a steep climb up to the deck, especially with the two weighty cartons from the chandler's. It must have been quite frightening for her, but she didn't complain. Nothing was as bad as having to stay in Poland!

Scouse and his mates were battening down the hold. 'Where have you been?' he asked as we stepped aboard. 'We thought we would be sailing without you.'

'No chance,' I laughed. 'You can cast off as soon as you like.'

'Who's your friend?' he called, as we walked on past him.

I looked back over my shoulder, dropped my box of groceries by my feet, then cupped my hands round my mouth to make myself heard above the noise of the winch. 'Long story, Scouse – I'll catch you later!'

We reached my galley without any more interruptions. We stepped inside and closed the door. The wonderful feeling of utter relief flooded our bodies. We held each other tightly, almost afraid to let go. But I had to break away. There was still danger while the ship lay in dock. I wouldn't rest easy until we were sailing out into the open sea. I glanced around the galley. I needed somewhere to conceal her until we sailed. My eyes rested on the pantry. Perfect! – she could hide behind the sacks of flour. I hurriedly pulled out a sack or two to allow her access. She squeezed in and huddled down behind them. I hauled the sacks back into position until she was out of sight. Then I stood on tip-toe and peered down on her. 'Hang on, my darling,' I whispered. 'It's only until we are clear of the docks, then you can come out and meet my shipmates.'

She gave me a resigned nod as I gently closed the pantry door.

Automatically, I put the kettle on to boil, then started to prepare the evening meal. The work had to go on, even though I moved as in a stupor. My eyes were being kept drawn to the pantry door. I heard no sound, but I hated having to keep her there. Perhaps she would take comfort in the noises I was making in the galley – at least she would know that I was near to hand. Above the sound of the singing kettle, I heard the low grating rumble of the gangway as it was pulled up to the deck. The Polish pilot must be on board and ready to take us out of the harbour. I couldn't contain myself, I opened the pantry door and whispered, 'Not long now!'

I didn't wait for an answer in case someone walked in and thought I was talking to myself. The *Alsovear*'s wailing siren told me we were casting off. I had to sit down; my legs had turned to jelly and I felt sick. I don't know why, I should have been feeling great. A delayed reaction, I suppose. After waiting twenty minutes I willed myself to look out, to see if any lights were following us. There was only the pilot boat and the fading lights of the harbour a mile beyond our wake. My nausea quickly passed; I was feeling better already.

I waited with baited breath as the engines slowed to let the pilot off then gradually built up speed as we sailed out into international waters. Elated, I flung open the pantry door and pulled the sacks away to release my Katrinka. She fell into my arms. 'Am I safe now?'

I couldn't speak, I could only keep on kissing and hugging her.

The galley door opened and Scouse came in. He stood still and looked at us, his mouth open in astonishment. 'So this is your reason for becoming a seaman.' He sat down heavily and rubbed his eyes, as if what he had just witnessed was a hallucination. 'I knew there was something – I just couldn't put my finger on it.' He stood up to go, then paused and shook his head. 'Oh hell, I almost forgot what I came here for. The Cap'n wants to see you in his cabin, pronto. I'll see you later.' He winked and smiled appreciatively at Katrinka as he left us to it.

The *Alsovear* was pitching and tossing with a vengeance now that we were in the open sea. Taking Katrinka's hand, I said, 'We had better go and face the Captain now; he doesn't like to be kept waiting.'

She pulled back, her eyes wide with panic. 'He won't send me back to Poland?'

'Of course not, my darling, he's a very understanding man. There's no way he would ever consider such a thing.'

She clung to me, unconvinced, and I kissed her again to allay her fears.

'Don't let go, I don't want to lose you now, Peter,' she breathed, gripping me even tighter.

'I won't. You know I won't. Come on.'

'I did not know you were a cook,' she said, as her resolve strengthened.

I laughed. 'No, neither did I, until this job came up!'

As we hesitated in front of the Captain's door, I asked her if she remembered my friend Albert.

'Albert, yes, I remember him – did he teach you to cook?'

'No, my darling, but he got me this job. It's through him that you're here today. He's Chief Engineer. You'll meet him after we have seen the Captain.'

I rapped on the Captain's door with my knuckles.

'Come in – don't stand there chattering all night,' boomed the

Captain's voice.

Katrinka shrunk behind me as we entered.

'So you have her at last then, lad, well done! Come along, stand where I can see you, lass.'

Still afraid, Katrinka moved to my side and confronted the Captain.

He looked at her kindly. 'Katy, is it? I can see why the cook is so smitten. A beauty to be sure. Yes, quite a beauty.'

Katrinka relaxed and smiled at him. 'Thank you, Captain. My name is Katrinka.'

He gestured for us to be seated, then lit his pipe and stretched out his long legs. 'Now, me boyo, are you going to tell me how you managed it?'

'With great pleasure, Captain,' I replied, and I knew that Katrinka, too, would benefit from hearing the full story of my determined search for her. I felt the pressure of her hand tighten as I related my experiences. I talked quickly, the memories still vivid in my mind. We were there for nearly an hour.

'There, that's about it, Captain,' I said at last. My mouth felt dry, but it was a relief to be able to talk about it.

The Captain noisily sucked air through his pipe. Somewhere along the way it had gone out, but he had been so absorbed in my story that he hadn't noticed. He reached for his tobacco. 'And where do you think this secret policeman is now?' Head bent, he carefully refilled his pipe.

'Still travelling throughout Poland, I hope, Captain.'

Without looking up, he murmured, 'And I hope so too.'

Satisfied that his pipe was working smoothly, he relaxed in his chair. 'When you reach home, will you start a career in boxing? I think you could do it.'

I told him, 'No, we will have to live in obscurity once we are back in Cornwall. I can't risk alerting the authorities again. I have lost her once – never again! I haven't made any plans; we will take things as they come. The main thing is that she is with me. If we can stay together, the world can look after itself.'

As we looked at each other, her eyes were brimming over with love and tears, the Captain said, 'You do realise that you will never be able to get married?'

His words shook me for a moment. I hadn't thought of that. Unless . . . a bright idea suddenly formed in my mind. 'Captain

Garrity,' I said with rising excitement, 'would you marry us on board the *Alsovear*?'

Katrinka's face was a picture of delighted astonishment.

I had clearly taken the Captain by surprise, too. His mouth fell open, and he almost lost his pipe. 'Hell no!' he spluttered, 'I have never married anyone before. Even if I did consent to it, the marriage would not be recognised under English law.'

'We wouldn't worry about that, Captain. We would be married in the eyes of God.' Excitedly, I turned to Katrinka. 'What do you say, darling?'

'I am so happy, my Peter. I would wish for nothing else.'

The Captain emitted a long, drawn-out sigh; he knew he was outnumbered. 'If I do this it will have to be entered in the ship's log.'

I wouldn't be deterred. 'We understand you have to do this, but it is what we both want more than anything else. Please, Captain, give us your blessing.'

He gave an embarrassed cough. 'I will think this over carefully, then I will let you know. Now I'm sure you can both do with some rest. We'll discuss it again tomorrow.'

'Thank you, Captain,' Katrinka and I said in unison.

We returned to the galley, oblivious to the bitter cold and the heavy swell of the sea. We were together! – that was all that mattered.

The galley clock warned me that I was running late. The men liked to have their evening meal on time. They were always starving.

Albert looked in as I was dishing it up. 'You have finally done it then, Pete. I had a feeling that this time you would.' He gave Katrinka a wink as he pinched one of my sausages. 'I heard it from Scouse – he was nearly as excited as you two.' Albert saw I was busy and moved over closer to Katrinka, so as not to be in my way. He put his arm around her shoulders. 'Just look at him, Katrinka, he's as happy as a sand-boy now that you are here with him.'

Katrinka put her arms around his neck and planted a kiss on his cheek. 'Thank you, dear Albert,' she said. 'Thank you for everything.'

His face was a picture. Pride, joy and embarrassment mingled together and slowly spread across his features. 'I'd better be off now, Pete,' he stammered. 'I see the meals are ready.' He picked up one of the laden plates, 'I'll take mine with me; one less for you to carry, mate.' He gave a short, nervous laugh as he disappeared through the door.

It was nice to have some help with the washing up. With Katrinka's help, the galley was cleaned and tidied in record time. My normal practice was to take a shower when I had finished for the day. I asked Katrinka if she would like to take one first, telling her that I would stand on guard, so she wouldn't be disturbed.

'I would like that very much, if you will guard me, Peter.' Then, glancing down at her drab clothing, she sighed and said, 'But I have nothing else to wear!'

I took her in my arms. 'It doesn't matter, you look beautiful to me. Tomorrow I will find something of mine for you to wear, then you will be able to wash your own things. We will manage, won't we?'

She looked up, her eyes shining. 'Yes we will.'

So I remained on guard while she showered. When the washroom door opened some ten minutes later, a flushed and shiny Katrinka stepped out. 'Now I feel good, Peter, I feel as if I have washed Poland away.'

I rested my cheek against her wet hair and savoured her clean, womanly scent. How I had missed her! – I don't know what I would do if I should lose her again. I quickly brushed the thought aside and vowed that I would never ever lose her again!

After escorting her back to the galley, I grabbed my talc and a clean towel and nipped back to the washroom. The hot water felt good. My muscles had certainly taken a pounding; I ached all over. All that running and carrying, and the policeman's dead weight over my shoulder, had taken its toll. Still it was all worth it. I would do it all again if I had to.

Katrinka was waiting at the galley door when I returned. 'The Captain wishes to see us,' she said worriedly. 'What can it be?'

I draped my wet towel beside Katrinka's, over the front bar of the stove to dry. 'Maybe he has come to a decision about marrying us. If he agrees, are you sure this is what you want?'

Without hesitation she gave me her answer. 'Yes. I want to be with you always, my Peter.'

'Come on then!' Playfully I shooed her out of the galley. 'We had better go and see what he wants with us.'

I put my head round the wheel-house door. 'You wanted to see . . .' I stopped in surprise. The Captain was there waiting for us, but so was the whole crew! I had to look twice at the Captain. Instead of his usual denims and thick jumper, he was smartly dressed in his official Merchant Navy uniform, complete with hat. He looked even larger than normal.

'Come on in, boyo, don't go standing there with your mouth open. Do you want to get married or not?'

As if in a dream, we entered the wheel-house, and as soon as I had closed the door against the biting wind, the men started to sing *Here comes the Bride*.

Katrinka clung to my arm. 'What does it mean?'

Joyfully I gripped her shoulders. 'It means, my darling, that we are about to be married!'

The Captain's voice boomed out. 'Are ye sure it's what you both want? – to be married on the *Alsovear*?'

We both nodded furiously.

He smiled. 'Very well then, I will marry you now – before I lose my nerve.' He motioned for us to stand in front of him. Scouse placed two cushions on the deck and the Captain invited us to kneel and hold each other's hand. Albert advanced and stood beside me.

The Captain drew himself up to his full height and cleared his throat. 'I am Captain Garrity of the motor vessel *Alsovear*. I am using the authority placed in me to join this couple in Holy Matrimony.' He then opened his prayer book at a marked page and proceeded to read the marriage service. First, he addressed me: 'Peter Rundle, will you take this girl to be your wedded wife?'

'I will.'

Then to Katrinka: 'Katrinka Wazda, will you take this man as your wedded husband?'

Her voice rang sweet and clear in the hushed wheel-house. 'I will.'

He turned back to me. 'You may now put the ring on her finger.'

My heart lurched; I had no ring!

Despairingly, I looked round at my mates for help. They were all grinning at my embarrassment. Then Albert took my hand and proudly placed a crude copy of a wedding ring in my palm.

'Compliments of Scouse,' he whispered. 'He's been busy.'

I threw him a look of gratitude. Bless him, this piece of jewellery would remain really precious to us. Gently but firmly I placed the ring on her finger. Nothing was going to separate us now.

The men started to cheer and Captain Garrity's voice rode above the din: 'I now pronounce you man and wife. You may kiss the bride!'

It was the happiest moment of my life. I took Katrinka in my arms, crushed her to me and kissed her wonderful lips. My crew-mates gathered round to congratulate us, and they were more than happy to kiss the bride, even though her bridal gown consisted of her old baggy trousers and jumper. Scouse said to her, 'I'm glad you're taking him away with you. Now I won't have to suffer the indigestion which always results from eating his tough old pasties.'

Katrinka didn't know what to make of that, until Albert stuck up for me. She smiled when he said, 'You lying toad, Scouse, you always eat two of them if you get half a chance!'

The Captain rapped on the table for silence. 'We will toast the bride and groom.' An assortment of odd glasses stood on a tray beside a bottle of the Captain's best Irish. His hand was shaking as he measured out the whiskey. Probably due to the ordeal he had just been through, I thought. When each glass was filled to his satisfaction, he turned his attention to Albert. 'Albert, as you are the best man, you will give us a speech.'

Poor Albert looked flustered as the Captain then invited all of us to help ourselves to a glass of whiskey. Albert swallowed half of his in one go, then raised his glass to us. Looking very self-conscious, he carefully cleared his throat, then ordered everyone to raise their glasses in a toast. 'To the bride and groom,' he said. 'We wish you every happiness, and we hope and pray that the authorities never catch up with you.' He drained his glass and looked at me. 'We are all sorry to be losing a good mate, even if he isn't much of a seaman. When we next sail into Liverpool and Scouse drags us to the fairground, we won't have anyone to shout for in the boxing tent. But I don't think any of us will forget the last one!' He dug his hand into his pocket. 'One more thing, I have a note from our good Captain . . . it's here somewhere!' Digging even deeper into his pocket, he finally extracted a crumpled ball of paper. He straightened it out and gave a puzzled frown. 'I can't read it, it's upside down!'

Everyone laughed, it was turning out to be just like a real wedding.

'I have it now,' he said seriously, and he proceeded to read the message. 'To the happy pair. As my wedding present to you both, you may have the use of my cabin for a honeymoon suite until we reach Cornwall.'

Everyone cheered, and Katrinka and myself were overwhelmed by the Captain's kindness. It was really something for him to give up his own quarters.

Albert held up his hand for silence. 'There's a PS on the bottom. He smiled as he read, 'As soon as we reach Cornwall, I will want my cabin back. Pronto! – signed, Captain Garrity.'

The crew whistled and cheered, they were almost as excited as us. I thanked the Captain for his present, and for the ceremony. We both agreed no bride or groom could have had a more wonderful wedding; he certainly did us proud. He tried to hide his embarrassment by gruffly telling the men that it was time they were back at their duties.

We thanked each and every one of them as they filed out of the wheel-house. They had all done their bit to make it special for us. Then Captain Garrity escorted us to his cabin.

The captain's cabin was modest but private. We stood side by side, not sure what to do with ourselves, while he busied himself picking up odds and ends which he would require. Last but not least, his favourite pipe and tobacco pouch were stuffed into his pocket. 'There, I think that's about it, I will leave you now, I'm sure you have things to do!' There was a wicked twinkle in his eye as he wished us goodnight and stooped to go out the door. I went to close it behind him and thanked him once again for giving up his sleeping quarters to us.

He started to walk away, then turned back and said, 'It's nothing, I started down in the bunks just like everyone else.' He paused, then added, 'After marrying you I might find myself down there for good!' The thought didn't seem to worry him too much. I could hear him laughing long after he vanished from view.

Alone at last.

I took Katrinka in my arms, and we rubbed noses like we used to do in Germany, nearly two years ago. The gentle nose-rubbing turned into passionate kissing. We broke apart to come up for air, then suddenly feeling strangely shy in her company, I felt I needed to say something light-hearted to break the tension. Adopting a serious expression, I said, 'I am very sorry, madam, but I am afraid your luggage has been lost in transit, along with mine, so we haven't any fancy night-wear for our honeymoon!'

That did the trick; she burst out laughing, and so did I. She looked on shyly as I started to undress. Then, very slowly, she began to peel off her jumper. My fingers became awkward thumbs as I tried to undo buttons while she slowly revealed her soft nakedness. They itched to fondle each perfect breast with its pink rosebud invitingly erect and waiting. It was as if I was seeing her for the first time. When we were alone in the army storeroom, it was different, it was furtive, everything was too quick. Now I wanted to take my time, to drink in her natural beauty.

She stood timidly under my gaze, then her hand moved self-consciously down to cover the soft blonde hair as she whispered, 'I love you, my Peter.'

I drew her warm body to mine. Her skin was so soft, it felt like sumptuous velvet. I had to touch her, to feel her, to kiss her all over.

The bed stood waiting.

I turned out the light and we lay down together, blending into one as our loving sighs joined forces with the screaming wind as it swirled its icy blast around the ship.

The next few days went by in blissful happiness. We still couldn't believe that we were together, and had to keep touching each other in case it was a dream. Working together, we cleaned every inch of the galley in readiness for the original cook's return. I wanted to leave it in the same spotless condition that I had found it; he deserved that much. I was beginning to wish that I could stay on the *Alsovear*. With Katrinka beside me, and with no serious worries, I felt I could have gone on like that for ever.

On our last day I asked Katrinka if she would like to cook the evening meal.

She turned to me, panic-stricken, and started to cry. 'I know nothing of cooking. I have lived in a refugee camp since I was a little girl . . . I have been a prisoner.' Sobbing pitifully, and with her eyes downcast, she said, 'I am not a fit person to have married you!'

I held her close. ‘I am sorry, I didn’t think. There are a lot of things that I don’t know either, but we will learn together.’

She smiled through her tears. ‘That will be good, I will enjoy learning with my husband.’

‘Me too,’ I said.

Chapter Twenty-five

The quay was lined with lorries waiting to be loaded with our cargo of steam coal as the *Alsovear* sailed into Par harbour. I had packed my bag for the last time and we were ready to leave when Captain Garrity and his crew came to the galley to say goodbye. I had a lump in my throat as I thanked them all for their help, and for putting up with me. When the Captain shook my hand and wished us good luck, I couldn't answer him; my heart was too full. I would never forget him. He had taken great risks for us – a father could have done no more.

Scouse was shaking his head in disbelief. 'What a queer lot you Cornish are,' he said. 'One minute you're in a boxing ring taking on the dreaded O'Driscoll, and next you're smuggling in a woman and acting like a sentimental lover.' He shook his head again. 'I will never understand the Cornish.'

I managed a feeble grin as Albert came across to shake my hand. 'You've done me proud, Pete, your mother taught you well.' He squeezed my hand. 'Good luck to the both of you, see you around!' He quickly turned away, not trusting his already croaky voice to say more.

I took Katrinka's hand and we walked down the gangway for the last time. At the bottom we looked back, but our friends had gone. I imagined them already engrossed in their duties, as for them time was precious. As we walked away from the *Alsovear* I noticed that its huge mechanical grab had already started extracting the coal from the hold and tipping it into the back of the waiting lorries. A cloud of fine black dust marked the scene of the action. We stopped to watch for a moment. No matter how many times I had seen this it still fascinated me.

'Pete!'

Someone was calling my name. I turned to see the driver of one of the lorries waving to me. It was Stuart, a local acquaintance of mine. We had grown up together in my home village.

'Long time no see. Pete.' He was talking to me, but his eyes were appraising Katrinka. He offered us a lift, if we could wait until his lorry was loaded with coal.

I accepted gladly; it would be much better and quicker than hanging around for a bus. The lorry in front of him had started to move. Stuart started his engine and prepared to follow it up to the *Alsovear*. 'Shouldn't be long!' he shouted. 'Wait for me at the gates.'

There was plenty of activity to hold our interest until he met us at the gates some twenty minutes later. He jumped down from his cab and ran around to our side, insisting on giving Katrinka a helping hand. I let him have his way; he always had an eye for a pretty girl. The Bedford lorry laboured in bottom gear. Laden down with seven tons of coal, and travelling uphill most of the way, it found it pretty hard going. The noise inside the cab was deafening; talking was out of the question. But that suited us fine. We were too charged with emotion for small talk.

'Here we are, Pete, all safe and sound,' he said, as he pulled up outside my home. 'I suppose you'll be playing football for us again now that you're home.' He looked leeringly at Katrinka. 'Or will you be too busy?'

I noticed with annoyance the sly wink he gave her as we climbed down to the pavement. Jealously, I took her hand. I didn't need words to tell him, 'Lay off, she's mine!' My face said it all.

He retaliated with a cheeky wave as the Bedford trembled into action, then slowly and laboriously went on its way.

We stood together on the pavement. Back where we started. A little bit older and a little wiser, I hoped. But we were there together and I was determined it would stay that way.

I led Katrinka through the warm, homely kitchen and into the living room. My mother was unaware of our arrival. She was intent on sorting out her insurance books in readiness for the collector when he called.

'Hello, Mum.'

She turned with a start. 'Pete! You made me jump. It's so good to see you!'

I lowered my bag to the floor and stepped to one side.

Mother's face was a picture. 'My God, you have Katrinka with you!' She dropped the endowment books and rushed to embrace her. The tears were running down her cheeks. 'We never thought we would ever see you again.' She looked at me in wonder. 'How on earth did you manage it, Pete?'

'It's a long story.' I gave her a big kiss. 'I will tell you all about it when Dad and Joe come home. But there is one thing you should know right now.'

She looked at me expectantly. 'Well?'

'You now have another daughter. Katrinka and I were married on the *Alsovear*.'

Her face registered shocked delight. 'Married!' she echoed, overwhelmed with joy.

Katrinka hugged her. 'I have a family now!'

Surrounded by my family at teatime, I related the entire story. Well almost. I omitted telling them about the dispatching of the secret policeman. I thought that part of the story was best left untold.

'Have you finished with the sea now, Peter?'

The unmistakable tremor in my mother's voice gave way to a sigh of relief when I answered, 'Yes, I'm not going to let Katrinka out of my sight again. We will try to earn a living by working together here.'

We left home as soon as tea was over. Fortunately for us, my other married sister, Jean, had called in to see my parents and had very kindly offered to put us up for a few days. She lived several miles away in the tiny village of Roche. I felt that we would be safe for a while there. I was sorry to leave the comfort of my home, but I wanted to avoid any official interference in our lives. I had been on tenterhooks all evening, dreading an unwelcome knock on the door.

It was some days later that an event occurred which was to map out our future life together. I had ridden over in the dark on my motorbike to see my mother and father, leaving Katrinka behind with Jean. I was afraid as yet to take any chances with her. I was happy and relieved to learn that no one had been there looking for us. So far, so good! Joe was engrossed in the local newspaper, when he suddenly peered at me over the top of it and said, 'Hey, there's something here which might be of interest to you two love birds!'

I stood up and looked over his shoulder to where he was pointing. *A fish and chip shop, situated in Plymouth, to be let with living accommodation!* I was interested.

He relinquished his beloved paper for me to read on. I would need a two hundred and fifty pound deposit, and the rent was three hundred pounds a year. It seemed a lot of money, such a risk, but we would be together, and out of Cornwall. We would be much harder to find if the authorities came looking. There was only one snag, we had no money.

In the end, and after much discussion, my parents and Joe offered to scrape up the money for us. All that was required now was Katrinka's approval. I felt really excited, and couldn't wait to get back to see her.

Joe carefully cut out the advert as I dressed up for my journey back to Roche. My mother looked at me thoughtfully, 'Are you sure it's want you want, Pete?' Not waiting for an answer, she added in an uncertain voice, 'Plymouth is so far away. We won't be able to see you very often.'

Joe handed me the cutting. 'Mother!' he said with exasperation. 'It's only just across the River Tamar, in Devon – fifty miles away at most, that's all. When Pete has earned some money, he can buy a car and then he will be able to visit us as much as he wants.'

She didn't look very convinced.

Later, after Katrinka had carefully read the advertisement, I told her that our family had offered to loan us the money, so that was no problem. Trying to hide my own eagerness, I asked her if she was interested.

She gave me a questioning look. 'Do you know how to cook these fish and chips?'

I gave her bottom a playful smack. 'No! – but I am more than willing to try.'

Early the next morning I walked down to the village. We had decided to go for it. But my hands were shaking as I stepped into the telephone kiosk and lifted the receiver. I spoke to the owner and arranged a meeting for the following day. He agreed to drive over to my sister's house.

So the following morning Jean and Katrinka polished and scrubbed the house in readiness for our visitor. We were all apprehensive; we were the first in our family to even consider running our own business – the mere thought of it was daunting. Katrinka wondered whether it would be best if I spoke to the proprietor on my own. 'No,' I told her. 'From now on your place is by my side. We will sink or swim together.'

When he arrived, we soon discovered he was a true businessman. He told us how he had rented his first shop when he came out of the navy. He was now the proud owner of four good shops, and without any modesty informed us that he was truly excellent at his job.

'If we decide to have your shop,' I said, 'I would deem it a great honour if you would teach us the rudiments of your trade.'

I had said the right thing. He proudly straightened his back and said, 'How right you are to ask. Yes, I will be happy to show you the ropes if you move into the premises three days before you officially take over.'

'Then we have a deal,' I told him, and we shook hands on it. The fate of two very immature people was thus sealed.

The next few weeks went by like greased lightning. At the end of each day I would thank God that we were still free and that no one had come searching for us. We hadn't realised there was so much to do when acquiring a business, but it was exciting and we were both floating blissfully along on cloud nine.

We finally made time to call at the big house to thank Mr Dawson for his help. Mrs Truscott let us in. As grumpy as ever, she managed a haughty sniff when her eyes rested on Katrinka. Not that it bothered us.

Mr Dawson was sitting in an armchair, gazing out over his beautiful gardens, when we entered his study. He looked startled for a moment, when he noticed Katrinka by my side, then he sprang from his chair and said, 'By jove, you've pulled it off!' He bounded over to us, took Katrinka's hand and touched it with his lips. She smiled as he said something to her in Polish, then she looked lovingly towards me as she replied in the same foreign tongue. I was none the wiser.

We were invited to sit as he rung the bell for Mrs Truscott to bring some tea. I started to tell him about my meeting with Jerzy, but he held up his hand to caution me as the housekeeper shuffled in with her laden tea-tray. Pointedly ignoring Katrinka and myself, she placed it on the low table beside her employer and walked out without a word, closing the door behind her.

Mr Dawson silenced me with his eyes. We waited for a few moments to ensure that Mrs Truscott was well out of earshot, then he told me to begin. I was grateful for Mrs Truscott's tea as I relived my past experiences. At times my throat felt as if it was lined with cotton wool, as in my mind's eye I was again faced with the sinister secret policeman and the treachery of the innocent looking priest.

Mr Dawson listened avidly, only interrupting me briefly at odd intervals to clarify some important issue which had appeared a little vague. He nodded thoughtfully when I had finished. 'You are two extremely lucky people. I have known many people who have been mixed up with the Communists, and some have lost their lives!' Placing his teacup back on to the tray, he regarded us gravely. 'You will need to remain on your guard at all times. The man you speak of is well known and dangerous. He may well seek retribution.'

I swallowed hard. It came as no surprise to me, but hearing it from him made it seem all the more real. He must have noticed my concern because he smiled and said, 'Things aren't so bad as they seem. It is in their capacity to send someone after you but it is unlikely. And if that should be the case, I will probably learn of it from my friends abroad. It would be prudent for you to keep me informed of your whereabouts.'

Katrinka and I both agreed. He made a fine guardian angel. I gave him his present of a fine bottle of malt, knowing that we had gained a valuable friend.

When I questioned Katrinka afterwards about their conversation in Polish, she told me that he had said to her, 'He is a very brave man and he must love you dearly.'

'And what was your reply?' I asked her.

She hugged me tightly as she said, 'I tell him I know of these things already.'

Epilogue

I looked at Garth and smiled. 'In the happy years that followed, we worked hard together. We laughed and cried together, but we made progress. Katrinka bore us two children – a boy and a girl. They both entered this world with a head of thick black hair, just like mine. Katrinka was overjoyed. We were our own complete family at last.'

I still wasn't sure if Garth had fully grasped the situation. But I was holding his interest.

I rubbed my sore leg and carried on. 'In spite of the business, we always managed to keep a low profile. It took us years to get out of the habit of looking back over our shoulder, and we were careful never to remain too long in one place. But as it happened, each move we made turned out well for us. We kept in touch with our friend at the big house over the years, and it saddened us when we received a letter, written in a weak, spidery hand, telling us that he was in poor health. Even then his thoughts were with us, as he had enclosed the name and telephone number of someone who, in his words, *would continue to be a helpful friend.* Shortly after receiving that letter we heard that our trusty old friend had died. Well, eventually we had saved enough money to realise our dream of owning a farm by the sea.' At this point I noticed a glint of understanding in Garth's tired eyes. 'The children were now both married with homes of their own, so there was nothing stopping us. We sold our business and came home to my beloved Cornwall.'

It was almost midnight. We heard movement in the kitchen.

Elizabeth popped her head round the door, surprised to see Garth still sat in the armchair. 'You look as if you two have been enjoying yourselves.' – she was smiling as she glanced meaningfully at the now empty whisky bottle. She warmed her hands over the dying embers of the fire. 'I'll put the kettle on, then I will make up a bed for Garth. I will not allow him to drive home tonight.'

While Elizabeth was out in the kitchen brewing the tea, Garth reached for his brown suede money-bag. He took out the cheque she had given him earlier and studied her signature. 'When did you start calling her Elizabeth?' he asked.

'A long time ago,' I said. 'It made us feel a little easier.'

Elizabeth returned with our tea and a saffron bun for each of us. 'What have you found so interesting to talk about tonight in my absence? – the usual farmyard tales, I suppose?'

Garth rose stiffly from his chair, crossed over to her, and kissed her hand.

'I feel honoured to know you, Katrinka,' he said.